RISE SIREN FIVE

By

SS DELAUNAY

Thank you

Thank you to everyone, ever, who cheered for creativity over conformity, power over subservience and freedom over fear. You are the true world shapers and the bringers of magnificent things.

Dedicated to

Dedicated to you, dear reader. You honor me in letting me share my stories with you.

RISE SIREN FIVE — TABLE OF CONTENTS

CHAPTER ONE

Debbie beeped.

Deep Space Debbie. Debbie for short. If Debbie beeps once, the arrays have picked up something with serious potential to be interesting.

If Debbie beeps three times, the arrays have picked up something real good.

When he first started working here, Nate Reynolds Jnr jumped into action at every solitary Debbie ding.

Tilds scoffed at him. But his eyes still tracked him, furtive and hopeful, all the same.

Debbie had just dinged three times. Tilds was maintaining his aura of cool detachment, but his eyes were glued to Nate at the OBO tracker.

OBO. Off-World-Black Ops. Uber level of security clearance required to be anywhere near this thing.

"Son-of-a-gun. This guy's a genius." Nate rested his hands on the desk and peered closely at the incoming stream.

"What?" Tilds said, aiming for casual. Almost making it.

"What?" he repeated, just a tad impatiently when Nate didn't answer right back.

"Cooper Pierce R9," Nate replied, easing back from the screen. "He's done it. He's off Moethiica."

Tilds whistled. "Well won't that make the powers that be happy. Golden boy on his way home again. Son-of-a-bitch." He picked up the phone. "I'll call it in."

"Who's picked him up?" Tilds queried Nate, while he cradled the phone against his shoulder. "Can you see them?"

He shook his head at the non-answering phone and held the receiver straight out in front of his face. "Hello? Earth to OBO Incorporated. Important news to report. Favorite son on his way home. Anyone want to freaking answer me?"

"No, I can't see them, but...." Nate leaned in close to the display again. "Fuck," he said quietly.

"What? What?" Tilds slammed the phone down and clumsily negotiated the exit route from his desk. Nate Reynolds Jnr, was a gentleman and a scientist.

And he never swore.

The bar had now been officially raised above real good.

"Holy fuck." Tilds skidded to a stop beside him. Unlike Nate, Tilds swore often. He was as much of a scientist. Definitely not so much of a gentleman.

"He's got her. He's freaking got her," Nate said eventually.

"I don't believe it," Tilds breathed.

"Believe it," Nate replied. He pointed to the screen. "She's right here in front of us. Heading fast our way."

Tilds' phone rang loud and sharp. They both jumped.

"Fark. Ok," Tilds exhaled deeply, cranking his neck and rotating his shoulders.

"Tilds, just answer the phone. Tell them he's got her," Nate rolled his eyes at him. Such a drama queen.

Tilds reached his desk and picked up the phone.

"This better be good, Array Boy." It was Jonassen. An arrogant bastard. But around Off-World-Black-Ops, you got that here and there.

"Oh, it's good, Jonassen," Tilds smirked. "It's more than good."

"Yeah, what?" Jonassen asked skeptically.

"Golden boy. Everybody's favorite, long off-the-grid, Off-World Agent, has gone all exit stage left on Moethiica on us."

"Pierce is off? You can see him?" Jonassen was excited now. And the best was still coming to him.

"Oh yeah he's off," Tilds replied. "And he's bringing you a little friend to play with Jonassen."

"Cut the crap, Tilds and spill it. Who's in transit with the Agent?"

"Siren5, asshole. Siren5."

There was dead silence. "You're shitting me," Jonassen said.

"No, I am not. Patching you to the Debbie data.... now!" He hit the last key with a flourish.

"Oh. My. God," was all that Jonassen could say.

"The most coveted freaking asset in the cosmos, Jonassen," Tilds gloated. "The most coveted freaking asset in the cosmos and we got her. Little low tech, bumbling baby earth just outplayed the lot of them. Yeah baby!" He pumped his fist excitedly and then recovered himself.

Nate looked up from Debbie to smile at him.

"Jonassen you still there?" Tilds put on his best serious voice. "Don't you need to go tell someone?"

"Yeah, yeah. I do and I'm out," Jonassen replied, shaking himself. He went to hang up and paused.

"Hey Tilds, you think she's hot as in smoking hot?"

"Of course, she's hot," Tilds replied. "She's a freaking Veil Portal opening Siren, Jonassen. Sex, wings and magic baby. Oh yeah."

"Cooper Pierce is a lucky bastard."

"Cooper Pierce is a freaking legend. And professional beyond all reason. He ain't gonna tap Priority One, Man. No matter how hot she is. She got important work to do down here."

Jonassen grunted, "I would."

Tilds laughed. "And that is why Cooper Pierce is on his way back from OBO Mission Moethiical with said Siren in tow, and you're still working a desk job."

"Fuck you, Array Boy."

"Aw, sorry Jonassen. I'm officially off the market. Gotta save myself for all that Off-World pussy that'll be coming through, once that little cosmic doorway opens"

"Tilds!" It was Nate. Looking pointedly furious.

"Gotta go. Gotta go. Go tell the big brass, Jonassen. Later."

Tilds hung up the phone and managed to look sheepishly apologetic. "Sorry Nate." He held up his hand to him. "Can't blame a man for getting a little distracted though."

Nate shook his head and turned back to Debbie. "You're depraved Tilds. This is huge. This is history. This is the gateway to the denied worlds. And we got her. We got the key. Which means we control it. We own it."

"No way anyone is going to cheapen this by trying to get laid by the Off-Worlders who come through it."

Tilds shook his head. "Nate, Nate, Nate. I admire your sentiment, brother, I really do. But I wouldn't count on it."

He winked at Nate and picked up the phone to make the next call.

CHAPTER TWO

Moethiica. Far, Far Away. 24 Hours Earlier.

"Hurry up," Marcs hissed behind her.

"Shut up," she laughed at him. "I want to savor it. It's my last time."

She settled herself again, drew a breath, and hurled the canister.

It was a good throw. The target was impossibly high. Impossibly angled.

When she was little she had practiced for hours on end, every day, for months for this.

Just for this moment.

It had to be perfect.

It was.

The canister hit true on the sensor, way, way above them. And the rock doorway to the run, slid open.

Rise turned and beamed at Marcs in delight. She eased herself through the narrow opening and felt him close behind her.

Marcs could not throw and hit that sensor. He had a cheek in rushing her. But this was the last time here with him too, most likely. And she would not let any small annoyances bother her.

She pushed through the next opening and came out on to the ledge, into the sunlight.

The sun was directly overhead now. It heat red rock and honeysuckle. Godds she loved that smell. She wondered if she would smell it after today.

"Unlikely," she said to herself, breathing deep, and stepping closer to the edge.

Her last run. She had come of age that morning. And that meant only one thing to a female like her on Moethiica.

They would come for her. They would take her to the Echelon.

And she would become their play thing.

They would take her wings away.

Tears pricked her eyes and she let the hot breeze take them.

What would come, would come, but it would come later. They would not spoil this last moment on Junar Run.

Because Junar Run was Paradise. Outlawed and abandoned.

A local street crew looking to loot whatever they could find from the long-abandoned weapons facility had found the entrance.

They got precious little in the way of loot. But they were an enterprising lot, many of them winged. They began to fly the old runs and hold races.

Only the best of the best, and those who could be trusted, were invited to join them. It became a profitable little venture for them. Rise had certainly forsaken many a meal to race here.

But it had been worth it. Oh, so worth it.

They were not here now, and she and Blake had the place to themselves. A bonus.

Blake had never beaten Rise on this run. No-one had beaten Rise on this run the last three years.

But they had beaten her enough before that. Years. Junar Run had been her life for some time.

Rise looked around her, savoring every precious detail of it.

Home. Freedom. Friendship.

The ravines of Junar are narrow.

And they bear the scars of war.

There are parts of Junar where the ledges have caved in from the blasts. And parts where the holes in the hard, red dirt floor have been blown through.

This was ground never meant to be disturbed.

Hot bursts of smoldering air erupt from the floor. They join with the warm eddies that rush through the ravine to form a wave of hot, fickle, unpredictable air. Eddies of hot winds that rise from the bowels of the earth and rush through the narrow passages of the ravines.

No-one knows where they come from or what causes them. But if you have wings and you catch one at the right time, you can ride them.

Ride them dizzyingly fast through the turns and twists of the run, and pray the eddy lasts until the end, where it will drop you outside of the rocks. It is an adrenalin rush like no other.

This is what they ride and race and fly.

Rock sprites live in the caves here. Other creatures as well. If you get caught on the run, it is a rock sprite who will come rescue you.

Pray it is a rock sprite anyway.

You would not want the other creatures who dwell here coming to your aid.

There is a stillness that is not stillness that comes over you before flight. It is being. It is fluid. It gives only the illusion of being still.

You become one with yourself and one with your surroundings.

The breeze stopped abruptly. The hot desert air hung heavy and dry.

Silence.

Rise waited. At one with herself.

The eddies came.

Soft, teasing, caressing. The first one lifted a tendril of dark hair from her forehead, already damp with sweat.

It was all she needed.

She dove.

And Marcs cursed, already half a second behind her. She had gone early and she sank dangerously close to the ground before the full force of the eddy caught her wings.

She surrendered to it. She was lifted. She soared.

She banked hard into the first turn. Her body and the elements one. In perfect sync with each other. Each lending the other to its cause.

The feeling through her wings was of ancient winds, hot earth, swirling air, rising heat, cool ocean mists. She felt all these things through her wings. She felt this air's journey. Felt where it had travelled. Felt where it had been. And now it was hers. Now she had become part of its journey. Now it was lifting her.

The third turn is sharp to the right and up after the comparatively gentle curved ease of the second left. It comes quickly upon you, and many a first and even tenth time traveler of Junar Run, comes to an early end of the ride here.

Of all places Marcs chose this particular turn to make one of his more outrageous passing attempts.

They slammed.

They slammed into each other hard. And before they could disentangle themselves from each other a freak up blast of a current propelled them up into the web of vicious overhangs above them.

That's the thing about Junar Run. The overhanging ledges stretch out far, almost touching on certain parts of the run. And their underside is a tangle of strange rock formations. Gnarled swirls and nasty hooks of rock.

As if some great giant knew to what purpose beings would come here. And added his own evil twist to the game, wrought in stone.

They struggled vainly, only making their situation worse and securing themselves even tighter in the overhangs.

There was nothing for it. They could only wait for the rock sprites. They would come rescue them eventually. All they must needs do is wait. And find some pieces of rocks they could cling to with their hands to take the weight from their wings to their arms.

The sun beat down steadily and Rise was saturated with sweat by the time Marcs spoke.

"Sorry," he grunted. Wincing as he shifted his weight.

They were saving what they could of their wings but their arms were taking some brutal punishment.

"It's Ok," Rise exhaled deeply through her mouth and adjusted her position slightly.

They waited longer in silence. The salty sweat poured into Rise's eyes and her biceps screamed with pain. She couldn't hold this much longer. But if she swung her legs up to try and get a purchase on the ledge above she would rip her wings.

And she really, really didn't want to do that. No matter what was coming later, she would preserve them as long as she could.

Rise closed her eyes and counted backwards from 100.

She could hold for another 100. A rock sprite would surely be here by then.

22.

It was no rock sprite.

Rise felt the base of her skull tingle, and the hairs rise along the back of her neck.

He came to sit cross legged on the rock face above them and rested his bemused head on his right hand.

It was a Pann Lord.

And he was magnificent.

His horns were enormous.

They were black obsidian but beneath them was a rainbow of color. The rich, jewel colors of the cosmos swirled, spiraled, spun. His deep brown eyes sparkled. Deep pools. Ochre, mocking, seeing, sensual. His lips were full of red promises. The beautiful, masculine face was framed with dreads pulled back high on his head.

His body was muscle. Lean, hard muscle. Muscle that could leap and bound and engage. There were braided bands of leather around his biceps. His ink was awesome. Symbols. Glyphs. Swirls.

His presence radiated. Depths of wisdom, ecstasy and exquisite sorrow. Laughter. Love.

Rise swallowed, wide eyed, feeling the rush of him.

"That was somewhat foolish." His voice was rich, dark, resonant.

With a fluid grace he was suddenly on the overhang directly above them. With gentle and expert hands, he untangled Rise's wings first, lifting her effortlessly on to the ledge beside him. Then he did the same for Marcs, setting him beside her.

He smiled at them. And pointed behind them. Showing them the entrance he had used and their way down.

And then in silence he settled cross legged on the middle of the ledge and closed his eyes.

Rise and Marcs stared, mesmerized.

Pann Lords are the kings of the land. Guardians, spell singers, keepers of mysteries. Masculine. That rich, deep, dark masculine that brooks no trivialities and is capable of the deepest joy, the most profound love and the richest laughter.

They initiate few outsiders to their mysteries.

They like to play.

And those who have been lucky enough to partake in the sensual arts with them have a knowing smile and a larger presence about them afterwards.

Rise had only ever seen one from a distance. Even then she could feel his vast presence. Feel how different he was from everyone else around him.

But never like this. Never this close. And never where one had his attention on her.

His attention was exquisite.

Rise stared transfixed until Marcs tugged gently but firmly on her hand to leave him be. Reluctantly she turned to leave but not before she felt the brush of the Pann's awareness against her mind.

He connected with her. Ever so gently, he connected with her. He was immensely powerful and immensely gentle and immensely pure. And in Rise he searched for some depth she was not aware existed.

This she felt. She did not understand it completely. But she was immensely honored. She turned to look at him. He was still as the rock which supported him and gave no acknowledgement of what had passed between them.

Marcs tugged on her hand once more and Rise followed him reluctantly into the mountain.

Light into darkness. The ground sloped away beneath them. Then the walls of the tunnel sprang to life. Crystalline sparkles. Rich walls teaming with gem told stories.

Slivers cut and set cunningly in the rock wall in the formations of the stars and nebula and galaxies. These gems of the sprites are sacred. They lit their path beautifully.

As they descended lower and their path spiraled more deeply into the depths of the rock, there were paintings. Images etched in rock in ochre and blood. Ancient stars and ancient giants. They told stories of things as ancient to them as they were to Marcs and Rise.

They told as best as they could of themselves, with the rules and materials afforded to them.

Marcs stopped suddenly and Rise crashed clumsily into his back. "Dead end," he whispered.

They turned to their left and as if on cue, the opening appeared to them. Narrow and hidden, the soft glow of blue light from whatever lay beyond it beckoned them in. Gingerly they eased their way through.

It was a cavern. And what a cavern. The vast sapphire blue lake was midnight depths of night sky and starlight. Sandy banks of white, golden grains edged back to rounded walls of gleaming obsidian rock. Jewel blue stalactites hung over the sapphire depths of the pool. It was a place to sing within yourself.

Rise felt the voice in her throat soar. She felt her mind quieten. She felt the endless chatter cease. She felt him again. The sunlight on him. On the rocks. As one with his surroundings. As one with the air. As one with the breath. There was no separation. The separation was an illusion. There was no he, no air, no breath. They were all one. And they danced together in endless spirals. Endless twirls.

Rise felt something in her awaken. And then he was lost to her. Gone. As if he had never existed.

"He wanted you to see this." It was an older female sprite. She touched Rise's arm and Rise saw the sadness flicker across her eyes when she turned to meet them.

Gently, she touched Rise's wings.

And then it hit her. Physical and not physical all at once.

She felt the foreignness of it, the shock if it. She screamed for Marcs. And then the pain hit her like a tidal wave.

And then there was blackness.

And she felt nothing at all.

CHAPTER THREE

He ran his torch over her from top to bottom. She was violet eyed, dark haired and exquisite. Smoking hot. A beauty. Whatever you want to call it. Winged.

L4 hated what those bastards did to the winged ones.

The sprites had dumped her and the guy on the outskirts of the run. The guy had come to just as they got close. He'd left her there the little bastard. Done a runner.

If he knew her, and knew what was coming to her, that made him a right prick.

But that was Ok. L4 had a good eye for faces. And the lights from their craft had illuminated his face nicely before he'd run. He would see the violet eyed beauty's friend again and teach him some manners.

L4 ran a hand through his hair. She had come to only seconds after the other had run. Instantly alert. Airborne. Straight up at dizzying speed. It had thrown him for a second. He'd never seen anything quite like it.

Two shots to take her. He didn't need two shots to take anything. C7 hadn't hit her at all. Her speed had taken them both by surprise.

"How the fark did she get up that far and that fast?" He mused.

"Determined little Minx," mused his fellow officer, C7. "Bind her. ID her. You know the drill. "

L4 deftly bound her. Wings, wrists, ankles. "She's a beauty," he said wistfully. Fark knows what those sick bastards would do to her. "She's only just come of age this morning according to her ID," he said to C7. Sure we just can't leave her somewhere?"

C7 hesitated, but then resolutely shook his head. "It's protocol. And she's already triggered the alarms on the Runs. They'll know something's up out here. They'll have ID'd her from that."

L4 grunted. "I know but…."

"I know," C7 agreed quietly. "But you feel like going up against the Echelon tonight brother?" he said pointedly. "I sure know I ain't no match for them."

L4 sobered at that. "They're wrong. They're just wrong."

"That they are," C7 agreed. "And there ain't one damn thing we can do about it. Come on. Let's get it over with."

L4 lifted Rise effortlessly in a fireman's carry and followed C7 back to their patrol craft.

It was the newest model. Sleek and highly maneuverable. It had capacity to fly as high as the first layer of the webs.

They had taken it up there just hours before. C7 was having problems with his girl, and had welcomed the distraction of checking into their designated night shift a couple of hours early.

It was a distraction alright, but creepy as fark. The rainbow-colored strands were duller then they expected them to be. Almost sickly looking. And they were few and far between. Most of them were a weird grey white. Off. Like they needed a wash or something. Thick and sticky too.

They could see the seemingly infinite layers of the webs beyond. Coding stations dotted in their midsts. Strange, unidentifiable creatures moving in the shadows.

"Fark!" they yelled it in unison as one of the shadow creatures appeared from nowhere and scuttled unexpectedly close.

C7 cursed repeatedly as he fumbled at the controls and got the ship further away from the web.

Creepy as fark.

But at least now they could say they'd seen them up close and personal. Moethiica's famed webs.

"What do you reckon it feels like being on one of those worlds that doesn't have this shit?" L4 gestured at the scene in front of them.

"Man! Shut the fuck up!" C7 hissed at him. "Don't be saying shit like that right up here and close to them."

"Doesn't matter where I say it," L4 retorted. "If these webs work how they say they work, they can hear me wherever I say it. Hell, they probably programmed me to say it."

C7 shook his head. "You can just never give it a rest. Can you?"

"I'd just like to know what it feels like, is all," L4 replied. "Hardly the stuff of rebellion and revolution."

"It's rebellion and revolution enough for her," C7 replied glumly and L4 grunted.

They sat in silence for a few more minutes and then C7 swung the flyer back in sharp descent to surface level. He had seen all he wanted to of the webs.

They had reached the flyer now and Rise moaned softly, coming to a little on L4's shoulder. "Steady on there violet eyes," he said.

As he settled her in the flyer he gave her a shot of sedative. It was a small mercy. But the best he could do for her.

"You're a softy for these winged hotties," his partner chided him.

"I'm a softy for everyone," L4 remonstrated light heartedly.

C7 snorted, swinging his hard-muscled bulk into the flyer. "Not likely," he muttered.

And L4 laughed in spite of himself, and where they were heading, as they took off into the late afternoon sky.

CHAPTER FOUR

The Black Gates of the Echelon. L4 and C7 stood reluctant before them, Rise still over L4's shoulder. They did not want to be here. No-one wanted to be here. Ever.

It was the Echelon's own compound in the city. Buildings on three sides around a large central courtyard. Smaller, private courtyards off the other, outer sides of the buildings. A maze of rooms and tunnels underneath the ground. The Entertainment Rooms are amongst them.

"We'll just leave her with you then," C7 was saying.

"The Upper now in session would have you deliver your gift to him personally," the Echelon Guard replied. "He is 'entertaining.' And would have you join him."

C7 opened his mouth to protest. But, knowing it was hopeless, thought better of it. One did not protest with the Echelon. One just did what they were told.

"Take them," the Guard barked at an underling.

He was identically clothed, gloved, booted and helmeted to his superior. Only the red insignia over his heart gave away his rank.

And he felt different. Not long in the helmets, L4 thought to himself. They connected themselves right into their heads these helmets. Programmed them. Linked them. Fed them. Made them even more freaking farked up than they were to start with. If that was possible. Old One soldier hybrids with magic tricks. Nothing better.

The Senior Guard tilted his visored head at him, regarding him steadily. L4 shook himself. They had mind-cept these bastards. Not only the power to read, but the power to steal. He stilled his thoughts to silence. The Guard moved slightly into him as they passed. It was a light touch but still felt like being jostled by a wall.

Icy, black tendrils washed over him. L4's skin crawled.

The underling led them to stairs at the rear, right hand corner of the courtyard. The entrance was straight out of the ground. There was suddenly a large, grey flagstone missing, and a gaping hole opening up before them.

They went down one flight of stairs in darkness. A small landing, and then the stairs headed off to the left. At the foot of these stairs, a dank, narrow, stone walled corridor ran into the earth. But there was a room on the right. Another small landing at the entrance and another small flight of stairs.

The underling herded them down into the room. And then turned and left.

It was long and narrow. Dark. A glittering bar with a huge black mask suspended over it took up the very far wall.

Ornate chairs and small black lacquered tables were pushed back against the walls on either side of the long room.

The trophies of the Echelon hung on the walls above them.

Huge. There were three on each side. And each contained a set of female Moethiican wings. Bloody and torn.

In the center of the room a circle of Echelon with their black cloaked backs to them, blocked the view of the current *'entertainment.'*

They had a woman in there now. The sound of her in the Echelon silence, unmistakable. C7 swallowed visibly and tried desperately to think of anything but the woman. He thought of their helmets. Like a living part of them, it was said they became. The rush of power they gave off when the needle passed through the brain barrier was supposed to be addictive.

"Would you like to try one for yourself?" C7 drew in his breath sharply as the sea of Echelon parted and the Upper walked through to stand close to him.

Arc.

He needed no insignia to identify him. But he bore it anyway. It was larger, more elaborate, more imposing, than any other Echelon here. Like his presence. Which identified him beyond question.

Dark Mage of the Old Ones. Echelon Leader of Moethiica.

He moved up close in front of them as the silent, unseen guards behind them, pressed in close from the rear.

C7 gasped. He looked down at his stomach, not yet believing. The tip of the Echelon blade protruded only slightly out.

The guard behind him kicked him off of it, and he fell dead, face first to the floor.

L4 began to struggle wildly, only then realizing they had injected him with something. He could move his upper body only slightly. He could not move his legs at all.

Arc stepped in even closer. He ran his black gloved hand ran down the still unconscious form of Rise.

He spun around to face the now attentive Echelon.

"Brothers, shall we see what our generous friends have brought us?"

There were soft murmurs of agreement.

L4 crashed to the ground as they withdrew their support from his weight. They cuffed his wrists and left him there to lay where he had fallen.

Two of the bastards had Rise upright now, arms stretched out hard between them. Another was holding something vile under her nose. Undoing the tranq and the sedative.

L4 tried to move, but he was paralyzed and could do nothing.

Rise coughed and came to, blinking rapidly.

Her vision was blurry at first and it hurt to look straight forward. She shook her head to clear it and the glint of light on glass caught her vision.

She looked up and beheld the bloodied wings in the closest trophy case. She looked about her and beheld Echelon all around her.

Rise screamed, struggling madly.

And the Echelon simply stood regarding her. Unmoving. Silent.

Arc had been standing off to the side but he stepped in close to her now, his black visored face the only thing in her vision.

And even Rise knew who he was. And she screamed even louder.

"Oh, please don't waste your screams now my dear. There will be plenty of time for screaming later."

He had a small, jewel handled knife in his hand.

He used it to cut her flight suit open. No rush. He was slow and deliberate.

He stepped back and took her in, up and down, just as slowly.

"Oh, my dear you are exquisite."

And then he stepped back and revealed her to the others.

"Behold my Brothers. What a delightful gift has been brought to us."

The silent Echelon all took one step forward.

Rise desperately tried to throw her wings open. Break through the bonds that held them.

But L4 had bound them tight as law demanded. They were too strong and she was powerless.

You are never powerless. The voice was male, dry, amused. It was almost always amused. A mind-voice. She had heard it since she was very young. Not with any great frequency. Just here and then. Random.

And every time she had heard it she had ignored it and schooled her mind to silence. Mind-voices here would have you killed very, very quickly.

The Echelon, Arc, tilted his black visored head at her. Curiosity emanated from him.

Rise swallowed hard with fear. Pray to all the godds he hadn't heard it.

He moved in close to her, pressing her chest in hard against the raised red insignia of his jacket. With a gloved hand he gripped her chin hard and painfully.

"There is something very different about you my dear, isn't there?"

Rise shook her head trying to free it from his grip. She pushed back, trying desperately to get her body away from him.

But they had her held fast and she cried out in frustration, her eyes furious and glaring at him.

"Shhhh." Still holding her chin, he traced the other gloved hand down her face. "Shhhh."

Down her throat. Her Down the side of her body. Over her hip. He stopped, his gloved hand barely touching her.

Horror, repulsion and terror pulsed through Rise and she braced for the worst.

He released her.

He stood back and gestured to the other Echelon.

They parted on cue and revealed the cleared space behind them.

There were more Echelon behind them. At the back of the room and to the sides of them.

And in the center of them was a winged female, like Rise.

Her wings were unbound. But they were broken. They moved jaggedly along the floor, leaving small dots of red blood in their wake.

Sickened, Rise spun her head away from the vision. But at a gesture from Arc, one of the guards behind her grabbed her head roughly in his hands, forcing it back again.

"Do you see what I take from her?" Arc looked from the winged on the floor back to Rise. His voice was cold, clinical, detached. Like he was giving a lecture.

"Not the physical," the Echelon continued. "The physical is but a Veil. I pierce the physical Veil for the gems underneath it. And they are much more interesting. Much more powerful. Much more fun to play with."

"Pierce her," he threw over his shoulder to the Echelon on the floor. And his gaze returned to Rise.

She closed her eyes. She would not watch this. Would not be a party to it.

"Do you see it?" His voice was a whisper, wrapping itself around her, compelling her eyes open and to the scene on the floor, in spite of herself.

The winged woman's eyes flickered open. Violet and stunning like Rise's own.

And Rise recognized her.

Soar. The rebel. The legend. The only winged in current times to have escaped them. She was believed to be in hiding in the desert, waiting for a sign. She believed she was the one. The one who would embody the Siren of the 5th, open the Portal, and raise the might of the Original Makers against the Old Ones. Against the Echelon. Against all like this and everything they stood for.

Rise looked at Arc and back to Soar in horror.

Soar moaned.

White mist danced on her forehead. Arc's outstretched arm was towards her, palm up. He drew his long-gloved fingers, upward, upright and together. The mist began to gather and form itself. And Rise saw it spinning. The size of a tiny egg. White gold. Glittering. Like a diamond.

He was drawing it out of her, from deep within her. From her mind's eye.

Essence. Power. Magic.

It moved up out of Soar and towards him.

Without a second thought, Rise willed the mind-diamond back to Soar with everything she had.

And the mind-diamond hesitated, wavering.

Arc merely twisted his fingers ever so slightly, and Rise felt his gloating satisfaction as the diamond flew toward him.

"No!" she cried, but the diamond tumbled over and over, unwavering on its path to meet him.

"No!" cried Rise again. This time more frantically. Still it sped towards him.

"To me!" she flung at it, just before it reached him. And the power of her voice shook the room.

The mind-diamond changed its course.

And slammed itself into her.

It felt like white fire cutting into her. Her entire head blazed with it.

Godds. What have I done? Only then did she begin to panic. Desperately she willed the thing back to Soar.

But it was having none of it. She felt it wash over her. Connect itself tight to her own essence, her own power, her own magic.

"I'm sorry," she whispered to Soar. But Soar smiled a small, weary smile at her. And Rise swore she saw another much dimmer light settle back into the woman's head.

And then wave after wave of undulating power broke over her. Sweat formed on her brow. She blacked out momentarily.

She came to with Arc's fingers around her throat. "Well you are just full of surprises aren't you, you little winged whore. "

"Bring me the Nephliim Blade!" he yelled, without turning from her.

A Nephliim Blade? Here? Then she felt him push into the base of her skull like the Pann and she forgot all about the Blade.

Because it was nothing like the Pann at all. There was no gentleness and nothing pure. He tore into her mind, seeking, searching.

He began to pull at her essence and her power. He would void her. She would be void to her Maker, void to the Creator. He would cut her threads to them and make her nothingness, but eternal and aware with it.

And he would feed his own power with hers. All of them here would have a taste of it. A taste of her. She would feed the monsters.

No.

She did not say it out loud this time. The walls of the room did not shake with the power of it. But her own walls did.

The Echelon tightened his grip on her throat until she saw stars.

And then the Nephliim Blade was brought to the room.

Amongst the Nephliim only a Prince could wield it.

And for the Portal to open a Veil Siren must be holding it.

A riddle. One that had never been tested truly. Because there had never been a Veil Siren at a Portal Opening with a Nephliim Blade.

And there had never been a successfully opened Veil Portal.

They had it wrapped carefully. Even amongst the Echelon only Arc did not seem afraid of it. But even he loosened the wrappings from the blade itself carefully. And took care to keep the handle well covered.

He held it before her now and the power from it shuddered through her.

And then he placed it flat against her bare flesh and the world turned golden.

That was all she could see. The gold and the light.

And the golden light illuminated the part of her the Echelon was searching for. Not to him, but to her.

And she knew instinctively that if he saw that part of her, she was done for.

The Echelon froze, sensing it. And the part of him that roamed inside her sped to it.

Rise panicked, not knowing what to do or how to block him.

But suddenly there was warm red rock. Sunlight. A cavern. Rise sat on the sandy banks of its shore, looked at the blue sapphire water before her, and waited.

She was safe here. Here was protected. Here was a haven.

The Echelon howled with fury. He stepped back from her and raised the Blade in both hands.

From her spot on the sandy shore, Rise looked calmly up at the Echelon and waited for him to plunge the Blade into her.

So be it. Here it would end. The others would not have what they wanted. But neither would these monsters.

And the Rise who sat on the shore thought it was ironic, that of all Blades, it should be this one that was used to kill her.

For she recognized it now. And a small smile played across her lips at its memory.

In the still ranks of Echelon behind the Upper with the Blade there was suddenly movement.

Arc whirled.

One of the Echelon was forward. Too far forward. He had broken ranks. This was unheard of.

"Do you have a problem, Brother?" Arc was now focused entirely on the Echelon who continued to move slowly towards him.

"Yeah. Yeah I think I do." It was a strange accent. He took another step closer to Arc. One step further away from his ranks.

As he did so, Rise leaned back into the ones holding her and kicked out straight and hard with her right leg, foot flexed.

The Echelon did not drop the Blade as she'd intended. But his head whirled towards her. It was enough. The Echelon who had broken ranks drew the gun concealed under his cloak and fired point blank into him.

He had other things beneath that cloak. Gas smoked the room. And Rise heard the sound of other small canisters popped and landing on the hard stone floor.

Behind her L4 staggered to his feet, hurling himself into the one remaining guard at her back and freeing her. The guard turned on him and lunged for her.

"Run!" L4 screamed at her before the gun shot took him. "Run!"

Rise did so.

CHAPTER FIVE

Up the stairs and into the night.

There was no time to think. She could see shadows moving across the courtyard towards her.

Rise sprinted for the building opposite.

She burst through an open doorway and skidded to a halt. The main passageway stretched before her.

Another passageway was just a little way ahead up on the right. She bolted to it and through.

There were explosions coming continually from underneath the ground now.

A huge echoing one shook the ground violently and sent plaster crumbling around her.

She shielded her hands over her head and ran the length of the smaller corridor.

She felt a rush of fresh air on her face and exalted.

Dead end.

The small, private courtyard she emerged into was old and cracked. Broken pillars were wrapped with creeping vines. Lush, green plants overran their pots. Huge statues lined the walls towering above her

Huge statues of Echelon.

Rise shuddered and halted, paralyzed with fear.

Statues. They're only statues, she said to herself, breathing deep.

But she was not alone in here.

She could feel it.

And he was stillness. Complete and utter stillness. He did not even appear to be breathing.

And then he was on her. So fast. He slammed her hard into a pillar. His hands were tight around her throat. His black visored face was a hair's breadth from her. He raised it back as if to head-butt her.

"Freeze asshole." It was another Echelon. The red tracer beam from his gun hit the black visor of the helmet. And for just a second, Rise thought she saw the eyes behind it. Dilated, pupil-less and cruel.

"You have no idea what you are dealing with here," the Echelon holding her said smoothly.

"Oh, I have a fairly good idea," the one with the gun replied. "Now back away from her, and keep your hands up or I'll blow your brains out. In 3, 2, ..."

The one holding her did as he was asked and took one small step away.

"Come here," the one with the gun held out his hand to her.

She bit her lip and hesitated.

The Echelon who had slammed her pulled a gun of his own.

Too late. The other guard shot true. But the charge on the gun was weak. The Echelon fell but rose again with speed. An explosion shook them. A large chunk of pillar falling hard on the Echelon attacker's bowed head.

"Nice," the other male muttered. He looked upwards. "I owe you one. Possibly several," he added as Rise made a desperate bid to bolt past him. He grabbed her with ease and she felt something heavy settle around her shoulder. With surprise she realized it was his cloak.

He threw her now securely bundled form over his shoulder.

The jolt when it came was unexpected. It staggered him for an instant. And he looked around for the source. It felt like her. But it couldn't be her, could it?

It shot through him again and then the auto-protect on his helmet kicked in, and he made haste out of the courtyard through the barely visible opening on the left wall.

He had to hurry. He had a ship waiting for him.

CHAPTER SIX

"Steady on violet eyes." Violet eyes. There was someone else who had just said that to her.

She stilled for a second.

The Echelon took the opportunity to inject her with a tranq and re-shoulder her.

He checked his wrist comms at the same time he used his mouth to recap the shot. The tranq was fast acting and he took a few precious seconds to readjust himself under her newly dead weight.

The opening from the courtyard led deep into a maze of corridors, twisting and turning.

Boom! Another explosion rocked them. It hid the sound of approaching boots until the very last moment. At least three pairs of them. The comms remained stubbornly blank. The approaching boots became increasingly louder. He had no choice. He had to move.

He went left.

He went left again.

The boots were louder now.

His pace quickened.

The comms clicked.

His eyes flicked to it.

Ah, so close. The door he needed was a mere ten feet up on the right. But they were on him. He couldn't risk it. His comms showed a concealed hold to the left. It would do. It would have to do. He tripped the override circuits as the first set of boots rounded the corner.

He slung Rise through, quick to follow and close down the circuit, tripping the door seemingly sealed shut from the outside once more.

Pressing his ear to the door he heard the boots move past. All but one pair. At a silent command, their owner had stayed behind, waiting.

And so, he would wait too. It was now officially a waiting game.

He hoped the ship had got the memo and was also down with that.

At least he had power. He could charge the gun. Not his first choice of firepower. But it had served its purpose and remained undetectable to them to the last.

It hooked seamlessly into the wall currents. He left it charging within easy reach and eased himself down to the ground to check the asset. Those startling violet eyes were closed now. Lips softly parted. She hardly seemed to be breathing. Gently he lifted her wrist and checked her pulse. Slow with the tranq in effect but she was fine.

He lost himself for a second, with the sudden, uncanny thought that he knew her. That he had touched her like this before. It felt almost intimate. To hold her wrist like this. He felt oddly possessive of her. He felt...

What the fark was he thinking! He didn't know her. He shook his head and dropped her wrist. It was the cloaking meds again. It had to be.

Ever since he'd been running on empty he'd been losing it like this.

The pain jabbed in his head again and he felt the momentary disorientation. The worlds flashed before his eyes like shards of glass. Shades of this one. Shades of others. Too many others.

His cloaking implant came with an expiry date. It could be topped up, but that option had dried up some time ago. He was running on an empty tank and it was farking with him. But this is what they trained for. Like Ghaniia12. It was like Ghaniia12 all over again.

Three's a charm. But three, in this instance, had not been so charming.

His first two Off-World Ops had been short and successful. He was the toast of the program. They had never had an agent do so well so early. He took to it like a duck to water. One of his Commander's joked he must have the blood of the Nephliim running through his veins. Cooper had laughed. He was a good height, broad shouldered, muscled, strong, but no towering seven-foot giant of the cosmos.

"We're a literal lot here on earth" his Commander had replied, a faraway look in his eyes. "We interpret everything through the physical. Big mystery, big actions, big ideas, big presence, big feet."

He had clasped him firmly on the shoulder. "Look past the physical Son. See through it. The real things happen behind it."

He left for Ghaniia12, six months later. Another classified Op to a place the majority of the good people on earth, did not even know existed. Hell, most of them wouldn't have believed him if he'd even been at liberty to tell them.

He would have been locked in a mental institution.

Maybe that would have been preferable to Ghaniia12.

It too should have been a short mission. This was still early days for Off-World-Black Ops. OBO. It was so off the grid Black didn't even begin to cut it. Noir Ops? Nah. Just didn't have the ring to it.

The ship to collect him had never come. For two years he had been forced to keep his cover on a supply of dirty, black market cloaking meds. The first lot almost killed him. The second, third and fourth lots weren't much better. But he built up an immunity to them.

The residents of Ghaniia12 were close enough to human forms that he could pass for one of them, barely. Still, he had to keep out of nice society and away from their security forces.

He worked the mines. Backbreaking work. Awful. Full of men like him, trying to hide. But a good place to make contacts and subtle enquiries.

He got back to earth on a string of promises. On a rebel ship under the alliance of Cortex. Cortex had been keen to make contact with the covert military operations on Earth for some time. If he could get them an Earth landing and in contact with his powers that be, they could get him home.

He did his best. Confident they would honor their promises. They honored none of them. Cortex and his rebels were forced to leave him at the Transitioning Station in the Webs. No landing granted.

He had been naive. He realized that now.

But at the end of the day it was one of Cortex's ships that had answered the call to take him home again.

Home.

Was it?

There were no heroes welcomes for OBO Agents. Few friends. No steady girl. No family. That he talked to anyway. They were ghosts. No-one knew they existed.

He'd seen things most people could not even imagine.

And he couldn't talk about it to anyone.

After Ghaniia12 he threw himself back into his work as soon as they cleared him. Mission after mission after mission. World after world after world. And then this, Moethiica.

He looked down at Rise. Potential. Potential and then some. As soon as they'd been prepared to kill Soar, he'd known she was no longer a Potential. The Echelon and the Old Ones needed the Veil Siren alive before the Portal as much as anyone.

But with Soar all they'd wanted was what she carried. And until they'd released it from her he'd been unable to ascertain exactly what.

Mind-diamonds. The Echelon knew more about the mind-diamonds than anyone. How they were linked to the sensual energies. How to mine them from those who knew they had them.

Mining them from those who didn't know they had them was relatively easy. If only people knew, they might be tempted to guard them more carefully.

But a mind-diamond that big, that distinct. This was ancient knowledge. Secret, sacred and powerful.

Secret, sacred, powerful. Echelon house specials.

Like the Potentials.

They knew. The Old Ones knew. Earth knew. Before the Veil Siren was revealed would come the Potentials. And in the end, the Star would know, or the Star would choose? Details were a little vague and foggy on that one.

Well they would know soon enough, no matter whether it was a choice or a knowing. Because the Star had risen and was hurtling at a rather alarming rate towards them.

She was in this corner of the cosmos. Whichever of the Potentials it was, they were here, or on a world close to it.

No doubt there were other peeps on those close by worlds who thought exactly like Cooper did now.

But they were wrong.

Because she was here at his feet. Siren5. Priority One. Freaking eventuated.

He just knew it. On some level he just couldn't explain, she sang it to him.

He felt the pulse in her wrist again. Still slow. She was still heavily under.

The world lurched, the shards of all the worlds cut like jagged bits of glass before his eyes. The pain in his head was unbearable and he futilely pressed his hands to either side of his black visor.

His comms lit up. They couldn't wait any longer. He had to move now.

Fark, the scout was still out there. He could sense him. He was going to have to take him out with Rise on his shoulder.

Bang. He tripped the override and burst through behind the cover of a steady stream of fire. The scout was down before he knew what hit him.

But there were more boots coming in this direction now. The first shot came fast as he tripped the landing door to the private port.

Rise jolted and murmured but stayed under.

"Cooper-Pierce-R9! Move directly to the flyer. I'll cover you."

The Second Mate who'd issued the command delivered on his promise. And Cooper was immensely relieved that the firepower now being unleashed on his pursuers was modern weaponry at its finest.

He was even more immensely relieved when the door closed behind them, and the flyer lifted instantly and smoothly away.

CHAPTER SEVEN

The flight to the mother ship was short and sweet. Incandesca3. The current pride of Cortex's fleet. An old deep space prison hauler.

Cooper was impressed. The ship was massive.

They took the flight deck cleanly and exited the flyer at speed. Cooper Pierce was still running on adrenalin. Rise was still unconscious in his arms.

"Targets secure and on board," the Second Mate relayed into his wrist-comms and then moved to take Rise from Cooper.

Cooper shook his head. He had strict orders not to let this asset out of his sight once secured. "I got her."

"Cooper Pierce you're shot," the Second Mate pointed to his arm.

Fark. He hadn't even realized. Still, he didn't want to hand her over.

But then the pain in his head jabbed, searing again. Shards of worlds like jagged glass through his eyes. The Second Mate caught him underneath the arms as he stumbled awkwardly.

There were several pairs of hands there now to take the asset.

The blackness took him and the hand that still clutched her fell loose.

"Sorry," he mumbled. As they took her away.

"Get him to the Med-Bay," the Chief Medic ordered as she took Rise's pulse. "She's fine to go straight to her quarters. A light shield grip only please."

"A *light* shield grip? Is that wise Chief Medic?" The voice was whiney. And offensive.

"Perfectly wise Celcius, and also humane," the Chief Medic, CM Gemini, replied sharply. "A value your father holds quite dear," she muttered under her breath.

"But she's a potential danger," Celcius, son of Cortex, protested.

"She is the being your father has searched the cosmos for," CM Gemini reminded him. "She'll have a light shield grip on her until we ascertain her awareness of herself and her intention. It is more than enough Celcius." She glared at him and the guards who blocked her path.

"Now, I have a patient needing surgery. If you'll get out of my way please."

Celcius stared at her, making her wait. Then he gestured his guards aside, giving the Chief Medic, and loyal serving member of his father's ridiculous rebel alliance a mock bow.

"Bitch," he muttered under his breath. Just before she passed out of earshot. But not quite.

CM Gemini ignored it. She had been called worse, and louder, in her time.

Again, she wondered how an apple could fall quite so far from the tree. Chief Medic Gemini had very little time for Celcius. They had all served his father loyally for years. But two more different men she could not imagine.

Still, he was the Commander in Chief on this ship. Cortex, declaring himself too ill to even make the flight. He was dying. They all knew it. CM Gemini pushed the thought from her mind.

"We'll take the service elevator," the Second Mate called back over his shoulder to her. He and another Aide had the stretcher with Rise.

"I'll be down to examine her as soon as I can," CM Gemini replied. The main elevator doors closed on her words. "Keep the pressure on that wound." She instructed her new Aide, Della.

She checked his pulse and nodded to herself satisfied.

"Shouldn't we take off his helmet?" Della asked, reaching for it with her other hand.

"No!" CM Gemini grabbed the woman's wrist sharply.

"This is an Echelon helmet. Connected straight through to his pineal. Not something you remove lightly or easily. He will need to calibrate from it when it comes off."

She studied it. "It certainly won't hurt his breathing. If anything, it will aide it. For all their horror, in terms of keeping someone alive and breathing under all manner of circumstances, there's no equal."

Della shivered. "It's scary looking."

"It's meant to be," CM Gemini replied. The elevator doors slid open on the Med-Bay.

The main theatre bed was already prepped. Mach, another Aide, with military field experience, took over from Della in applying pressure to the wound once he was on the bed.

A Med-Bot scanned the length of him. CM Gemini read its output and drew in her breath sharply. "How on....? That can't be right."

"What is it?" Della was at her side in an instant.

"Prepare an interim Generic Cloak and an implant unit STAT. The bullet wound's simple. But we're going to need to replace that cloaking implant."

"Oh, my godds." Della stood staring open mouthed at the screen. "How is he even......?"

"STAT Aide!" CM Gemini cut her off and moved quickly to her patient's side. The Med-Bot hovered nearby ready to anesthetize.

The visored head turned CM Gemini's way. The body on the bed began to buck and struggle.

"Bot!" CM Gemini backed away and the MedBot was on it while Mach held him down.

She scrubbed in quickly while the anesthetic took hold. They would do the bullet wound first. It wouldn't take long. Standard procedure.

The cloaking implant though. And where and how they'd inserted it. She'd never seen anything like it. CM Gemini frowned at Cooper Pierce while she took his pulse. Boy, what have they done to you?

"Aide, is that implant ready?"

"Just one second," Della drew out the words. "Ok. Ready now."

"Give it to the Bot. Bot configure to patient scan."

She looked at both Aides. "Alright, scrub in and then let's get started people. We're going to be here for a while."

CHAPTER EIGHT

They were there for a while.

It was many hours later when an exhausted Chief Medic Gemini checked on Rise.

She was still out cold which was odd, even for such a heavy tranq. "Has she come to at all?" CM Gemini asked the ship's guard watching over her.

"No," the guard shook his head. "And one of us has been here the whole time."

"She's a little warm but not too bad. Pulse is fine." She stood. "She'll keep until I've had some sleep. May as well get some of your own. I'll instruct whoever's on night watch to keep an eye on her via the flight deck monitor. If she's not woken by now, like as not she'll sleep through to morning."

The security guard nodded gratefully at her. "Thanks, Chief Medic. It's been a busy couple of days."

CM Gemini gave him a small, exhausted smile. That was an understatement. Lifting the pair of them off of Moethiica had been no easy task. They were all exhausted to the point of ridiculousness. They'd probably had six hours of sleep between the entire crew in the last forty-eight hours.

CM Gemini detoured through the flight deck on the way to her quarters. The ship was on auto-flight. The First Mate had had some much-needed sleep and was taking second watch.

"Was there no heavy pursuit from Moethiica?" she asked him. She was often not aware of such things when she was operating.

"Token., he grunted in reply. "We took some small damage to the rear left of the Hold. But Cortex is right. She's a beauty." He patted the deck console before him appreciatively.

"Were you able to repair it?" She shivered. The ship was a beauty. And the fact that they'd been able to penetrate the Moethiican webs with it and remain completely cloaked and shielded, no small feat. She liked its capabilities. She just didn't like its history. Prison haulers were evil beasts.

"We can't get down there," the First Mate replied. "Celcius's got the Hold completely sealed off. Only he's got the codes. He took a look at the damage assessment and said not to worry about it," the First Mate shrugged. "Can't argue with the Commander."

He patted the console again. "She'll hold until Vade5."

"Hmmm." Ridiculous on this particular flight they should even think about stopping on Vade5. But Celcius was adamant. Other business, equally as important, was all he'd say.

CM Gemini yawned. Gave the First Mate strict instructions to wake her at the first sign of movement from either of their two new passengers.

She took herself to bed and fell instantly asleep.

Three hours later and the ship was quiet and still. The First Mate rechecked the monitor. The winged Moethiican female was still asleep. In-fact she didn't even looked like she'd moved since he'd first looked at her.

The Earth Agent was still out and still in that damn helmet. They all had strict instructions not to remove it. Not to even touch it. Under any circumstances.

"Not that there's anybody who'd want to touch a damn Echelon helmet," the First Mate muttered to himself and turned away from the monitor to busy himself with some minor repairs on a malfunctioning comms unit.

~~~~~

It was the heat that woke her. She was so warm. Blinking her eyes, she kicked off her blanket. Blanket? Where had she gotten one of those from?

Rise sat up and looked slowly around the room. Her head was ridiculously groggy. Even the smallest movement seemed hard.

She knew that heavy feeling. They had a shield grip on her. She began to panic. And her heart began to pound.

She'd had a heavy one on her once when she was younger. Hideous things.

Technology designed to adapt itself to your essence and link to your very core. Transparent, virtually invisible, the weight of a shield grip is like mountains bearing down on you. Physically, emotionally and mentally it weighs you down and drains you.

They make the smallest movement hard. And painful. And escape impossible. This was a light one. But even with a light one, the same rules applied.

Escape.

Memories of recent events came flooding back in, vague and disordered.

She drew her knees up and hugged her arms around them. The heavy fabric encasing her was course against her arms.

There was a shuttered window beside her. She reached out cautiously and tested the mechanism. Locked but un-lockable.

Coming on to her knees in front of it, she unlocked it quietly and eased it up a fraction.

It was dark outside. Strange lights. She waited, heart pounding and counted to ten. Nothing. There mustn't be anyone out there. She pushed the rest of the shutter up.

Rise's mouth dropped open. "Oh, my godds." It came out almost as a whisper.

Desperately she blinked her eyes and shook her head. She shut her eyes tightly for thirty seconds and reopened them. Slowly. But it was still there. No mirage. No illusion.

Her heart was beating so loud and so fast she thought it would burst out of her. She put both hands on the thick glass pane and looked out at the scene before her in wonder.

Stars and moons and nebula and meteors and rocks, and the odd bit of space junk, moved gracefully before her in an exquisite dance on the background of an ink black sky.

Space. She was in space.

As high as she flew on Junar Run was as far as she'd ever been from the surface of Moethiica.

She was in space. How long had she coveted this? Rise smiled.

She was so distracted by what was before her, she didn't feel the pain.

It was the light flashing in the reflection that caught her eye. Because it was coming from inside the room, right behind her.

There was heat too. Right on her back. Pain. Twisting and turning she scrambled from the bed to the small adjoining bathroom.

Rising up out of her cloak, the upper tips of her tightly bound wings were glowing. And the visual on the pain knocked everything sharply into focus. They were burning. Her wings were burning. And she had to get this cloak off of her.

She pulled at it and screamed in agony as her melted wings came with it.

Rise flung herself into the shower, and blasted herself under a torrent of cold water.

It did nothing. If anything, it felt like the water was making her wings burn hotter. When she looked in the mirror there were flames shooting up about her.

She hit the cabin door. Locked. She pounded, kicked and screamed for help while her wings burned. Over and over again.

The small view hatch opened.

A pair of eyes stared in at her.

"Open the door! Godds! Help me! Please help me!" Rise screamed.

But the owner of the eyes did nothing. Just watched her. Desperately Rise tried to reach her hand through the hatchway.

The owner of the eyes stepped back. Smirked at her. It caught her hand. Painfully.

Rise screamed again and then she heard a door explode open. A man's voice yelled, "Stand back!"

The hand released her. A male voice answered. "I was trying to comfort her. All the doors are stuck."

He moved to the side out of her vision. Another face appeared in his place, his eyes growing wide and a little panicked at the site of her. "Get away from the door. I'm going to blast it."

Rise stumbled back into the bathroom doorway. She was in so much pain now it was hard to stay conscious.

A goodly portion of the door exploded in the blast. There were more voices and footsteps out there now. Someone threw a fire blanket over her.

Two of them lifted her from the room.

Her head lolled. The pain was too much. Rise was getting mighty sick of people injecting her with all types of shiz, but she would have welcomed any form of oblivion now.

It came, but her own body supplied it. She was safe. It let itself shut down completely. The body is clever beyond all reason and merciful like that at times.

CHAPTER NINE

In an ancient tunnel on Moethiica, two beings passed each other silently. The stones under their heavy boots were well worn over many thousands of years.

The roof of the tunnel curved gently over them. Above that roof, above the many layers of hard packed earth it rested under, snaked the inner sanctum of Moethiica's power hub.

The silver enclosed tunnels and corridors zigzagged and curved and connected the various levels in a maze-like formation. One had to know exactly where they were going to get there successfully.

That above however, was all for show.

It was beneath the surface, in these ancient tunnels that those with real power walked. And where real decisions were made.

One of these beings wore the uniform of a Moethiican Echelon. The other did not, but he was also disguised. The mask that covered his face was more ancient than these walls and used only for meetings such as this and for ceremony.

He breathed in the power of it as he walked. And it was even more intoxicating and addictive than the ceremonies themselves.

The two beings passed each other.

They did not stop.

Only one of them spoke.

And he spoke in a tongue that was as rare as those who had access to these corridors of power. Who even knew they existed.

It was a very Old Tongue.

A magical tongue. Able to bind and render.

But it was not used for magic here. It was used simply to convey and disguise a message.

It was a message many had waited for and would set a chain of pre-planned actions in motion.

"The Siren of the 5th has awoken."

There was no acknowledgement.

But the Echelon felt the power contained in the mask lash out at him as he passed it.

A feeling of nausea and revulsion washed over him as it touched him. Fear prickled his skin.

It knew. Somehow it knew she had eluded and escaped them. But the man behind the mask did not need to know that.

He winced slightly, still in pain from the spy's gun wound. He was lucky to be alive at all. But the man behind the mask did most certainly not need to know about any of those events either.

A wild night gone awry. They had explained away the entertainment room explosions.

He closed his mind on those thoughts and pushed his way through the fear. He sent the power behind the mask images of what his men had done to the bitch winged rebel, Soar.

The power behind the mask was pleased with that. It responded with a heady rush of power that was intoxicating.

The power behind the mask was hungry and eager for the coming war.

It was imperative that when the Veil opened, it should be them in possession and control of the Siren.

He would leave on the morrow.

But first, there was other business to attend to. The rebel, winged whore was still a little bit alive. Not enough to do much but enough to feel everything he had planned to do to her. He smiled to himself. He must stop thinking of her as winged. Because those had long been torn from her.

She would suffer for passing the mind-diamond to the Siren. And she would plead for her death before he gave it to her.

CHAPTER TEN

When Cooper Pierce came to he could feel the scars. The old ones. And the fresh new ones.

It hurt to move. But he was conscious, he was breathing. It was a vast improvement.

"I need this helmet off."

Chief Medic Gemini had looked at him doubtfully. "Are you sure you're up to calibrating? It will take a lot out of you."

He shook his head. "I don't need to calibrate straight away. So long as I do it within the next seventy-two hours I'll be fine. But they are tracking me. I can feel them. I need it off Chief Medic. Now."

The eyeless visor had fixed her with a stare. If that was possible. It was creepy. You sensed the face as clearly as if you were seeing it. But it was amplified. Every nuance of the face amplified in emotionless blankness.

CM Gemini shook herself. They were designed like that. It was meant to.

She looked away, letting the Bot watch over patient and process. It seemed a private thing to remove something so intimately attached to you.

She heard a hiss as the final part of the mechanism released. And then a grunt as he removed the pineal needle.

"No. I'll keep it with me." CM Gemini turned as the Bot beeped and moved back. It must have reached for the helmet.

She had dealt with a similar type of helmet used on another Old Ones world. Even without it on he would still have its energy running through him for a time. And he would be possessive of it.

It would be better for all of them when he had calibrated and the thing was well and truly off. Or as off as something like that could be. He was like to be a tad aggressive until then. They had best tread carefully.

As for the helmet, it was a CyTech living thing. She did her best not to look at it.

But she could not miss the blood on the pineal needle as he retracted it into the helmet before settling it beside him.

CM Gemini shuddered. She would not look at the helmet. She would look at Earth Agent Cooper Pierce instead.

Because he was a vision.

Chiseled face. Square jaw. Strong brow. Close cropped, dark, sandy blonde hair. Masculine. Military. He looked every inch a soldier. A drop dead gorgeous soldier though, to be sure.

CM Gemini stood gazing at him too long for just the tiniest of seconds.

And then those penetrating eyes shot up at her, alert and ready for action.

And food. "Any chance of a meal CM? I'm pretty hungry."

"You'll be sick this soon coming out from being under," she cautioned him.

She was rewarded with a smile. "I've been under and come out the other end ravenous many times CM. Never been sick. Not gonna happen now."

"Ok." She turned to Mach.

"I got it," he replied without being asked, leaving Cooper to the administrations of the Bot and CM Gemini.

"When can I get up?" He asked her when they were done with their scanning and testing.

"When I say so," she responded drily.

She had explained already what had happened to his cloaking implant and how they'd fixed it.

He got how serious it was. But he was like many soldiers she treated. Once something was fixed, that was the end of it. He was not going to spend a whole lot of time thinking about it and fussing over it.

It was an admirable sentiment, but in the case of most of them, and especially the impatient one before her, could have done with some tempering.

"Rest," she had commanded him as she left him. "You'll not leave that bed until I say so."

"Aye, aye, Chief." She had been rewarded with another smile.

Jackdaw was hovering outside. He and Cooper had a history and a friendship, that much she knew and no further.

"Can I see him?" Jackdaw asked. He was a nuggety fellow with a wizened face and farseeing, somber eyes. He was an exceptional pilot, a recruiter, a jack of all trades, a loyal soldier of the rebellion.

More Cortex's son than Celcius, CM Gemini thought to herself. And not for the first time. It was a thought echoed by many of them.

It had been a shock to all of them when they boarded the ship and found Celcius there.

Not only there but in command. She wondered how Jackdaw was taking it so well and smiled at him.

"Yes. But only for a few minutes. And absolutely no mention of the girl."

"I promise," Jackdaw nodded.

"Alright. A few minutes," CM Gemini reminded him and then went on her way.

"Cooper," Jackdaw grasped his hand. "Friend, it's good to see you."

"And you, Jackdaw." He raised his eyebrows. "Not the way I would have expected though."

"Happens to the best of us," Jackdaw smiled. "You'll be up and about in no time." He settled back in a chair close to the bed and folded his arms. "From what I can gather you're a bit of a miracle man. Gemini has no idea how you managed to keep cloaking yourself on Moethiica of all places."

"Practice?" Cooper shrugged. "I've had to do it before."

"Yeah, but Moethiica?" Jackdaw said incredulously. "Amongst the Echelon? That's got to be the toughest gig in the Cosmos."

Cooper grunted. "It wasn't easy, especially towards the end."

Jackdaw shook his head again. "But you did it. You still did it. I can't believe you… How did you find her?" He leaned forward intently.

Cooper grimaced. "I'd infiltrated but only as a lower. Towards the end I knew one of the Uppers was on to me. He confronted me one night. Alone. His mistake."

He paused and took a sip of water, the effort to talk obviously wearing on him.

"I took his Helmet. His uniform. His place amongst them. I kept my mouth shut. Right place, right time. They brought her into an Upper Meet and I was there."

Jackdaw whistled and looked at him appraisingly, knowing that this version of events was a greatly simplified version of the actual events that had actually transpired. But as much as anyone was like to be getting. Typical Cooper. He didn't press him further, simply commenting. "You are one lucky son-of-a-bitch. Someone up there likes you."

Cooper smiled grimly. "You don't know the last of it." Confirming his suspicions.

"And the Blade?" Jackdaw asked him.

Cooper shook his head. "Did my best. Couldn't get it."

"A shame," Jackdaw mused. "But at the end of the day, she's the most important part." He smiled at Cooper. "And they'll have to bring it with them to Earth now anyway."

Cooper grunted. He looked suddenly grey and tired and Jackdaw reached out a strong hand to lay on his arm.

"You're exhausted. I'll leave you to rest." Jackdaw rose to leave but turned back suddenly to him.

"It's good to see you friend. Now rest up. It's a while before we get to Vade5."

"Why are we stopping on Vade5?" Cooper asked curiously and suddenly very much more awake.

"Picking up some essential cargo," Jackdaw replied, rolling his eyes. He raised his hands in the air when Cooper looked mutinous. "Out of my hands friend. It's Celcius calling the shots here now. Rest," he added pointedly.

He was almost out of the door when Cooper asked, "How is she?"

Jackdaw cursed silently before he turned back to him.

Cooper pounced on the pause.

"How is she, Jackdaw?" he repeated, a little bit more forcefully.

"She's fine, friend. She had a bit of a rough patch first night on board but she's going to be fine," Jackdaw said brightly. He turned quickly in the direction of the door.

Cooper's voice grew quiet. "Jackdaw. What's going on? Talk to me."

"Nothing's going on, Cooper Pierce. And you need to rest. Gemini said I was only allowed a few minutes. I'll come see you again tomorrow."

"Jackdaw!" Cooper called angrily.

But he was gone and it was the Chief Medic who poked her head around the door. "Everything all right?"

"Fine," Cooper replied steadily. "Everything's fine." One cheek muscle twitched just a little as he said it.

"Alright," she replied a little hesitantly, not sure whether to believe him or not. "Well, rest Cooper Pierce. And lots of it."

"Yes, Chief Medic."

She pursed her lips and looked like she was going to say something else, but then just rolled her eyes and disappeared out the door. It had been a very unconvincing 'Yes Chief Medic.' But she knew his kind. There was little point in arguing with him. And she had a remote comms consult to get to re Rise.

Adrenalin is a wonderful thing. And the adrenalin of knowing something was seriously fucking wrong was coursing through Cooper's veins.

It would not be the first time he'd left a Med-Bay bed early and against a Chief Medic's wishes.

He pulled the IV from his arm with practiced efficiency.

He wondered where they had his weapon. It wasn't much but he would rather be with it than without it. He'd back himself against anyone and three of their closest friends hand to hand any day.

But weapons were always handy when everyone else was carrying them.

He eased himself from the bed and made his way cautiously out the door.

The ship appeared to be standard Federation design.

Cooper wondered idly how they'd gotten their hands on it, and was thankful that they had.

The Federation were not much into design innovation or deviating from the plan in the layout of their ships. And Cooper was more than familiar with said layout.

He had been in room three. There would be only two other Med-Bays like it on this ship. He would check these before he headed for the quarters.

He could hear CM Gemini's voice in the second room. It sounded like she was consulting with someone via remote comms.

The first room then.

An Aide turned suddenly into the corridor and Cooper concealed himself quickly in a small supply and gurney alcove.

The Aide was in and out of the first room quickly.

She did not look happy.

The golden yellow glow of a Stasis Chamber glowed as she shut the door quietly.

The Aide knocked quietly on the door to the second room, and entered at CM Gemini's bidding.

Cooper moved quickly across the corridor and into the first room containing the Stasis Chamber.

He shut the door quickly and quietly behind him.

He moved in close and looked down into the chamber.

He clenched his fists, taking a well-schooled deep breath and exhaling deeply.

"Who did this to her?" He got it out low and a rumble, almost like a growl, between clenched teeth.

He had heard someone enter the room behind him.

"Who did this to her? Don't bullshit me." He repeated.

"We believe it was the Echelon Cloak," Mach, the Aide, replied cautiously. And not convincingly.

"What else?"

Mach hesitated and then squared himself. He was going to see the footage anyway.

"Her room was locked on the outside. She couldn't get out. Celcius was there. But he didn't open the door. Said he couldn't. They blasted it open eventually. But when they ran the data it was his over-ride code that had locked the doors and taken out the cameras."

"He watched her burning." Cooper said it briskly, business like.

"Yes."

Cooper nodded. "Where do I find him?"

"His quarters? The bridge?" Mach shrugged. "I don't know. Cooper Pierce, he's Cortex's son and Commander in Chief of this ship. And you should be back in your bed. You can't do anything to him. We just have to watch over her."

"Thank you." Cooper looked up at him from Rise. "Where is my gun?"

"I don't know. Cooper Pierce, you can't. He's his son."

"Thank you," Cooper replied. "I'm well aware of who his father is. I know him well. Stay with her. I don't want her left alone again."

The way he said it was cool, calm, matter of fact. The look on his face was thunderous.

"Oh, fuck," Mach cursed as Cooper stormed past him.

Shit was about to go well and truly down.

CHAPTER ELEVEN

Cooper found him on the bridge.

Cooper was not at his best.

But it's hard to be at your best when you should still be in your Med-Bay bed and have no business being up and about and in people's faces.

It gave Celcius false confidence.

He stayed close to the Third Mate. He'd stayed close to the crew since the 'incident.' Mainly because it prevented them from talking about him. Now it was more about safety in proximity and numbers.

Cooper Pierce was sans helmet and sans uniform. And when all was said and done he'd been an imposter in the helmet and uniform anyway.

But you don't get to imposter a Moethiican Echelon, without being a little bit all sorts of dangerous and scary on your own. Sans uniform, sans helmet, sans anything.

But substance is as substance does and people with little of it, too often judge the world in their own likeness.

Celcius judged Cooper poorly. And not only that, he smirked.

The hit was guaranteed. The smirk simply made it land harder and truer.

The bridge stood in conscious, stunned silence.

Celcius lay in unconscious, stunned silence, on the ground.

There had been no conversation before the exceptional right hook.

There was no conversation now.

Cooper simply left the bridge and returned to Rise's side.

When neither the Chief Medic nor the Aides could persuade him back to bed, they bought him food and clothes. It took some doing, but the CM Gemini made him have a shower before he put on the clothes. He did so only after one of the Aides brought him his helmet. The CM had put it in a Med-Box.

He opened it, satisfied himself that all was in order and set it on the floor underneath his chair. Because the chair beside Rise was his chair now. He took the shower in the small bathroom off her room. It was barely two minutes. He left the door open.

There is a contact-port on modern stasis chambers that lets you rest your hand over the hand of the chamber's occupant. You're not touching but there are senses. You can feel something. And on waking, many occupants say they were aware of the contact and found it soothing.

Cooper was less concerned with this than he was with being instantly aware of any change in her condition.

But Chief Medic Gemini had seen many times, the excellent affect this could have on healing. This could be good for the girl. So, propped up with pillows and covered with a blanket, she was happy to leave him there.

Jackdaw had secured a guard loyal to him to take turns with him standing watch at the door. CM Gemini came and went. But for the most part, he was left alone with Rise in relative peace and silence.

He was beyond exhausted and his chair was comfortable. He stayed stubbornly awake for many hours. But eventually, with no immediate drama presenting itself, he closed his eyes.

Gemini looked up from her monitors. "She knows he's there," she observed quietly. "Her activities changed dramatically since he's been sitting there. Had they known each other before this I wonder?"

"I asked him that earlier when he was awake, and no, not at all. He'd never even seen her before," Mach replied tiredly, stifling a yawn.

"You should get some sleep yourself," the Chief Medic observed mildly. "I'm here now and he'll wake up if she's in danger you know." "I've seen this sleep before on types like him. It's like a system going into sleep mode until it needs to do something."

"I know," Mach replied. He made no move to get up though. Staying lost in his own thoughts for a time.

"Why now?" he said suddenly, breaking the silence. "Why Celcius? I know he's his son, but how can he not see through him? How could Cortex put him in charge of this ship? I don't get it Chief Medic. I just don't get it."

"Blood ties make us do funny things," CM Gemini replied. "But there's more to this than that. Cortex believes in the Foretold. That those who accompany the Siren to her destination are vital to it succeeding in their favor."

"But they're so vague," Mach said doubtfully. "I don't know how you'd ever tell who was who. And I certainly don't know how you'd get Celcius out of it."

"It's different from that though," Gemini said thoughtfully.

"That's more what it's watered down to be. But the purists see it more about who's there at the time, rather than deciding in advance who that should be." She shrugged. "Maybe Cortex hopes that by placing him here, it will be the catalyst for change within Celcius."

"I know he sees the best in everyone, but sometimes I think his faith in some people is misguided," Mach replied glumly. "He's not regained consciousness?" he asked Gemini kindly, suddenly mindful of the Rebel Leader's own status.

He knew they were close. Had a long history.

"No," Gemini replied with a small choke in her voice.

"I'm sorry," Mach said.

He gestured at Rise. "Do you think she'll wake anytime soon?"

"No," the CM replied. "And nor would I want her to with burns like those." She checked the readouts again. "He's having a mighty effect on her though. She's coming along in leaps and bounds."

Mach halfheartedly stifled another yawn. "You know Celcius will try to have him thrown into a cell when he's brave enough."

"I'm rather surprised he hasn't already," The CM replied, with a tinge of worry. "It's strange we've heard nothing from him. I don't like it. I'd almost prefer one of his usual tantrums to this strange silence."

"Maybe he's too frightened of Cooper Pierce," Mach replied hopefully.

"Hmmm," CM Gemini replied doubtfully. "I rather think it's more likely that he's plotting something."

She was about to add something when the bulk of Doon, the trusted ship's guard, brought about a partial eclipse of all light coming through the door.

Mach stood. "Ok, that is my cue to get some sleep. I'll be back after some shut eye."

CM Gemini smiled at him. "Get a good sleep. We'll be fine here."

"Will do," Mach replied. No matter how tired he was he would not have left CM Gemini alone with Cooper asleep and no Doon at the door.

"Any sign of the oxygen thief?" Doon asked him as he left.

"None," Mach replied and Doon grunted.

Prior to joining Cortex's Rebels, Doon had lost everyone he cared about to Old Ones' atrocities. The winged beauty in the stasis chamber in the room he was guarding was the key to the end of their reign.

And the man sleeping beside her had knocked the little oxygen thief unconscious with a single blow.

He, like most of the ship's crew, worshipped Cortex, and despised Celcius.

The Siren of the 5th was the hope of the Cosmos. But Cooper Pierce was their new local hero.

CHAPTER TWELVE

Cooper grunted. His body jerked in that half sleep, half waking state, and he woke.

The Med-Bay was quiet and dark. The only lights coming from the stasis chamber. It threw an eerie red glow on the gleaming equipment and walls around him.

His hand still rested in the contact-portal. And it was hot. Almost unbearably so, but not quite. He had a strange compunction to leave it there regardless.

The thought struck him that a stasis chamber like this one usually glowed yellow. But his hand continued to glow red with the rest of it. He could see the bones of his hand now underneath his hot, red, skin.

Rise's hand was raised, pressed up to meet his own, against the roof of the contact-portal.

Her hand glowed like his and her wings burned, even in the chamber.

The pain in his hand was suddenly excruciating. Desperately he tried to pull it free but a vice like grip held it trapped there.

He looked at Rise.

And the jolt ripped through him as her eyes opened.

Just like when he'd first picked her up. But times 1000.

She turned to look at him and from her lips came a whisper for his ears only.

Except the whisper was a crescendo and he thought his head would burst with it.

He screamed and pulled back. And suddenly he was awake. Both hands cold and safe. Pressed tightly to his ears.

The Stasis Chamber glowed yellow. Rise was still, the Med-Bay was lit and humming gently with quiet, efficient machines.

"Bad dream?" Della's voice made him jump. When he turned she was leaning against one of the gleaming medical cabinets. Had she been watching him?

He shook his head, trying to clear it and stood abruptly, putting a little distance between himself and the chamber.

Chief Medic Gemini swept into the room. She through Della a glance as if surprised to see her there. The Aide moved quickly and quietly to the far side of the room.

"You're awake," Gemini said to Cooper brightly.

He ran his hand through his hair. A habit. A nervous gesture. It came away soaked with sweat. "Yeah. How long have I been out?"

"Two shift changes," CM Gemini replied briskly, moving swiftly to her readouts. "I told you, you should still be in bed and not sitting up like this." She looked thoughtfully at Rise's readings. "Although I must say you're still having a remarkable effect on her healing."

She walked over to the chamber and her eyebrows shot up in surprise at the state of Rise. "More than remarkable."

Cooper leaned forward and peered cautiously into the chamber. "Fark," He said quietly. He had just looked at her. And no matter his dazed state, he would have put good money on the fact that she did not look like this before.

Rise's cheeks were pink and glowing. The skin on her body almost healed. Her ruined wings were re-sprouting. Not only lush, sleek, black adult plumes, but here and there, soft violet baby feathers.

"She's sprouting baby wings," he said quietly.

The Chief Medic nodded. "Complete regeneration where the damage was too much. On its own that's enough. But the speed of this." She shook her head. "I've never seen anything like it."

"Trouble coming." Doon was suddenly in the room. He took up a protective position at the foot of the stasis chamber. The impressive looking blaster he wore constantly across his chest was now pointed at the door.

Jackdaw came through it. "I'm sorry," he said to Cooper. Anguish on his face. "I'm sorry."

Cooper moved swiftly, but the room was already a swarm with guards, guns drawn.

And these were new guards. Celcius's own. No-one had even been aware they'd been on the ship.

The specially sealed prison hold, CM Gemini thought grimly.

She placed a protective hand over the stasis chamber. "If any of you fire anything in here and hit this chamber we're all done for." She said sharply. "This thing will blow and take us all with it."

Not entirely true. But worth a shot that none of them knew any better.

"Move!" The voice was whiney, imperious. Celcius marched up to stand before Doon. "Get away from that chamber you big lug."

The only movement which emanated from Doon was the play of the nasty things he would like to do to Celcius from his steady eyes.

One of the guards placed his gun against CM Gemini's head. Another pointed her gun straight at Rise.

"Easy," Jackdaw spoke quietly but authoritatively. "Let's not anyone do anything silly here. Celcius, you don't want to do this. Think about your father. Think about the movement. The alliance."

"Fuck the alliance. Fuck the movement. Fuck my idiot father." Celcius rolled his eyes and threw back his head and gave a short bark of laughter.

"Godds I've been wanting to say that out loud for the longest time."

CM Gemini's voice shook with anger. "You are mad, Celcius. Out of your mind. Your father will never forgive you for this."

"My father is dying you stupid bitch. And his ridiculous movement with him."

He looked her up and down. "It's quite lucky for you that Lok still believes in this superstitious nonsense and wants you all alive. If I had my say in things, you'd be enjoying a slightly different fate."

"Take them to the Prison Hold," he commanded sharply.

Jackdaw motioned Goon to stand down. Goon did so but not without a deep throated growl. He knew the name. They all knew the name. Lok was Cortex's sworn enemy. Selling out his own father to the enemy. The little oxygen thief had outdone himself.

The guard nearest to him took his gun.

There was a guard with a gun at all their heads now. The one pointed at Rise had not faltered. Cooper glared at her and she stared back at him impassively.

"The prison hold," Celcius repeated contemptuously, then turned on his heel and exited the room.

While his guards supervised the move of his father's fools to the hold, Celcius made his way hurriedly to the bridge.

Too long he had been dragged along in this pathetic game of Cortex's. Too long been derided and dismissed by the sad sycophants who followed every word the man said.

Pathetic.

And all for some ridiculous superstition about some winged whore and a Veil Portal.

Celcius didn't like superstitions. He had no interest in the unseen. He liked things he could touch and use and spend.

Money. Celcius very much liked money. And all the delicious things that accompanied it.

The bridge was quiet when he entered it. There were more of his own guards here. The old crew kept their heads bowed.

Yes, you'll all show a little respect now, thought Celcius smugly to himself as he sat down at his console.

It had all gone so beautifully. The false vid feed showing an empty prison hold and sealing the locks with the over-ride code had worked superbly. A pity about the whore's wings when he'd jammed all the doors and feeds inadvertently.

He hoped it wouldn't decrease her price.

Oh well, getting to watch her burn like that, had been a reward in itself.

And it was hardly his fault they'd been too stupid to take an Echelon cloak off her when she first arrived here.

He keyed the sequence into the comms unit.

"It's done," he said as soon as Lok answered.

"Excellent. Well done Celcius. You are cleared to land on Vade9. Proceed to this address" - he sent it - "and wait for me there. "Lok instructed calmly.

"Affirmative." Celcius's whiney voice sounded self-important and pleased. He shut down the comms link and looked out at the magnificent expanse of space before him. He would set himself up nicely on Vade9 with the riches awaiting him. Godds but he couldn't wait to be done with this shit.

Lok turned slowly and cautiously to the Moethiican Echelon resting deceptively casually on the counter edge behind him. "It is done," he said.

"It most certainly is," replied the Echelon and gestured for him to lead the way out of the room.

When they put the gun to his head Lok was not surprised.

Just glad that he had had the sense to get his children and wife out the minute these bastards had contacted him.

Or so he thought. And it was a comforting thought to die on.

The reality of what actually befell them he was better off not knowing.

CHAPTER THIRTEEN

The prison hull was vast.

A grated, narrow metal corridor ran its length, twenty-five feet up, suspended by heavy steel cable from the ceiling above.

It was the same level as the cells which were no longer cells. Now they were used for storage and cargo of smaller items.

In the main floor area, the larger cargo crates, some of them fifteen feet tall, were pushed back against the walls. Some of them had been dragged into position to section off areas of the main floor of the hold by its most recent occupants.

This was the old rec space. The bolted down tables and chairs had been ripped up. In their place, old steel camper beds had been moved in and secured for the use of Celcius's guards.

Who would no doubt enjoy the contrast of the vacated private quarters of those now down here.

Cooper secured his Echelon helmet back on top of his uniform in the Med-Case. At least he still had these. They could prove invaluable studies on Earth. Plus, he still need to calibrate and completely shut down the helmet. Smart of the Chief Medic to put these items in a Med-Case. Even smarter to seal it for quarantine while he'd been out. There was more to CM Gemini than met the eye. Cooper was sure of it.

Their beds were in the middle of the area. There was a sizable communal bathroom, a small Med-Bay and a galley area all down one end of the space.

The door to the Med-Bay was too small to maneuver the stasis chamber through. And it was already jam packed with a bed, a single chair and med equipment of its own.

But there was a partial wall to form a waiting room just outside of it. It would do. It would do nicely. Gemini and Della positioned the chamber in the alcove, Doon and Jackdaw helping them. Mach was not amongst them and Gemini prayed for his safety.

When they moved back to the main area where the camper beds were, Rise was hidden from sight, only the yellow glow of the stasis chamber showing.

That and the green Exit lights were the brightest lights in the hold.

There were other lights, high up in the roof above, and the occasional remaining working one along the cell corridors. But apart from that the hull was a gloomy, hulking darkness.

Della inspected the bathroom and galley. Both were basic but stocked with at least a few days supplies.

She told the others as much.

"How long will she be in there?" Jackdaw gestured back to Rise.

"The move doesn't seem to have upset her too much. I would say at least another two days, but at the speed she's recovering she could come out of it at any time now to be honest," Gemini replied.

"She had better be out of it before we need to change ships," Cooper muttered matter-of-factly, engrossed in a small device he had procured from his Echelon uniform.

CM Gemini looked at him sharply. "All deep spacers have stasis chambers and Lok's is no different. Surely Celcius doesn't mean to have her change chambers? Surely they will just swap for an empty one from Lok's?"

Cooper said nothing, just shrugged, poker faced.

Jackdaw looked at his shrewdly. "Know something we don't know, Cooper Pierce?"

"Why would I?" He regarded him steadily, giving away nothing.

Jackdaw looked at him questioningly, but didn't push it further.

"Now, time for food I think," the Chief Medic said.

Cooper rose. "I'm going to scout this place and give it the once over," he said, already looking around him. "Then we eat. Get some shut eye."

He moved off in the direction of the far end of the hold.

"I'll come with you." Doon trotted off after him.

Jackdaw smiled and placed a hand on CM's arm. "It's alright Doc. I'll go with him, make sure he doesn't over exert himself."

"Thank you, Jackdaw," CM said gratefully and turned to Della. "Now come on, let's see about fixing something eat-worthy."

"#Stereotyping," Della muttered. Staring off after the men. "Will we be expected to cook for her too when she wakes up?" She gestured, almost dismissively at Rise.

CM Gemini found both her tone and her question off and looked at her sharply. "No-one expects you to cook anything for anyone Della," she replied. "I thought it might help you take your mind off things. I'm quite capable of preparing anything I find in there by myself. As are any of the men here. Perhaps you'd best take a lie down."

The Aide tried to protest but CM Gemini waived her away. Della was new on the last few trips and still didn't sit quite right with the Doc. She would have much preferred that Mach be down here with them. And right now, she wanted some distance from her.

While CM Gemini put a modest meal together in the galley, and Della sulked on her bed, the men worked in companionable and efficient silence.

Before they re-joined the women, Doon posed a question to Cooper. "What do your Earth bosses think of this Foretold business?"

It was a smart question. If Cooper was in his position he would do the same. Try to find out just how expendable or valuable he was likely to be, when crunch time came.

It deserved an honest answer.

"Some believe it. Some think it's a crock. 50/50 split I would imagine. Still, if it keeps us all alive buddy, I'll sing its validity from the rooftops."

Doon grunted. And they joined the others to eat.

CHAPTER FOURTEEN

Cooper and Jackdaw met in the mines on Ghannia12. They were both there seeking the same thing. Cover, questions, answers, a way out. Jackdaw had ended up there on a rebel mission gone horribly wrong. He joked that Cooper had ended up there for the same.

Cooper had laughed but responded that Earth were no rebels, just wanting to get to know their neighbors a little better.

Jackdaw had given him that look. Raising one eyebrow at him, but letting the subject lie.

Jackdaw had saved his ass many a time in the mines. He was that shortish, nuggety build that proves the better of many bigger opponents. He was good in a fight and knew how to end them quickly.

He also knew how not to start them in the first place.

Cooper was still young, but already wise beyond his years. There were not many young men - on Earth anyway - who had undergone the training he'd undergone, and seen the things he'd seen, done the things he'd done.

But he was still young enough to get into fights he could just have easily avoided. And still young enough to enjoy some of them. Just a little.

But then again, Cooper was no slouch in a fight either.

Jackdaw watched him for a time, on instinct took him under his wing, and taught him to pick his fights carefully.

He also secured a better line of cloaking meds.

They were still black market and still disgusting. But less likely to be fatal. And that was 100% improvement.

"Barbaric fucking method," Jackdaw had muttered about the implant, the last time Cooper had collapsed from a particularly nasty batch.

Too weak to inject himself with the replacement Jackdaw had found, he let the other man do it for him.

Slowly he withdrew the small syringe and quickly gave Cooper a medi-swab to hold against the needle's entry site.

There were all sorts of airborne delights in the mines of Ghaniia12. And any sort of open wound could fester quickly.

Cooper laughed weakly. "It might be barbaric to you but this is high tech for us. Beyond the realms of what's even considered possible."

Jackdaw had just shaken his head. He had questioned Cooper once, and once only, on the true intentions of the good people of Earth behind him.

Cooper was steadfastly loyal to his world, his commanders and his people. It was the only sore point between them, and to Jackdaw, not a fight worth picking.

Besides, Jackdaw's next port of call was supposed to have been Earth's outer webs. It would be impossible for him to get there now without assistance. His leader, Cortex, had long sought a meeting with those Earth leaders who stood outside of the game. To contact them from the outer webs was the first step towards it.

Jackdaw put it to him. If Cortex came, could Cooper get him audience?

If they could get him back to the transitioning station in Earth's outer webs, Cooper could get them audience, he was sure of it.

He knew they had the capability to land Off-World ships on Earth. He was just not privy to the finer details of it.

But that was history now. The right messenger had been found. Cortex had come. They had got him to the transitioning station. But no landing and no audience had been granted.

Still, they held no grudges to Cooper.

And if he found himself in a pinch or a tight spot it was still these men he called.

And these men who came to him.

~ ~ ~ ~ ~

Jackdaw spun her through the air and she giggled in delight. "You have to let her fly. She's got wings," he said to her mother, holding the child high above his head and fixing her with his best Jackdaw smile.

Her mother was not 100% convinced on this subject.

"But she's so little," she said.

"She's adorable," Jackdaw said, throwing her up in the air so her wings unfurled while her mother suppressed the urge to snatch her away from him. Catching her quite securely, Jackdaw turned to her mother with that serious take to his eyes that she seemed quite partial to.

"She'll be full grown before you know it. And she's just going to try it by herself at some stage anyway. Better she learns properly now while she's small." He paused. "You don't even have to come along. I know it would kill you to watch her. I'll take her."

The child regarded them both, feeling like she was going to explode with anticipation if they took more than five seconds to work this out. Explode with disappointment if her mother said no. And explode with excitement if she said yes. When she ruefully shook her devastatingly beautiful head and said yes, all the child actually did was remember to breathe again.

She remembered her young self being deliriously happy and content with all around her at this time. And then Jackdaw took her on her first flying run and her world got even better. It was a baby run with soft corners, wide spaces and lots of room for error, but in her eyes, it was the center of the Cosmos. It was magnificent.

Jackdaw had been a fighter pilot when he was younger. He got it. He never said a word. He didn't have to. Just held her small hand tight, all the way home.

She adored Jackdaw. He didn't live with them. But he was a constant fixture in her early years. Strong and nuggety, he had the kind of handsome, weathered face and farseeing eyes that told everyone everything would be alright. Jackdaw was here. He had everything under control. She guessed that was one of the reasons her mother liked having him around. Regularly.

She had stood in the doorway the night it happened. Witness. As these two people ripped her world apart.

But she was not a factor.

Merely witness. Audience.

Heartbroken.

Silent tears flowed down her chubby, rosy cheeks. Innocent cheeks. The cheeks of a child.

She saw one tear fall from Jackdaw's eye until he brushed it away.

Such pain in his face. She wanted to run to him. She wanted him to pick her up and make everything Ok again.

But it was not an option.

Silently, she watched him leave.

He never turned back. Never saw her.

She did her best to comfort her impossibly beautiful mother while she sobbed hysterical tears at their small kitchen table.

As she grew older, she came to realize that she would often be expected to comfort the hysterical tears of her impossibly beautiful mother.

She also came to realize that her mother was incapable of offering this or any other type of comfort in return.

There were reasons for it.

But there are always reasons, aren't there?

When she left, she had no-one to tell about it and nowhere to go. But she left anyway. Her impossibly beautiful mother's scathing remarks ringing in her ears. "He won't want anything to do with you, you little fool. You're the reason he left. You're the reason they all left. No-one wants a woman burdened down with such an ugly child. You've held me back all these years! I've given up everything for you!"

She had heard it all her life. Since she was very little. But for the first time now she heard it with a heartbreak edged with clarity rather than guilt. And she thought to herself, No. No, actually I have given up everything for you. Friends, my childhood, my self-worth, my sanity.

"Well I will hold you back no more mother. Perhaps you will be able to find happiness without me." She left for good.

She regained her sanity.

The self-worth came on board grudgingly.

The friend thing she just found too hard.

The childhood? Well adults should know better than to take someone else's to replace their own.

It just doesn't work that way.

She knew better.

But it didn't stop her setting out to search for it. She made it to Jackdaw.

Or rather he found her. Turning up front row in one of her first fights.

She had done well. She had done very well.

And Jackdaw had followed her career with interest. And then one day, when she was near the top of her game, he told her a secret.

Told her a secret about how parts of the cosmos really worked. About what many believed would go down in the next little while. And what some few were planning to do about it and were working towards.

He explained that her fighting career would, by its very nature, have a finite or limited lifespan. But that it would serve perfectly, both now and post it, if she wished to join them.

She did. And like the child she'd once been, she trotted trustingly along.

But after GhostSong5 she had lost a little of that trust.

It was only marginally late to pick her up as these things go. But still, it had meant an extra day and night in the desert. She had rationed her water to last. One does not survive long in the desert if one does not learn to ration their water for the worst possible scenario. But she had run out of food.

One of the packages she had been forced to buy hurriedly from an unknown street vendor had proved inedible. Sand for the most part.

She had committed his face to memory. One day, no doubt, she would return to this hell hole, and on that day, he would learn to regret his decision. Deeply. Until then she had bigger fish to fry.

The GhostSong5 flyer was small and sleek, able to land easily, and take off quickly. Still, it did not land completely. That was only asking for trouble in these parts. It hovered. And sent down a chain link. These ladders were incredibly strong and kind of stable. But with the down force from the flyer as it hovered, and the winds playing their havoc with both the underside of said flyer and the sorry state of her wings, the climb was unpleasant.

The Second Mate grabbed her by the underarm and helped haul her aboard through the small underside hatch. The feathers on her right wing caught for an instant and she grimaced as she felt them catch and pull. But then she was through and up and in.

The flyer was airborne. Instantly. Which was just in time. If the titanium shields had not been in place, Lilt and the Second Mate would have seen night-horsemen pounding over the hills towards the ship. One of the leaders shouldered a substantial and nasty looking rocket launcher. It fired and exploded silently and gracefully against the invisible shields activated in front of the titanium ones.

Lilt sat back in the co-pilot's chair and pulled a crooked and torn feather from her wing.

The Second Mate glanced at her as he flew them speedily away and back to GhostSong5. "Doesn't that hurt?"

"Yes," she replied matter-of-factly as she pulled out another. "But once their hex-chromed they'll never regain their shape. Toxic as hell too. Better to grow a new one."

She finished running her hands over her wings and satisfied leaned back with her feet up on the flight console. "Ok I'm ready. Take me to your leader," she said which made him smile.

She had been on many missions with this lot but not on this new ship yet. They landed cleanly within the flight deck and exited quickly.

"This way," the Second Mate pointed. They made their way to a large elevator in the middle of the long wall of the launch deck.

There was just one other flyer that Lilt could see. The two tiny ships looked even smaller in the vastness of the deck. They could take a sizable ship in here, Lilt noted. Plenty of room for even a couple of mid-size craft.

The Second Mate leaned back against the elevator wall as it made its ascent and studied her. She was impressive. Even covered in desert and clearly in need of a good wash, she was impressive. Chiseled. Her arm muscles put his to shame. "I thought hex-chroming was outlawed," he said. "Even on Venus12," he added. Lest she think him a totally naive fool.

She looked at him properly for the first time, taking his measure out of clear, dark brown eyes. "I wasn't fighting on Venus12, I was fighting on Bella3," she smiled. "Your leader point blank refused to come and pick me up from Bella3."

He swallowed hard. "Bella3?" he said incredulously. "You were fighting on Bella3?"

"Yep. And I gotta tell you there ain't much that's outlawed on Bella3." She cocked her head to the side. "And even if it is, you do what you need to do to survive."

"Ah, um, yes. I can imagine," he stammered, still reeling from the fact that she had fought - not only fought but fought and survived - on Bella3.

"No, you can't," she smiled. "You can't even begin to imagine it. But that's OK."

They exited the lift and they took her immediately.

The Old Ones had taken the ship. They ripped out her wings before they even asked her a question.

They dumped her body in front of the only Rebel Base they'd got her to disclose. It was worthless information. Due for evacuation soon anyway.

She had lived, miraculously she had lived. A long time in surgery. And an even longer time in rehabilitation.

Lilt no more.

Della ate her meal in silence remembering the fighter she'd once been and the type of missions she'd run.

And now here she was. A Medic's Aide. Her past glory completely unknown or long forgotten.

But CM Gemini had been kind to her and she was ashamed of how she'd behaved earlier.

But no mind, she would make it up to her tomorrow.

CHAPTER FIFTEEN

They turned in shortly after they ate. Cooper woke just a few hours later. The hold was in darkness. Save for the emergency lights and the glow from the stasis chamber.

The green of the emergency lights looked sickly against the violet of the chamber.

Since when had it glowed violet?

Cooper rose from his bed. Bare foot. Bare chested. His ink glistening in the strange lights.

He was there already. His hand on the contact-portal. How had he gotten here? He did not remember walking here. He did not remember.

He had a moment to realize that it was panic he was feeling. An emotion that had been trained out of him years ago.

And then the connection with her through the contact-portal jolted through him like a laser bolt.

And she was looking at him. With sapphire eyes. The chamber was a sea of violet.

So fast. She was so fast. It was just a blur of movement. The lid of the stasis chamber shattered.

Her hand was on his chest, dark nails pressed into his flesh. Godds it was ecstasy. The essence of her washed over him. Worlds swum in her eyes. She opened her mouth to say something and it was too much. Cooper pushed away from her and the worlds in her eyes were replaced with sorrow.

She fell back against the bed of the stasis chamber. And now she swam in darkness. Bathed in darkness, bathed in blackness, bathed in death.

He had killed her.

With a gasp, Cooper sat up in his bed. He was dripping with sweat.

Nightmare. Another one.

He looked around the room, getting his physical bearings, calming himself.

The hold was dark. Green emergency lights. Yellow stasis chamber.

Cooper let out a long breath. Everything was normal.

He was going to take a shower.

As he passed the stasis chamber, he forced himself to look. Rise slept a deep stasis sleep. But there was even more color in her cheeks now. Her lips were full. Her long dark hair glistened. She was framed in the inky blackness of her folded wings. Their depths contrasted with the violet feathers dotted amongst them.

Her eyes were closed.

Her breasts were barely covered by the sheet, the upper swell of them clearly visible. He had a sudden memory of them. Of all of her in the underground room of the Echelon. The reaction in him was immediate. Ok now he had to move away. Maybe he better make this shower cold.

He heard the sound just as he reached the door to the bathroom.

He whirled back in the direction of the stasis chamber. Something glistened in the darkness as it flew quickly away from it.

Flew?

Edging slowly back to the chamber, Cooper searched high and low but found nothing.

Doon snored loudly. All of the others were still sleeping soundly.

Great, he thought. Now I'm seeing things while I'm awake too.

Cooper shook his head. Had to be the new meds. He would ask the CM when she woke up in the morning.

He pushed open the door to the bathroom. Took the closest stall and turned on the water. It was pleasantly and surprisingly warm.

All thoughts of a cold shower were quickly forgotten. The mirrors above the sinks misted over with steam. The pounding of the water echoed off the tiled walls.

Balia, Minx Fae, the creature he'd sighted by the stasis chamber, hesitated.

She was going to turn off the silly glowing machine. The pretty heifer in side of it was well and truly cooked. But hot delicious was naked in a shower. Surely that should take priority as worth investigating.

She sniffed the air, and flew on silent, glistening wings to the bathroom, eyeing the door with increasing disapproval.

No buttons. It was one of those handled things.

She flitted up to handle height and pulled on it. To no avail.

Too big and heavy. When you are one and a half feet tall, the big heavy doors of the heifers with handle mechanisms, can prove problematic.

But there was a smoked glass section in the top of the door. Rippled.

Perhaps she could still catch a glimpse of him.

"Get away from there!" CM Gemini made a lunge for her and missed. Della made a better lunge and got her.

Holding her expertly by the neck and straight out from her.

Minx Fae horns are nasty. It makes catching them and keeping them difficult.

"A cage. We need something to use as a cage," Della said. Doing her best to control the madly struggling Fae.

"I'll be right back." Doon took off at a run to the rear of Hold. He had seen something that would do nicely earlier.

"What is going on and what the hell is that?" Cooper had burst from the bathroom when he'd heard the shouts. He stared incredulously at the small, winged, horned creature still struggling wildly in Della's outstretched arm.

"Ooh, hot delicious." The creature stilled at the sight of him and eyes him approvingly from top to bottom. "Please feel free to drop the towel."

"You behave yourself!" Della gave her a little shake.

Cooper secured the towel more firmly around his waist as Gemini did the explaining.

"She was perched at that bathroom door window there trying to get a good look at you."

Cooper turned to look at the creature pointedly, and was met with an extremely unapologetic look of her own.

"You're not the least bit embarrassed by that?" he asked her.

The creature laughed. "Only dumb heifers get embarrassed by normal things."

"There's nothing normal about spying on people when they're taking a shower Missy!" CM Gemini told her sharply.

"I'm only spying on hot delicious because of the stupid door!" the creature exclaimed exasperatedly.

She looked at him with eyes that held all sort of bad promises. "If I could have gotten in the door, hot delicious would have known I was there for certain."

She smiled at him knowingly and Cooper had the grace to color a little.

And then she turned, quick and sharp as a whip, using her horns to slash open a gash on Della's forearm.

Della cursed, but did not release her. Blood from the cut dripped on the floor. The creature huffed sulkily and folded her arms over her chest.

"Doon?" Jackdaw called. "Any luck with that cage?"

"Yeah I got something." The mass of Doon reappeared at a trot, bird transit cage in hand. "I've even got something for her horns. He held up the tiny horn mittens in his other hand.

The Minx Fae could not see them, as Doon was behind her, but she howled loud and long at his words.

"Someone needs to hold her head still," Della advised.

"I will," Jackdaw replied, stepping in behind her. The Minx Fae hissed at him revealing a pair of long, sharp, pointed teeth like a cat's.

Jackdaw held her head in place. Della still had her firmly by the neck.

Doon got the mittens on her horns with only a few tiny scratches. At the same time, he used some rope he'd found to bind her wings.

He stepped in front of Della with the cage and she threw her. The small creature hit the back of the cage hard. Doon closed and locked it.

The Minx Fae recovered from her hard knock at the back of the cage almost instantly and threw herself at the cage bars in a fury.

She gripped them hard and tried to rub the mittens off of her horns on the bars. "Off my horns!" she shouted angrily.

"But they look so pretty on you," Della said to her as CM Gemini deftly cleaned and bandaged her arm. "I think pink really is your color.

"The creature looked at her in horror, open mouthed. "Pink?"

Della tilted her head considering her. "So pink. In fact, that's the pinkest pink I've ever seen."

"You cannot put pink things on my horns!" Simultaneous foot stamping and fist shaking came from the cage.

"Oh, but you look so cute," Della replied.

"You do. I think it really is your color," CM Gemini added. "Now, I am going to find a nice dark cloth to cover this cage with so you can go nigh nighs."

The Minx Fae hissed at her and sat down sulkily on the floor of her cage, arms crossed, glaring out at them.

Cooper was still staring incredulously at her, speechless at the entire scene which had unfolded before him.

"And you put some clothes on!" CM Gemini admonished him. "We'll never get the little monster settled with you running around like that."

"Ok, Ok." He held up a hand. "But could someone please tell me exactly what the little monster is?"

"It's a Minx Fae," CM Gemini replied. "I'm surprised you never encountered one on Moethiica. They're most commonly found amongst the Pann Lords."

"It's rare to see a Pann Lord on Moethiica now. And they hate the Echelon," Cooper replied absently. "And it's called a Minx you say?"

They all nodded in unison at him.

"It behaves like that and it's called a Minx. Gold. Absolute gold." He began to laugh. He began to laugh and couldn't stop.

As he finished his interrupted shower and dried and dressed afterwards, he was still chortling.

He hadn't laughed quite like this since before Ghaniia12.

It felt good. It felt damned good.

And when he thought about the fact that a flying Minx with horns had brought about its manifestation, it made him laugh even harder.

CHAPTER SIXTEEN

"That's quite a grip you've got on you," Cooper remarked to Della next morning as he poured himself a coffee.

Ah, coffee. He was extremely glad to find out it was a cosmic addiction. They might call it different things here and there, but it was still coffee.

He breathed in the aroma appreciatively. Nothing like it.

"Yeah, I noticed that too," Doon commented. "Saw you catch her too. Impressive. You're quick. It's not easy to catch a Minx Fae."

Della shrugged. "I've had some experience with them before is all. There were a number of them about the place where I was…grew up." She got up quickly from where she'd been sitting contentedly at the Galley. "I better go see if CM Gemini needs me for anything."

"Short and sweet," Doon grunted.

"Yeah, she really didn't want to talk about that one," Cooper agreed. "Know much about her?"

Doon shook his head. "Not really. Been assisting the CM on the last couple of missions. Keeps to herself. She looks familiar though," he added. "I've thought that since the first time I saw her."

"Interesting," Cooper mused. "I was just thinking the same thing. Girl's got a mighty set of forearms on her, I'll give her that much."

The day was spent in relative calm. They moved the Minx Fae's cage to the far end of the hold. There were some war wounds on Doon and Jackdaw from supplying her with food and water.

Sans horns, it seemed her nails were more than capable of reaping some nasty damage.

Cooper smiled and shook his head, still fascinated by the small creature. He needed to calibrate but there was a problem with his helmet. He spent most of the day tinkering with it, trying to fix it.

"Gotcha," he said in satisfaction. It was well after their evening meal and only he and CM Gemini were still awake.

"Will you calibrate it now?" she asked him concernedly. "You'll need to do it sooner rather than later you know."

"First thing tomorrow," Cooper replied, yawning. "It'll take a few hours and then I'm done with it."

"It's Ok. I feel good," he reassured her at her disapproving glance. "First thing tomorrow is plenty of time."

"It's quite normal to not want to do it you know," she replied, regarding him steadily. "Its been part of you for a time now. This sort of bio-technology. It can feel like you're shutting down a part of yourself. It can be hard to let go. But you must."

Cooper opened his mouth to protest and then realized she was right. There was a part of him that didn't want to let go of it. And was finding it very hard to do so. The Echelon were despicable. Monsters. But powerful monsters. There was a heady rush to their dark magic, no matter what he told himself.

"You're right," he conceded, "But not now. Not tonight. Tomorrow morning."

"Good." She laid a hand on his forearm. "I'm here if you need me. Right, I'm off to bed."

"Chief Medic," he said as she made to move off.

"Yes, Cooper."

"Is there anything in those new cloaking meds you've given me that would cause nightmares? Like really crazy bad, real feeling nightmares?"

"No. I wouldn't think so. What are your nightmares about?"

"Her." He gestured in the direction of the stasis chamber. "Always her."

"Ah," CM Gemini said as is that explained everything. "So that's why you've not been near her since we've been down here. A pity. She flourishes. Heals at twice the speed when she senses your presence." She looked at him quizzically. "Are you absolutely sure you've never seen each other before? It's quite a connection you have the pair of you."

"No. Never." Cooper shook his head and exhaled. "Thanks anyway. Must be this weird 'connection' thing doing it."

CM Gemini smiled and bid him goodnight.

Cooper sat for a while longer in the galley lost in thought. Before he crashed for the night he steeled his nerve and paid a visit to the stasis chamber.

Tentatively he laid his hand on the contact-portal. He tensed, half waiting for the jolt of his dream, but the connection when it came was soft and gentle.

He relaxed and let out a breath. Godds she was beautiful.

And also an Asset. He reminded himself sharply. *The* Asset. The Mission. Siren5. Priority One. The only living Siren. The only one who could open the Veil Portal above Earth and let the Original Makers through.

It was this that the highest levels of authority on Earth, and much of the Cosmos, was counting on.

That she would let through other things the Old Ones and the Echelon were equally counting on, was just part of the bargain. The unfortunate part.

"She may or may not know who or what she is." He had been briefed. "If they run true to form since the Siren of the 3ʳᵈ she will not look like a typical Siren. But never forget, that she is a Siren. And as valuable as she is, so she is powerful and dangerous."

"When she truly realizes her own identity, she will be powerful and dangerous beyond reason. Certainly, beyond your ability to contain and command her."

"Establish control and establish it quickly."

"And remember also the Siren's charms and the Siren's power of seduction."

"An Asset. Think of her always as the most powerful and dangerous Asset you have ever had to manage."

Cooper remembered his briefings and trainings. He withdrew his hand from the contact-portal.

Yeah, so she was beautiful. He had dealt with beautiful before. Really, when it came down to it, on Earth, and across the Cosmos, beautiful looking females were a dime a dozen. There was no need to get hung up on the ones who were wholly inappropriate.

He turned abruptly away from the stasis chamber and took himself to bed.

Cooper slept soundly. No nightmares. Not even a dream he would remember.

They all slept deep and well.

And as they all slept, Balia, the Minx Fae, who had observed them all with interest since their arrival in the prison hold, plotted silently.

The first thing she plotted was her escape from the cage. A given really. Idiot heifers. She could have been out of there some time ago.

But there were further travel plans on her mind and as this particular lot of heifers didn't seem intent on trying to kill her - epic lolz if they did - they might just be worth hitching a ride with.

Which meant she might have to play it nice for a while.

Hmmm.

Decisions. Decisions. Decisions.

They *could* be useful.

And she had been on this ship forever such a long time now.

Ever since that unfortunate incident with that ridiculously angry man.

It had been a grand night until then.

An all-night hookah bar, a particularly potent batch of sprite beer. She had been having the most marvelous time. Dancing dreamily in the acrid fumes of the black-market smoke machine.

At the end of the day it was the smoke machine's fault! One minute dancing. Next minute squishy. Well not her squishy. But what was suddenly on the end of her left horn rather than still firmly attached to its owner, definitely squishy.

Then it had all descended rather quickly into name calling and threats of vile retribution.

Anger management issues indeed.

Godds, he had another one didn't he.

And it was her that had to get his disgusting squishy human eyeball off the end of her horn.

Ewwww. So gross. It sent a shiver through her now just thinking of it.

She had barely gotten away. And then of course Seth was nowhere to be found.

It was so extremely disappointing that she had to do all of this by herself. She folded her arms and huffed sulkily.

At least they had one pretty heifer with wings.

She preened her own wings smugly. They were well free of their bindings. And hers were Fae silk. Glimmering, fine, transparent, mesmerizing. Tough as steel, barbed and poisonous.

Poor heifers with their ancient feathery wings.

Mmmmm. Heifers. They were going to Blue Earth. Blue Earth had lovely heifers from all accounts. Even four legged ones with big brown eyes and hoofy ankles. And there was nothing like a bit of warm, bleeding, juicy heifer meat first thing in the morning.

And cats. Blue Earth had cats. And unbeknownst to it, their Queen. So, all she had to do was get to Blue Earth with this motley crew and make contact with her.

She would smuggle herself in one of their packs. Or even better, in hot delicious's pocket. She only had two of the shrinking invisible vials left. But it was a potent batch and would last her a time.

She liked the head rush when she shrank invisible. It was like snorting Arcadian shroom dust. Now there was a worthy past time.

She didn't like coming out the other side though. No, that wasn't very nice at all. Made her very grumpy.

She settled back against the cage and closed her eyes. Happy with her plotting and content to sleep herself for a time.

She smelt it rather than heard it. She had a very sensitive nose. Balia cocked her head in the funny machine's direction and drew in a sharp breath.

She had no idea why they were cooking the pretty one. But they had best stop, because bitch was done!

She listened, but there was nothing. No noise, nothing to indicate that they knew what was going on outside of there.

Drawing the sharp pointed needle from where it hid in her wealth of hair, she used it expertly on the lock on the cage to free herself.

Carefully, she drew back the covers and peered out into the hold. Excellent. All was quiet. They were sleeping.

Carefully, carefully, carefully, she made her way on silent wings out of her cage and across the room.

When she got to the funny machine she sat atop it for a while considering its occupant.

There was something different about this one that she couldn't quite put her finger on.

Oh well. Whatevs. She was most certainly done. Time to stop cooking pretty heifer!

Gracefully, she flew around the machine. Once more she drew the sharp, shiny, pointed needle from her hair, and stuck it in the small metal hole receptacle she had found the other day.

The stasis chamber exploded in a shower of golden sparks.

The sound was enormous.

CHAPTER SEVENTEEN

Cooper emptied the first fire extinguisher on it and started on another.

Doon and Jackdaw lifted the now foam-covered body away from the wreckage. For surely it was nothing more than a body now. It was sort of amazing that it was still even a body, and not just a collection of tiny pieces.

CM Gemini motioned them hurriedly into the Med-Bay. The door to it had been closed thank goodness. This being an ex-prison hold, its walls and doors were built to withstand all kinds of violence, including blasts. The Med-Bay had escaped relatively unharmed.

Cooper put down the fire extinguisher. The fire in the stasis chamber was out. Ruined but no more threat to them.

Cooper hurried into the Med-Bay where Della was clearing the last of the foam from Rise.

CM Gemini was already at her chest working frantically to resuscitate her.

He had a deep, sinking feeling in his chest.

CM Gemini stood back.

Rise did not move.

Della looked crestfallen. CM Gemini looked determined. "Come on now Missy," she said. "I know you're in there. Enough of this."

She started again. This time with paddles. The lasers shot through Rise, jolting her whole body from the bed.

Again, she lay still as CM Gemini stood back from her.

And then she coughed.

She coughed.

CM Gemini and Della went to work about her in a blur of motion. He wanted to stay, but CM Gemini shooed him from the room. "I'll let you know when she's stable and you can speak with her," she said and turned all her attention to her patient.

Jackdaw led him out and closed the door behind them.

Cooper ran his hand through his hair in frustration, but there was nothing to do but obey the Chief Medic's orders.

"She's conscious," Cooper informed Doon as they walked back to where he held the Fae.

"Thank the godds" he said and then shook her roughly. "No thanks to you."

"You did this?" Cooper tried to very, very carefully put a lid on his anger as he marched towards the Fae. "Why?" he demanded.

"She was cooked!" the Minx exclaimed at him, struggling furiously.

"What do you mean, cooked?"

"Done! Enough in the silly machine. Could you not smell her? Ready to come out! Cooked!" She gave up struggling and crossed her arms, pouting at him. "Hot but dumb," she muttered under her breath as Cooper crossed his own arms and stared at her hard.

She met his gaze, defiantly.

Jackdaw had retrieved her cage and was holding it ready.

"Cuff her first," Cooper said coldly. "Wrists and ankles. Wings tight. Horn Mittens. Secure this time. Link everything to her wing bindings." He added and she glared at him but said nothing.

Jackdaw did so while Doon and Cooper held her tight and unmoving between them.

Then Cooper swapped places with Jackdaw and searched her thoroughly. He found a multitude of arsenal on her, some of which he was quite pleased with. No doubt, it would all come in very handy. When he was sure he had everything, he held the cage for them.

She hissed and flashed her dainty little cat fangs when Doon shoved her inside the cage, but apart from that she went in quietly enough.

They had found more rope. Good and thick and coarse. Cooper bound it tightly round the cage using a series of intricate knots. If she could pick them undone with her tiny hands good luck to her.

They settled the cage on a low crate and he pulled up the chair from the Med-Bay in front of it.

"Talk to me," he said to the Minx Fae. "Start with your name." He leaned back in the chair, folded his arms and stretched his legs out.

She narrowed her eyes at him suspiciously.

He yawned at her. He had all the time in the world for this.

"Balia," she sniffed eventually. "My name is Balia."

Doon came over to him and then and whispered something in his ear. Cooper nodded his agreement. "Do it," he said quietly and then turned his attention back to the Fae.

Her eyes followed Doon's movements suspiciously, but came back quickly enough to settle on Cooper when he said her name.

"So, Balia, tell me exactly why you did it and what you meant by 'cooked.'"

The Fae was exquisite he realized, looking at her. Miniature, exotic, horned, fanged, perfection. And then shook his head in disbelief at his own thoughts. Oh, how the years away from Earth had changed him.

"She cooked. Done," Balia sighed. Exhausted now after all the excitement. "She longer in that machine and you ruin her. Like meat." She added helpfully as if that would explain everything.

"What would be ruined if we left her in there?" Cooper pressed.

"Diamond," Balia responded. "Pretty heifer has two inside. Means she cooks quickly."

Cooper sat forward, his memory of the mind-diamond passing into Rise that night still fresh. In complete defiance of Arc's magic. He had never seen Arc's magic thwarted, ever.

The power of her voice had called it. But there are a lot of powerful beings who know the true power of the voice and how to wield it.

"What are the Diamonds and what does it mean that she carries two now?" he asked the Fae.

Balia looked at him like he was mad. "Same as your Diamond. Same as mine. Except she got two. And one a big one." She peered at him closely. "Hmmm. Curiouser and curiouser. Same as you."

"What do you mean, same as me?"

"You got two too, Hot Delicious." She tilted her head at him. "Where you get your other big one from?"

He opened his mouth to ask her what she meant, but then closed it. This was ridiculous. She was a Fae and she was answering him in riddles. Jackdaw voiced his own doubts.

"Be careful, Cooper. These ones are experts at telling you what you want to hear. She'll lead you in circles all night with this nonsense."

Balia hissed at Jackdaw and her eyes held real hatred.

Cooper sighted. Jackdaw was right. She could be telling him anything.

Doon appeared then, nice long syringe in hand and looked at him questioningly.

"Do it," he said, standing suddenly and pushing back his chair.

Doon moved quickly to the cage and injected the Fae in the neck with the tranq. It was human strength, only slightly modified for her, and she sagged immediately.

Problem solved. They would keep her tranqued all the way to their next landing and set her loose there.

Cooper sighed and rotated his shoulders. They were all exhausted. Could all do with some more light tranqing.

"I spoke to Celcius," Jackdaw told him as they headed for their beds. "Convinced him that was just the way she came out of stasis."

"Good. Thanks," Cooper grunted.

The door to the Med-Bay opened and Della appeared.

"She's conscious, stable and not to be disturbed by anyone for at least the next 24 hours," she announced to them all.

"Fair enough," Cooper grunted, relief flooding him. He could not wait for the green light to talk to her. But first things first, as soon as he woke up, and with a day now up his sleeve, he would calibrate that damn helmet.

CHAPTER EIGHTEEN

Rise awoke in a small room, feeling rather wonderful. Like she had been asleep and rested for a very long time.

She stretched contentedly and felt two things. The first was the large mind-diamond. It fluttered and shimmered with warmth at her waking. Its movement sent golden waves of pleasure pulsing through her.

The second thing she felt was that her wings were unbound.

Punishable by death on Moethiica. And the raids could happen by day or night. The only time her wings were unbound was when she flew Junar Run.

Moethiica. She sat bolt upright. She was no longer on Moethiica. She remembered she had been in space, and then something had happened. How had she got on the ship again?

She searched her mind but could not remember it.

No mind, she had the mind-diamond. It moved lazily within her again, making her feel even more wonderful.

There was a woman in a chair beside her bed, soundly sleeping. She had red bobbed hair. Rise stared at it. It was the most beautiful color. The woman had a kind, mature face. Exhausted. Rise hoped she rested well.

Easing herself cautiously out of the bed she slipped past the woman without waking her. Holding her breath, she tried the door and smiled delightedly when she found it open.

She slipped quietly out of the peaceful little room into a vast hulking blackness.

She looked around, hoping to get another glimpse of space, but there were no windows here. Oh, but look, there was another door. Perhaps the windows were through that way.

There were more people in here, sleeping. She could not see them all, but she could sense them and hear their quiet breathing.

Moving on tiptoe, ever so quietly, she made her way over to it and pushed open the bathroom door.

No windows.

But room a plenty to stretch her wings. And showers. Rise snapped out her wings and twirled about in circles of happiness. It was the violet flashes in the bathroom mirrors above the sinks that caused her to stop.

She moved towards the sinks and studied her wings carefully. She did not remember having violet in her wings before. Not since she was a baby.

Oh well, no mind. She twirled again and headed for a shower.

It felt beyond wonderful.

The only thing that tempted her out of it was the thought of the drying machine. The sensation of it through her sleek ebony and violet wings was exquisite.

She felt so contented. Safe, warm, clean, free.

Naked.

Rise pursed her lips and looked about her for clothes. There were towels. She guessed one of them would have to do.

Ah, no someone had left a shirt behind.

She would need to cut some holes in the back of it for her wings. But she was well used to adjusting walker clothes to fit her wings. And she was sure the owner of the shirt wouldn't mind.

No scissors or knife though. Perhaps her nails would do. They seemed awfully long and strong now. She had no memory of ever seeing them like this. She held the shirt up and tested it with a nail.

It tore apart with ridiculous ease. Mmmm. Handy.

She tore two openings in the back of it large enough to fit her wings through. Lifting it close to her face, she breathed in the scent of the shirt. Delicious and masculine.

Expertly and with practiced hands she contracted and worked her wings through the newly fashioned openings. The shirt settled perfectly around the foot-long joints at her back, and she let her wings fan out again, out the other side of them.

The shirt was big on her, like a little dress, covering her to mid-thigh. Perfect. Now for food. She was suddenly ravenous. She hoped they had a well-stocked kitchen.

Forgetting all about being quiet, Rise burst happily through the bathroom door into the main area.

The black visored Echelon head turned slowly towards her. He was barely ten feet away from where she now stood, frozen.

Rise forgot every sense of happiness and wonderful and screamed.

She whirled madly about her looking for an exit.

"What the fuck! I thought that was the Chief Medic in there." As the monster lunged for her she remembered her wings were free.

She dodged him expertly and launched herself.

There were metal beams some fifty feet up. She landed perfectly on the first one and perched there.

There were others below her now. They had come running from everywhere. The small room she had been in opened suddenly and the red-haired woman came out of it.

"Oh, my godds," she muttered when she saw Rise perched above them, wings free and lashing in and out behind her somewhat menacingly.

"Rise."

"Ah." The red-haired woman knew her name. Someone amongst them had ID'd her.

"Rise, it's alright. My name is Chief Medic Gemini. You're perfectly safe here. I've been looking after you."

Rise heard her words but everything was not alright. She flexed her wings with a sharp snap, making them all jump. All except the Echelon. The reason everything was very much not alright.

She fixed him with her gaze and would not take her eyes off him.

"Rise, it's alright," CM Gemini called up to her. "He's not an Echelon. He's been undercover with them. This is Cooper. Agent Cooper Pierce. From Earth. He's the one who rescued you."

CM Gemini turned to Cooper and hissed at him. "Take your bloody helmet off for goodness sake! She'll never come down with that on your head."

"I can't take it off, it's calibrating," he hissed back at her. "And what the hell is she doing awake and well and flying around?"

"I don't know," CM Gemini responded. "I honestly don't know."

She turned back to Rise. "Won't you come down and talk to us Rise. Honestly, no-one here means you any harm."

Rise cocked her head at Cooper, still not having taken her eyes off of him.

"Tell the Echelon creature to remove his helmet and prove he is who you say he is."

"He can't take it off right now Rise. It's calibrating. Once he's finished that, it will be off of him for good."

"Echelon lies," Rise spat.

"Rise, these are no lies. This man rescued you from the Echelon. Please, Rise, I beg of you. Come down and talk to us."

Rise hesitated, considering.

Cooper put his hands up in a peace gesture. "She speaks the truth. I am not an Echelon. I was undercover with them. I did rescue you. And I mean you no harm. Once I can safely take this helmet off, I will do so."

"If you lie to me Echelon pretender, I will kill you." She was not too sure of the finer details of how she would do this. But her conviction was strong on it. She was quite sure she was capable of it and could work out the exact how's of it later.

"I will come down only if that thing is no longer present." She gestured at Cooper who had to count to ten to control his anger before he turned to CM Gemini.

"I am going to walk away now and I will stay away until I take this thing off and have finished calibrating. Bind her wings as soon as she's down. I don't care if you have to tranq her to do it. Bind her."

He spoke barely above a whisper but CM Gemini saw Rise narrow her eyes at him suspiciously and shooed him away impatiently.

"It's alright Rise. He's going now. He won't be back until he can take off his helmet."

The Echelon helmeted thing walked away to the far end of the hold, disappearing behind some large crates.

Rise considered. A real Echelon would not be shooed like that by the red-haired woman. A real Echelon would not be shooed by anyone. Perhaps this one was just an Echelon pretender.

It made up her mind.

And she dropped instantly, vertically, impossibly, exquisitely to the ground, making them all gasp and frightening the hell out of them.

It took every ounce of courage CM Gemini had to put a smile on her face and walk towards her.

CHAPTER NINETEEN

Back in the Med-Bay room CM Gemini eyed Rise carefully as she examined her. What a presence she had. And her eyes. It was like starlight shone through them.

She was perfectly healed. Perfectly healthy. Her wings were perfectly reformed.

"You're in remarkable shape." CM Gemini commented. Knowing the words to be inadequate but not knowing any other way to put it.

"My nails are very strong. Look." She proffered one hand to the Doctor who quailed at the sight of them. The girl she had first taken into her care had short nails, cut square and blunt. She knew she had taken samples from just underneath them.

These nails were the same nails. But twice as thick. Long. Pointed. They glistened pink and white and beautiful. CM reached out and tested one tentatively. Hard and sharp.

"Is that what you cut the holes in the shirt with?" she asked, trying to keep her voice light and casual.

"Yes. It ripped very easily. I like this shirt. I like the scent of its former owner."

CM Gemini was about to remark that she was quite sure that it was Cooper's shirt she was wearing and then thought better of it.

When she turned around the star like eyes were regarding her intently. This was so not the same girl who Cooper had first boarded the ship with. But then she checked herself. How did she know this? How did anyone know this? Rise had been unconscious. They had no idea how aware she was of herself, or how much the Siren in her had awakened.

For looking at her now, Chief Medic Gemini agreed wholeheartedly with Cooper Pierce. This was no Potential. This was the real thing. This was the Veil Siren.

And none of them really knew her. He was right. She was an unknown quantity. Potentially more powerful and dangerous than any of them could imagine. She needed to be bound and restrained somewhat until they knew exactly what they were dealing with, and had established some relationship with her.

"Are we done?" Rise asked. "I am very hungry."

Ah perfect. CM thought. I can put the sedatives in her food. "Yes. Of course. I will fix you something."

"Thank you," said Rise simply. Trustingly.

CM Gemini moved to the small cabinet and retrieved the sedative. She felt Rise's eyes on her back and a sweat broke out on her forehead as she did so.

She schooled herself, turned brightly and smiled at her.

"Right you are then. I'll be back in a jiffy."

When she returned with the sedative laced porridge, Rise wolfed it down hungrily and asked for another.

Relieved, that her plan had worked, CM Gemini obligingly went to get it.

Jackdaw, Doon and Della were all in the galley this time.

"Smart," said Jackdaw approvingly. "That will knock her out till nightfall."

"Do you think?" It was Rise. She had moved silently into the galley behind them.

They all froze. CM Gemini was in the midst of pouring the sedative into the bowl before her. There was no disguising it.

"I trusted you," Rise said to her. "You have deceived me. This shall not be forgotten."

"Rise, I'm sorry. It's for your own good. Please believe me," CM Gemini said. Ashamed of herself and her actions suddenly.

"It is not for my own good. It is for your fear. You are all controlled by the Echelon. I will find him and kill him."

She turned on her heel and launched herself.

"Fuck me. Get a tranq shot loaded now," ordered Jackdaw and CM Gemini ran for it.

"Doon. Della. Find something strong enough to bind her wings with. I'm going to get Cooper."

And he took off at a run down the other end of the hold.

But Cooper was not down the other end of the hold.

Unbeknownst to them all he had witnessed Rise's equally quick, silent and ridiculously magnificent descent from the beam. He knew what it meant. He was fully briefed, when she came fully into her own, of just how dangerous she would be. There was a good reason for this procedure.

Once Rise was in the Med-Bay, he had worked his way up, unseen, to the first floor. He did not want any attention drawn by anyone to the fact he was up there.

He would have one shot at this if she flew again before they bound her.

He had calibrated some ten minutes back. Had heard the conversation in the galley. He crouched now on the metal beams running down the length of the hold and waited for her.

Rope in hand.

He felt the rush of air at the approach of her wings. He timed it perfectly. The rope caught and tightened over her chest, rendering her wings useless.

Rise screamed and desperately tried to free her wings. Cooper held tight to the vertical beam the rope was secured to and lowered her as gently as he could to the floor.

They all came running, and Jackdaw moved forward with the tranq shot.

"Stay back," Cooper called. "I got this." He still had control of the rope when he made it to the floor. Pulled tight, binding both her arms and wings to her.

"Give them to me. I'll do it." Cooper took the bindings from CM Gemini's outstretched hand and moved purposefully towards Rise.

With brutal efficiency he pushed her on to her stomach on the floor. He bound her wrists tight behind her with some more rope that Jackdaw proffered to him.

He bound her wings expertly and quickly. Tight and hard up against her back. She cried out in pain as he pulled on the final adjustment. He did not need to pull them that hard but he had a point to prove and a power dynamic to lay.

CM Gemini and Della both winced at his roughness. CM Gemini thought to point out that he may still have the energy of the helmet working through him.

And he looked at her as she thought it. Piercing eyes, hard, cold and frightening. And she knew then he most certainly did have the energy still coursing through him and that he had heard her.

Satisfied she was secure Cooper gave one final vicious tug on Rise's bindings and pulled her roughly up from the floor.

He propelled her forward to their bedding area, and sat her down forcefully on his bed. He tied the ropes holding her wrists and the rope holding her wing bindings to the metal base of the bed.

Cooper's discarded Echelon helmet sat on the bed beside her.

The others stood back in silence, not knowing what to say or do.

Cooper stood in front of her, safely out of kicking range, legs apart, arms folded.

"Now," Cooper said. "In a few minutes the sedative Chief Medic Gemini gave you is going to start working. And you and I are going to have a nice little chat and get to know each other."

"There will be no more talk of killing and no flying. Chief Medic Gemini is right when she says no-one here means you any harm. But if you mean any of us harm, then make no mistake, I will stop you. With whatever means I have to."

"Do you understand me?" he demanded.

Rise narrowed her eyes and glared at him.

"Do. You. Understand. Me?" he demanded again, emphasizing each word.

"I understand you perfectly," Rise responded.

There was just a hint of a threat in her tone when she said it.

And her starlit eyes shone.

CHAPTER TWENTY

The small abandoned courtyard within the Echelon compound afforded a magnificent view of Junar.

It rose above the ancient statues of the giant Echelon. Perhaps that's what made this place peaceful for him.

Because it was odd, that when he first infiltrated them and bore witness and sometimes sickened participant to their atrocities, that this place is where he came to regroup.

The ancient statues stared down at him. And Junar stared down on them all.

Desert. Rock. Mystery.

Another atrocity. Another need to regroup.

But he would need to stop this practice. The Uppers were too aware of him now and too skilled at mind-cept for him to cloak completely against them. He could feel one of them grow suspicious of him already.

Ok. He steeled himself. This would be the last time then.

It was the cooler months now. The moons shone brightly, illuminating his path. It was windy.

And the wind hid other sounds.

Shadow. He was suddenly in shadow.

His heart lurched.

The beat of wings. Huge wings. Behind him. She was suddenly overhead.

Her energy hit him in waves. Undulating and breaking against his own. Which suddenly seemed small and insignificant. His heart continued to skip beats. Sweat broke on his forehead as the warmth of her swept through him.

He had a longing to feel her wings enfold him and breathe close to her magnificent heart.

He felt the tingle at the base of his skull as she connected with him. And just that, slight, brushing touch rippled through his body. It felt like the promise of the most intense pleasure he had ever known.

He steadied himself on a statue of the Echelon, and the cold rock brought him somewhat back to the version of himself that had existed before her presence.

She descended to perch above him on the high rock wall of the courtyard.

They knew that he came here. They had been watching him.

She was terrifying. Exquisite. Divine. Her wings spanned 20 feet or more. Black wings. Tiny golden horns protruding from a wealth of long, dark hair. Her face and body were the most exquisite face and body he had been fortunate enough to gaze upon.

And he had gazed upon a few. More than usual of late. Hardly in the most desirable of circumstances, but still his body betrayed him. Ah, Moethiica, he thought to himself, what have you done to me.

Her dark golden eyes stared into his. A silent challenge in them.

Her voice when she spoke, was like a star song of ecstasy, encased - barely - in the necessity of words he would understand. The scent of honeysuckle filled the night air.

Incongruous in the cold.

But he could no longer feel the cold.

He felt those ripples of ecstasy break over him again and he clutched the statue tighter, gripping fiercely to an anchor that was not her.

"She will come to you." She looked at Junar and then back at him. "Here."

His voice when it came was hoarse. "When?"

Her voice was amused then. "When she comes."

Again, she looked at the mountain, and then back to him. She inclined her head to him. And then took off as suddenly as she had come.

When her two companions took off with her, his heart skipped more beats. He had not even been aware of their presence.

Cooper Pierce waited. He waited a long time. Beyond the expiration of his cloaking implant. Well beyond what his Earth Commanders expected from him.

Not that he had contact with them. Too risky. But they could see him. Disguised as a tiny space probe in their tracking systems.

And then one day, against all the odds, and like nothing he had expected, she had come.

Cooper Pierce left Rise tied to his bed and took a shower. She didn't look like them, but she felt to him very much like the Sirens who had descended on to that courtyard wall.

She felt magnificent. And no good could come from it. He had been briefed to shield against this power they wielded.

This shower was cold.

CHAPTER TWENTY-ONE

"One hand. And one hand only," Cooper said firmly.

CM Gemini opened her mouth to push for more, but saw the look in his eyes and knew that was all she was getting. Her shoulders dropped and she nodded, "Thank you."

Cooper beckoned to Doon as he strode towards Rise. "Hold her while I free one of her hands."

Doon obliged and Rise's left hand was freed. Her right hand and bound wings were still tied firmly to the bolted metal bed.

Cooper moved around in front of her and drew up the chair.

At his earlier instruction Doon stayed behind her.

Did she know who and what she was? Well, if she didn't know now, she would know by the time this little chat was over. Cooper was well briefed in the perceived mistakes of the handling of the first four Veil Sirens. He was not about to repeat them.

He sat back in the chair and folded his arms. He started with the basics. "What is your name?"

"What is yours?" She retorted.

"Cooper Pierce R9. What is your name?"

"You know my name. You have already ID'd me," she replied pointedly.

"I know what you've ID'd as but what do you call yourself?"

"The same as the ID."

"And nothing else?"

"Nothing else."

"Rise, where were you born?"

"Moethiica."

"How long have you lived there?"

"All my life."

"Where else have you lived?"

"Nowhere."

"How do you know Soar?"

The mention of Soar brought it all flooding back. Her face clouded, her beautiful violet eyes shone with tears, and a deep sorrow cloaked her.

She used her free hand to angrily dash away the tears.

"Soar was a legend amongst the winged. A rebel. We thought...." She took a steadying breath. "We thought she had escaped them."

"Had you ever met her?"

"No." She dashed another tear away. "Yes." She remembered. "Once. When I was young. Only briefly. Before she escaped to the desert."

"Who crossed to the desert after her?"

"No-one. No-one crossed after her." She glared at him icily. "You were there. You saw her. You saw what they did to her. You saw me."

She pulled violently on her restraints, so obviously distressed that both Della and Gemini moved towards her.

Cooper held up one hand, halting them. He had not even turned to look at them, but he had sensed them move.

"Did you try to cross, Rise?"

She blinked rapidly at him, remembering. Not just the pain of falling short and hitting the shields. But the punishment afterwards. How ironic, that being female, underage and promised to the Echelon had saved her from harsher treatment.

"What happened?" he persisted.

"I failed."

"Are there Sirens amongst the rebels in the desert, Rise?"

"I would not know. I failed."

"Was the Veil Siren amongst the rebels in the desert, Rise?"

She hesitated. Soar and her supporters had been so sure of themselves.

"I do not know. I failed," she repeated eventually.

"Was Soar the Siren of the 5ᵗʰ, Rise? Was she the Veil Siren?"

"She believed that," Rise replied cautiously.

"But you are not so sure," he said quietly.

She was quiet for a long time before she replied, "No. I am not so sure."

"Did you know the Echelon had the Nephliim Blade before you were brought there?"

Rise looked at him like he was mad. How on earth would she know such a thing?

"The Nephliim Blade, Rise," he said again. "Did you know it was there?"

"No. I did not know," she replied. The memory of her reaction to the Blade, and it's to her rose to the surface. Not breaking yet, but hovering tantalizingly close underneath.

"And did you know Soar was there?"

"No." She had already answered that. He was trying to trick her.

Desperately she sought the memory of the Blade. She was less sure of herself now and wished she could remember.

"What did you take from Soar?"

The mind-diamond rolled within her at this, making her dizzy. She pressed her free hand to her head to still it. "I did not take it. I stopped the Echelon Mage, Arc, from taking it."

"How, Rise? Are you also a Mage?"

"No."

"Then how? How did you do this?"

She honestly had no idea. And for some reason that annoyed her. Like she was stuck somewhere with some essential knowledge being denied to her.

She glared at him. "I don't know."

"What is it Rise? What is it that you took?"

"I don't know," she said again.

Cooper sat back and sighed, heavily, feigning disappointment.

"It's very disappointing, Rise. You know after all the hype, you don't know much about anything do you?"

The anger flared in her and her eyes shone. "How dare you!" She spat at him.

He smirked at her. "What are you so offended about Rise? You're just some Moethiican winged, come of age, female, the Echelon picked up to have a bit of fun with. I didn't really expect you to know anything."

He heard some gasps from the ones behind him at that.

Rise's gaze was locked on him. She stared at him in silence for some time before she replied.

"I am not," she said eventually.

"Not what?" Cooper sounded almost disinterested.

"I am not just some come of age female from Moethiica," She replied icily.

"Really?" Cooper sounded doubtful. "Then what are you?"

"More than you will ever know. What are *you*?" She retorted.

"I am Agent Cooper Pierce R9. I work for the US Military of Earth. Black Ops. Undercover," he added and then paused.

"What are you Rise?" he asked again.

She stared at him in deep confusion. This was ridiculous. Why should this question confuse her? She knew what she was.

Bu suddenly she didn't.

And then the ground fell away from her as the mind-diamond she had seized away from the Echelon righted itself on its point and began to spin.

It was egg sized when she had taken it. It seemed bigger now. Like it was growing inside her.

And it was shaped like a round, cut diamond. The point lodged deep in her pineal. The top surface of it opened up to everywhere.

The mind-diamond began to spin more slowly, happy with her awareness. The ground righted itself.

And some lost knowledge within her, clicked into place.

"Where are you taking me, Cooper Pierce?" she asked. And the confidence in her voice was back again.

"To Earth. I am taking you to Earth, Rise."

"To the Veil Portal," she stated.

"Yes," Cooper nodded. "To the Veil Portal."

"You believe that I can open it for you."

"Yes."

"You believe I am the Veil Siren."

"Yes."

"You are not an Echelon," she said suddenly. Like she had just made up her mind about this.

"No. I am not."

She relaxed just a little then. And as she relaxed, the memory of the Nephliim Blade came back to her. And as the memory settled in her, she wondered how ever she could have forgotten it.

A memory of Cooper shot before her. Not of that night amongst the Nephliim, but another time. But it was gone again. As quickly as it had come.

She looked him in the eyes. "I am something, Cooper Pierce. But whether I am the one you think I am, I do not know."

He nodded. It was enough. He sat forward and addressed her intently.

"Rise, I believe you to be the Siren of the 5ᵗʰ and by the power vested in me by The Confederation, I have taken you into military custody of the United States of America, Earth, to be transported to Earth, to open the Veil Portal."

"The Confederation are opposed to the Old Ones," Rise said. It was not a question. It was like she said it out loud to reassure herself.

"Yes, we are," Cooper replied quietly and matter-of-factly. "I'm here to escort you safely Rise, and we are already in transit. We can do that with you bound, kicking and screaming, or we can cooperate and do it together. I would prefer to do it together."

She regarded him steadily for a time and then nodded her agreement.

"Good." Cooper gave her a small, tight smile and rose from his chair. He nodded at Doon.

"Leave her wings bound as they are. Untie the rest of her." He folded his arms and regarded Rise coolly again. "One fraction of an inch out of line and you'll be completely restrained again. Are we clear on that?"

"Yes," she said. Her tone giving away nothing.

She looked up at Cooper as Doon untied her.

"You have seen Sirens," she said to him suddenly.

He hesitated, then nodded, "Yes, I have."

"Where did you see them?" she demanded and her gaze was hungry.

"On Moethiica," he replied. "At the Echelon compound. In the very courtyard you ran to."

She stared at him open mouthed. "Where you took me."

"Yes," he replied.

"What did they say to you?" she gasped.

"That you would come to me there. It's why I waited so long amongst them." He walked away from her then, the memory of the feeling of the Sirens too much with the feeling of her right in front of him.

He felt the weight of the eyes of the others upon him as he walked past them. Rise was not the only one he'd surprised.

CHAPTER TWENTY-TWO

"See. He's not so bad. And you did threaten to kill him." CM Gemini finished readjusting the bindings on Rise's wings. Cooper would kill her if he found out. But he had put them on cruelly before. They were still firm. They would do. She had put some salve on her wrists where the ropes had cut into her too.

"I thought he was an Echelon," Rise said. Even knowing that he wasn't, he was still unsettling. And he had seen her.... she pushed the thought from her mind. She did not want to think about that.

"Do you still think that?" CM Gemini was asking. "Even a little bit?"

"No," Rise replied, hoping they could change the subject soon. "But there is something about him."

"He had just come out of that helmet when you first encountered each other. It takes a while for all the energy of them to begone."

"Have you ever seen them?" Rise asked her. "The Echelon. Up close and personal?"

"No." CM Gemini looked far away then. "But the stories of them are well known. Let's just say, I have been unfortunate enough to have encountered similar." The Chief Medic shuddered and Rise looked at her curiously.

"A long time ago now," she said just a little too brightly. She looked pointedly at Rise. "That man out there rescued you. Against all odds, he rescued you from them. Be thankful for that."

She turned back to packing away her medical supplies and she had a cheeky smile on her face now.

"And of all the worlds and rulers and governments who have been looking for you to make sure they are the ones to bring you before the Veil, I can think of worse ones to have ended up with."

Even Della smiled at that. "He is hot. Even when he's angry."

"Too hot for you, dumb heifer," came the snigger from the cage.

They all turned in unison. The Minx Fae. In all the excitement, they had forgotten her. But they had moved her covered cage into the Med-Bay while she slept off the tranq.

It appears she had slept it off rather quickly.

Rise, looked around the room, wondering where the voice had come from.

"And he got two Diamonds," continued the voice from the cage. "Like her. Easy to tell not Echelon. Echelon don't have any Diamond. Except he got one missing. Maybe they keep it. Bah." Balia was a little groggy still and rambling.

Rise looked pointedly now in the direction of the covered cage. "What is that?"

"Oh, my godds, Balia. I'd forgotten all about her," Gemini exclaimed.

"Queen Balia to you, dumb heifer."

Gemini rolled her eyes and strode to the cage, whipping back the cover. "I see your little sleep has done no improvements to your temperament.

"Rise, this is Balia. Balia this is Rise."

She turned to Rise apologetically. "Balia is the one responsible for your rather early exit from the stasis chamber."

"No early. She cooked!" Balia exclaimed excitedly. She looked at Rise appraisingly. "See I told you she was done and ready!"

"What does she mean I was cooked?" Rise demanded, peering in the cage at her. "And what is she?"

"I'm right here!" Balia shook her fist at her feebly in her restraints. "Don't speak like I'm not, pretty heifer!"

"She's a Minx Fae," Della replied drily. "And not to be listened to or trusted."

"A Minx Fae," Rise mused and then rounded on them. "The Pann. Minx Fae are the companions of the Pann. Why is she restrained like that?" She demanded. "Who did this to her? What is wrong with you people?"

"Yeeessssss. Go pretty heifer!" Balia egged Rise on delightedly from her cage. "They have been mean to me. So mean to me."

"Oh no." Della rubbed her forehead wearily.

CM Gemini bit her lip but turned her back on the Fae, addressing Rise earnestly. "We've been nothing of the sort. She's been treated more than fairly. Especially considering the fact she almost killed you," she said pointedly.

"Don't speak like I'm not here!" Balia yelled at Gemini, stomping her foot in frustration and baring her fangs at her.

"And opened up Della's arm with her horns," CM Gemini added, and Della raised her still heavily bandaged arm as proof. "They're not exactly harmless little creatures." She shot Balia a disapproving stare.

"What horns?" Rise asked. "All I can see on her head is funny pink things."

"Mittens," Della told her. "We had to put horn mittens on her."

"They're horrible." Rise screwed up her nose.

"Yes horrible!" Balia was jumping up and down in her cage. "Pink things on my horns. Horrible! Horrible! Horrible" She was working herself into quite a state.

"Rise, now don't you be taken in by her."

"Rise, she's not to be trusted."

They each laid a hand on her arm, both of their voices rising in a cacophony of protests.

"Release her!" Rise commanded, shaking off their hands and stepping towards the cage.

Balia stopped her tantrum to regard her shrewdly.

"Release her now!" Rise yelled.

"Oh, we can't do that."

"No, best we keep her in the cage."

"You don't know what she's like."

The cacophony of voices and protests again.

Rise strode to the cage. Ripped the ropes. Wrenched on the lock. Shattered it.

She tore the restraints from Balia. Tore the bindings on her wings like they made of paper. Discarded the mittens with a small noise of disgust.

She looked at Balia and Balia looked back at her, wide eyed and silent.

Then Balia reached out and lifted Rise's chin in her tiny hand.

"Ah," the Minx Fae said. "Pretty heifer. You the Siren."

And then she span around and around in midair circles of delight, whooping and smiling fit to burst.

Rise pulled back, narrowly missing being gouged by one of her newly mitten emancipated horns.

"Are you right there?" Della asked Balia drily when she eventually came to settle on top of a pile of not-to-be-settled-on Med supplies.

"Oh, I am more than right," Balia purred. My Master is going to be so pleased with me."

"Why?" Rise asked.

"Because my Master is Seth, King of all Pann Lords," Balia replied smugly "And he been looking for you everywhere."

"What the hell is going on in here?" The door burst open to reveal angry Cooper back in play.

"Ooooh, Hot Delicious," Balia crooned. "See." She flew to Rise and laid a hand on her forehead. "Two Diamonds here." She flew to Cooper and laid her hand in the same spot on him. "Two Diamonds here." She looked up at Cooper. "But one missing. Maybe it down lower." She said mischievously as her small hand headed south.

"Ow!" She squealed as he grabbed her hand roughly and held her away from him.

"Don't you hurt her you big bully." Rise rounded on him.

He ignored her. "Tranq her. Then bindings back on her and back in her cage," he ordered Della and CM Gemini. Holding the small Fae ready for them.

"Noooooooooo!" Moaned Balia and struggled furiously.

"You are a monster," Rise yelled at him.

"Yeeeesss monster!" Balia wailed. "Pretty Siren heifer help me!"

Rise took a step towards him but stopped short at the look in his eye. "Enough!" Cooper yelled. "Enough out of both of you."

"Tranq now," he ordered CM Gemini. The Chief Medic had it ready and obliged.

Balia sagged instantly and Cooper looked at Rise pointedly. "And don't think I won't do the same to you."

"You will do no such thing!" Rise stamped her foot at him angrily and stormed out of the room.

Cooper shoved the unconscious Fae at Della to re-cage her, and took off at a furious pace after Rise.

She was all the way to their sleeping area before he caught her by the arm. "Nice adjustment to your wing bindings. Come here." He held her easily when she tried to struggle away from him.

He pushed her up against his bed so her knees were locked with his body weight against them. With deft hands he pulled the bindings tight. Not as tight as he'd pulled them before but enough.

Done. He moved abruptly away from her, stalking back to the Med-Bay and Galley to have stern words with all of them about loosening the bindings on her wings.

"I hate you!" She turned and yelled at him, shaking with impotent rage. "I would rather be back on freaking Moethiica than here with you!"

It was silly. He had saved her ass. But the way they'd treated the Fae had upset her. And she was so angry it was the best she could do.

He turned back to her and his eyes and tone were icy. "I can assure you the feeling is most definitely mutual," he said. "On both counts."

"I liked you better when you were unconscious," he added, folding his arms and staring at her threateningly.

"You would. You Echelon poisoned bastard," she yelled furiously at him.

"Children please!" Jackdaw tried to calm things down by making light of them.

Rise looked around wildly for something to throw. Throwing something always felt so good when you were angry. The only throwable object in sight was his disgusting Echelon helmet. How appropriate. She lunged for it, quick as lightening and hurled it at him.

It missed him. Just. And only because he moved very, very quickly.

Jackdaw held his breath, expecting the worst. But Cooper simply turned on his heel and walked away from her, leaving Jackdaw to retrieve his helmet and pacify a still furious Rise.

CHAPTER TWENTY-THREE

The rest of them walked around on tiptoes after that. The tension between Rise and Cooper was so thick you could carve it with a knife.

They both had tempers.

The rest kept quiet and tried their best not to set either of them off.

When an hour or so had passed with nothing but the uneasy silence, CM Gemini and Doon gathered in the galley and let out sighs of relief.

Perhaps the worst of it had passed.

Those thoughts were immediately rewarded with the vision of Rise marching purposefully to the Med-Bay and retrieving Balia's cage.

"Oh godds, where is he?" Doon hissed.

"I don't know. I'm too old for this," CM Gemini said wearily, preparing to rise. But Doon put his hand on her arm halting her.

Rise had merely set Balia's cage down on a small metal ledge protruding out of the wall on the side of the hold.

She peeked underneath the cover and one hand was concealed underneath it for a time. And then she dropped the cover back in place looking well pleased with herself.

"She's unlocked that cage door, I'll put money on it," CM Gemini whispered under her breath.

Doon sighed. "I'll almost be glad to land on Vade5 at this rate."

"How far off do you think we are?" Gemini asked.

"Another 48 hours at least."

"Ok, folks, slight change of plans." Cooper's voice boomed across the hold as he strode towards them. The small device they'd seen constantly in his hand, was glowing intently.

The rest of his words were lost in the wrenching sound of great sheets of impossibly strong metal tearing, and a sudden ten-foot shower of sparks arcing into the hold.

Della screamed. Jackdaw, Doon and CM Gemini swore. Rise said nothing but looked a little wild eyed at the scene before her.

There was a split second when breathing lost its optional status, and they were all reminded quickly and completely of how precious that option was.

Then the flare of sparks subsided and something large and circular clicked into place.

The banging on the other side of the elevator entrance was loud and furious. They could hear the frustrated shouts of Celcius's men. They could not get through.

"Been busy?" Doon grunted at Cooper.

"I'm a light sleeper," Cooper replied with a small smile.

"Move to the nice big new hole in the ship, people," Cooper directed them. "We're jumping now."

"A ship jump. Are you serious?" Della asked him disbelievingly, but he had already moved away to where Rise was standing.

Rise was staring doubtfully into the nice big new hole he had ordered everyone to. Whatever was clicked into place was moving slightly. It looked neither safe nor stable.

She turned back to where Balia's cage rocked precariously on the ledge close by and hoped she had done enough to free her.

Cooper grabbed her and pressed her close and tight against his chest.

He didn't even hesitate.

He jumped.

And they were spiraling. Spiraling down a moving, rocking shaft. Their feet dangling in nothingness. Her wings tried to open instinctively, but the bindings held them safely closed.

There was so space for wings in the tight space. They would have torn to shreds along the sides of this thing if she'd opened them.

Regardless of the bindings, which she was suddenly grateful for, Cooper had them held closed and tight against her perfectly.

It was so quick. And the pressure on her body was so strong she felt she would burst.

And then something caught them. And the stillness was as bad as the movement, and it took all Rise's effort to hold down the bile in her throat.

She heard Cooper swear and felt him struggle with something.

Wisely, she determined that the best course of action at this point in time was to shut her eyes and keep them firmly closed.

And then whatever they were caught on released and they shot down again. Thank the godds it angled sharply at the bottom shortly after that and ended.

She felt Cooper ease her into other pairs of hands.

"Take her. I'll help the others," he said. And then two of them had her gently by each arm and she felt them moving up a gently sloping ramp.

When they arrived at their destination just a few minutes later, Rise still had her eyes tightly closed.

"You can open your eyes now," one of them said to her. It was a male voice. A nice voice. She did not recognize the accent, but the voice sounded like it was smiling.

Still, the opening of eyes seemed premature and foolish.

"'I think I just need to sit for a little while," she said quietly.

"Ok." There was a reassuring hand on her shoulder. "You sit. We'll be right here close by if you need anything."

Rise nodded and sank back into the chair, gripping the armrests tightly and pressing her feet as solidly as she could into the floor.

It was only a matter of minutes when she heard some familiar voices, as the others were brought to where they'd stationed her.

By the sounds of the cursing and swearing, the trip had not been popular with any of them.

"Are you Ok?" Chief Medic Gemini asked her, concern in her voice. She turned to shoot daggers at Cooper with her eyes as he strode past them both unawares, deep in conversation with another man Rise didn't recognize.

"I think so," Rise nodded, cautiously opening her eyes. "I didn't really like that," she added somberly. "Do you do that often in space travel?"

"No!" CM Gemini snorted. "And no-one likes it. Well maybe some." She looked pointedly in the direction of Cooper, but he was still lost in conversation with the other man. He did look kind of glowy and exhilarated though.

CM Gemini shook her head and turned her attention back to Rise.

"I'm going to check on the others," Gemini told her. "You going to be Ok here for a while?"

Rise nodded, all of a sudden touched by the woman's concern. She had never had that. Most winged on Moethiica are throwbacks. And abandoned or orphaned young. Rise had been abandoned. Had looked after herself. Other people showing concern was very new to her. CM Gemini patted her arm and moved off.

And the full view of the ship's panorama opened before her.

They were at the rear of the bridge. It was huge. A massive flight control desk dominated the center of the room. From the midpoint of the room and back, system arrays lined the walls.

The front half of the room, or at least the top half of it, was all window.

And the view out of it was magnificent.

The colors of the cosmos swirled outside the ship. Nebuli, Nebula, stars, moons.

In the sheer beauty of it, the fright from the ship jump was forgotten.

Rise felt a pulling, like a gentle tug on something within her. Something was about to happen. Something was calling to her.

She looked around to see if anyone was looking for her, but the ship was a blur of activity.

The others were still slumped, recovering from the Jump.

Cooper seemed to have forgotten she existed. He had his back half turned to her, and was pouring over a large image screen with two other men.

No, no-one was taking any notice of her for the moment. Rise made her way quietly and surreptitiously to the front of the ship and stood before the massive windows.

And The Star rose.

It swum up from underneath the ship and then it was everything. All she could see before her was The Star. Like a huge blue jewel suspended right in front of her.

Rise stumbled as the force of it hit her physically.

The Star's massive awareness pushed into her, vast and majestic. She felt very small in comparison to it.

It drove suddenly deeper and more forcefully into her then, and Rise gasped in pain. The pressure in her head was brutal. And she could not breath.

She doubled over in pain and fell to her knees. She looked up at The Star to beg for mercy, but there were strange shapes swirling in its depths, and she felt its anger.

Rise felt the chill creep over her. They were wrong. She was not who they believed her to be. The Star did not recognize her.

And then Cooper was suddenly there beside her. His hand gripped her upper arm. He lifted her to her feet. He stood her up in front of the angry Star and steadied her.

The Star went out completely.

And the entire cosmos plunged into blackness. Blackness and silence. And all but those on the Forgetting Worlds saw it and felt it.

Breath caught in Rise's throat and she gasped on it, suddenly alive, suddenly breathing again.

Cooper's strong hand was still on her arm. He stood before the blackness with her and held her upright.

And she heard the song.

And it was an old song. One she'd realized she'd known and not known for as long as she could remember.

And The Star was singing it.

Rise began to hum it softly under her breath, in time with The Star. And even at that pitch, her voice was magnificent. Full of promises and power and the birth of new beginnings.

And The Star appeared once more before them.

And it whispered something to Rise, underneath its song, just before it sent the Cosmos back in motion again.

And then there was suddenly searing, burning pain behind her eyes, and ever so slightly they changed color.

And the blue of The Star now intermingled with her startling violet.

The Star moved then. Suddenly passing beneath the underside of the ship. Rise could feel it underneath them and she turned, with Cooper still steadying her, to follow its journey.

But the sight before her stopped her in her tracks.

Every occupant of the ship stood gathered on the bridge looking at her. And as she looked at them, as one they dropped to their knees, hands on their heart, and bowed their heads to her.

CHAPTER TWENTY-FOUR

Rise stood staring, not sure what to do.

The crew remained, heads down, kneeling.

A flash of light in the windows caught her eye. She turned back to them as Cooper pushed her quickly to the ground.

An armada of ships hung in the space vacated by The Star.

The first gun fired and the shot flared against their shields, breaking in a booming wave against them. The entire ship vibrated with it.

"Battle shields down." The order was given. Rise was forgotten. The crew were back in their positions, a flurry of activity behind screens and controls.

Cooper waited until the titanium shields were in place and then lifted her by the arm, propelling her quickly to the rear of the ship.

"It's underneath us now." A ship's officer suddenly stepped into space beside him. "It's almost like it's covering it for us. As soon as it moves again it will be open. We can hover you over it in one of the deep flyers and drop you straight into it."

"You'll cover us?" Cooper questioned.

"We'll cover you," the officer affirmed.

"How much more of this can you take?" Cooper queried, still undecided as another blast shook the ship.

"More than you'd think," the man smiled. "We'll drop a disperser in over you. Nothing will follow you through. Well, nothing you can't handle," he added, still smiling. "Some of their smaller craft may slip the opening before the disperser takes full hold."

Cooper whistled. "Some ship you got here."

"Some ship," the other man agreed, still smiling.

Cooper thought about it only half a second longer. "Ok, let's do it."

He had never taken his hand from Rise's upper arm and he propelled her forward again. They moved quickly down a rear corridor and down another level.

Through another short passageway they came to a set of airtight doors.

They stopped and the men shook hands, quickly and efficiently.

"Is she stocked?" Cooper asked, adjusting something on his wrist. It was something new. Rise had never seen it on him before.

"Everything you need," he affirmed. "Godds speed friend."

"And you." Cooper clasped the man's shoulder.

The Ship's Officer punched in the code. The airtight doors hissed open.

The passage beyond looked dark and uninviting. But as Cooper stepped forward, some isolated panels on the walls lit slowly. The Ship's Officer pressed a small charm into Rise's hand. "From all of us. For luck," he said, closing her hand over it. "I promised all of them I would give it to you."

He stepped back. The airtight doors slid shut, and Rise was alone with Cooper in the small, dimly lit passageway.

Beyond it there appeared to be nothing. Just a big black emptiness.

It was quiet in here too. And cold.

"Where are the others and where are we going?" Rise asked, suspicion and the first faint glimmerings of alarm beginning to grow in her.

"We need to board a smaller craft," Cooper advised, placing her firmly in front of him and moving her swiftly forward.

"There's a hatch opening at the end of this passageway. I'm going to drop you through into it. You need to grab hold of the ladder. Dropping you through in 3, 2 …"

He dropped her, and she forgot all about the ladder. Rise landed hard on the ship's floor and grimaced at the pain that flared in her right ankle.

Cooper was down quickly behind her. Of course, there was no hard landing for him as he used the ladder.

She glared at him, ruefully rubbing her ankle, steadying herself on a strange looking transparent cylinder poking out from one wall as she did so.

"Get in," he indicated the co-pilot's seat.

It was the only adjustment they'd made to it that Cooper could tell off the bat. This was a one-man vessel with slight configurations.

Not seeing a great many alternative options available to her, Rise sat. Cooper buckled her in tight and jumped enthusiastically into the pilot's seat.

Rise watched him flipping switches, punching in commands, taking the manual controls and looking way too excited about things.

"Ready?" He asked her.

Rise sighed resignedly and nodded unhappily, gripped the arms of the chair and prepared for the worst.

Correctly she had figured out they were in the bulking hull of the ship where they must launch smaller craft from.

Wrongly, she had surmised that they were only going a short distance because of the size of the craft.

"Are the others in ones like this?" She asked, peering out into the darkness but not seeing anyone.

The others, Cooper thought. It's funny how some people you can know for the shortest amount of time and bond with. Whereas others you can know forever and you still wouldn't piss on them if they were on fire.

"Not exactly," he replied noncommittally as the hull opened beneath them and the light of The Star flooded everything around them blue.

He was aware of Rise gasping, and then The Star moved, revealing the drop, opened and waiting beneath it.

Cooper let out a "Fuck, yeah!" under his breath and drove the flyer deep into the drop. Their Confederation mothership, Savana9, immediately launched a disperser over their passage, as promised.

Two of the armada made it through before it took full hold of the opening. Closing both the way into the jump and any way back out of it.

CHAPTER TWENTY-FIVE

The fighters that had followed them in, lost no time in their attack. They were fast too. Maneuvering themselves quickly past Cooper and Rise, and turning round to face them head on.

Rise tensed, thinking they were done for, but Cooper took out the first one instantly and sent the other one spinning quickly away from them.

Rise got a brief glimpse of its occupants before they spun away. One human, one hybrid. Their eyes locked on hers, their expressions intense.

Cooper accelerated suddenly, diving at breathtaking speed after the spinning ship and taking them out completely in one singular, spectacular explosion.

"The firepower in this baby," he murmured appreciatively. And then it was all just one, big sickening blur.

Rise was forever grateful when whatever they were in spat them out into the relative calm of normal space. A passing asteroid shower which Cooper managed to rather skillfully maneuver around seemed relatively peaceful in comparison.

As Cooper made various adjustments and studied all manner of systems and read outs, Rise thought about how much she had always wanted to space travel.

Who knew how much it truly sucked.

She prayed they would be landing soon. A big ship like the one they'd just been on would suffice. A large solid planet would be preferable.

"You Ok?" Cooper asked her, looking unreasonably happy with himself and their situation, unbuckling his restraints and reaching over to do the same with hers.

She shook her head and slapped at his hand. "No! And I would like to leave the restraints on please."

"Um, you can't," he looked at her carefully, trying to gauge her level of hysteria.

She seemed alright. So, he continued with the facts as they stood.

"We need to get out of these seats and into the Stasis Chamber."

"Stasis chamber? What do you mean stasis chamber?"

Her voice was getting that dangerous rise in volume. Maybe he had not gauged her as well as he'd thought.

"Not like the one they had you in when you were injured," he reassured her hastily. "A deep space one. There are two jumps to Earth from here. We need to be in stasis for both of them. It's to protect us," he added. And then wished he hadn't when he saw the look on her face.

"What do you mean jumps to Earth!" Rise looked around her wildly. "In this thing! You must be joking!"

"This 'thing' is worth a freaking fortune." Cooper shook his head. "This is state of the art." He took a deep breath, calming himself with some effort. "We're quite safe." He looked at the control panel. "But we need to get in the stasis chamber *Now*."

He reached over and unbuckled her restraints and guided her gently but firmly up and out of the co-pilot's seat.

"But who's flying?" Rise stubbornly gripped the seat with one arm, refusing to move.

"Auto-flight." Cooper said it, and looked at her as he said it, like she was incredibly stupid.

Rise felt herself start to hyperventilate.

"You can't put this thing on auto-flight!" She cried. "You have to fly it! I want you to fly it! I can't believe this thing even has auto-flight! Oh, my godds I hate this."

"That's it. Enough," he muttered angrily to himself. Prying her fingers with ease off the chair, he picked her up around the waist like she was a child and moved her swiftly into the strange transparent cylinder thing she'd noticed earlier.

He moved in quickly after her. It was a tight fit. The side she was pressed against was padded. His body pressed against hers as he keyed commands into a controller above her head. Like on the mother ship, the front window was suddenly encased in steel. A dizzying amount of readouts before it.

The fact that she could no longer see just how close she was to deep space reassured Rise somewhat. That and the calmer pumping through the activated stasis chamber was making her feel a little better about their state of affairs.

Cooper placed his palms and forearms on either side of her and shifted his weight somewhat. But it was impossible for their bodies not to touch at least a little, the space was so small.

"Where is Balia?" Rise asked Cooper suddenly, her words starting to sound a little slurry and sleepy as the stasis chamber began to fully activate.

Cooper shook his head. "Don't know. Shoosh now," he said. "Let the stasis take you."

Rise nodded and closed her eyes, close to stasis sleep already, sinking into the padded cushioning behind her.

Cooper deftly fastened her in place and then secured himself. The stasis gas would keep them upright on this short jump, and there was barely room to move at all with both of them in there but better to be safe than sorry.

As the stasis gas began to fill the chamber in earnest, he looked down at the now completely still form of Rise.

Some people were lucky like that. The stasis took them out instantly.

He was not so lucky when it came to stasis. He never had been.

It was strange. He got to experience the transition. Feeling his finely honed, finely trained mind having to slowly relinquish control. Give himself over to the stasis.

The oddest of thoughts came to him at this time. The strangest of feelings.

And this time was no different.

But the thought that came was not a thought he liked. Or one he was even allowed to be thinking.

She was his.

He breathed deep, trying to shake the thought loose with his breath. It was the Echelon energy still pumping through him.

He was very much aware that even now, this long out of the helmet, this long away from them, his thoughts still oscillated between theirs and his own.

He was the first to go undercover on Moethiica. The first to infiltrate the Echelon that he knew of. Jackdaw had warned him. Said that CM Gemini had experience with others like the Echelon. Like them but not even close.

No-one really knew how long it would be until he was completely free of them. He had to be careful. He had to be oh, so very careful around her.

But godds. That Siren energy of her broke against him every time he got near her. But that's what he had to remember. That she was a Siren. And this was some of the power they possessed. To drive a man crazy with it.

Was she doing this on purpose to him? Did she even know how? Did she even feel it?

She had felt the Star when it had marked her, he knew that much. He had felt it with her.

Which was another hangover from the Echelon and another very bad sign he had gotten too close.

He would need to keep his distance. Watch her carefully.

He stared at her exquisite face until the stasis took him, fighting thoughts that he told himself over and over again were not his own.

CHAPTER TWENTY-SIX

On GhostSong5, the Echelon Mage, Arc, was bored. And angry.

He had been deceived. The Siren of the 5ᵗʰ had been right in front of him. Helpless. Bound.

Only a few more precious seconds and he could have wielded the Nephliim Blade properly on her. Who she was would have been revealed to him.

But a traitor in their midsts had ruined everything. Shot him. Killed many Echelon. Saved her.

Saved her, and the little Siren bitch had taken the Diamond with her.

Arc seethed, fresh waves of anger emanating from him. A black glass goblet on the large desk cracked with it and shattered.

He picked up one of the large sharp, black shards thoughtfully.

The liquid from the goblet oozed over the desk, wetting the sleek blonde hair of the Cybriid lying on the desk before him.

Perfect hair. Perfect skin. Perfect Cybriid.

But manufactured to be so.

The most advanced CyTech form in existence.

He knew that there were nerve endings in her perfect Cybriid flesh that triggered receptors in her brain.

He knew her pain was real enough when she felt it.

And she would not die. There was that. He could do things to her over and over again that no organic flesh and blood being could survive.

But they just could never perfect the fear on these things. The memories. For that was where the real satisfaction lay. To keep them barely alive and thrumming with fear. Let them heal a little. Let them hope a little.

Then bring them back. And do worse, much, much worse than before.

Stop as they began to beg for death. Keep their ruined bodies and ruined souls hanging by a thread. Send them away. Bring them back again. Repeat the cycle again, and again and again.

That is how the fear became palpable and exquisite. He licked his lips and felt his mood begin to lift again.

He remembered how long he had kept the winged deceiver Soar alive. Her wings were now encased in the new entertainment area. He had let her see them hanging there before the end.

And the mind-diamonds. The Cybriids had no mind-diamonds. And that was the most exquisite part of all, capturing those. The power, oh the power. And the waves. You had to free it in the peak of their waves. And the sensations of the waves stayed with the power, thrumming you with it constantly.

Arc groaned and slammed his fist into the desk in frustration.

There were no other females on this ship. And he grew so bored after a time with the Cybriids.

He sighed, running the large, black shard of jagged glass almost absently down her cheek. Blood welled beneath it. Cybriid blood, but still red and satisfying. He cut deeper and harder, making her cry out. That pleased him.

The comms unit on the desk beside her hip sounded. Incoming. He pressed the screen to take it.

"Yes?" His voice was slightly hoarse.

There was a slight pause. "Clumsy miss. I hope you have plans to rectify it."

The Echelon grimaced and turned his attention away from the Cybriid. "There are more jumps to Earth."

"Yes, but none as quick as those," the voice replied. "They will be there before you," it added pointedly.

Arc grunted. "It will not matter. I will make up the time lost when I land."

"Yes. You will," the voice replied sardonically.

There was silence for a time and then the voice asked. "Who is he? And who is he to her? Do we know this yet?"

"Him?" the Echelon scoffed. "Some pathetic human Earth spy. He is nothing. And nothing to her."

"Not so pathetic," the voice mused. "To have done what he has done so far."

"Luck." Arc grunted. "Luck he will pay dearly for. I will enjoy killing him. And I will make him watch what I do to her first."

"You know you cannot kill her until she opens the Veil, Arc," the voice commanded him sternly.

"Yes." he growled reluctantly. "But I can still have some fun with her before...."

"No!" the voice cut him off. "After she opens the Veil you may do what you wish to the Siren whore. Prior to that Veil Opening she is off limits. Well, off limits to your more exotic tastes anyway."

The voice paused. "We must be in control of her when that Veil opens. It must be our own who come through first."

"Of course, we will control her. We have the Blade," Arc replied, as if that settled everything.

"Do not dismiss the might of the Original Makers or the Nephliim amassing behind that Veil. Even those Siren bitches in their full glory. All of them wait to come through and wipe us from the cosmos," the voice chided him. "You are young, Arc. You have not encountered our true foes before. They are worthy enemies I can assure you."

"But we will have our own come through the Veil first." Arc closed his eyes as he thought of it. Old Ones, even stronger than the ones who ruled the cosmos now. All that power. They would pour through, join with those of them already here and crush the Confederation and the rebels. They would crush everyone. All who stood against them. The thought almost took him over the edge.

"Yes," the voice mused. "It will be a magnificent and bloody final war. And we will prevail, young Arc, have no doubt of that. But do not grow complacent!" He snapped. "And leave the Siren whole until I say so."

"You are right as always," Arc smiled, as he thought of Rise splayed and bleeding before him, instead of the Cybriid.

"What are you playing with while you speak to me, Arc?" The voice did not sound disapproving, just curious.

"Just a Cybriid," Arc replied. "There are no other females available to me on this ship," he spat angrily.

"There was one," the voice said. "Oh, Arc."

"I was angry," Arc replied. "And she was more fragile than I am used to." He turned to the ship's guard who stood behind him, leaning back against the wall "Bring me another." He licked the Cybriid's cheek. "A different flavor. Godds why can they never get the taste right on these bitches."

"Yes, but they make them look so delightful," the voice on the other end of the comms unit said.

Arc sighed and sat back in the chair. At least they would reach earth soon and his real mission could begin.

"Do you have another one coming?" The voice on the comms unit asked.

"Yes," Arc replied absently.

"Excellent. Now why don't you amuse yourself by pretending she's that little Siren that got away from you so easily. And when you're done with that, you can pretend she's her little earth boyfriend who deceived you under your very nose."

Arc howled and smashed the comms unit with his fist.

The Cybriid did not return to service on the ship when he was done with her.

CHAPTER TWENTY-SEVEN

The first time the recruiters came to visit, his dad shut the door in their faces.

Cooper Pierce heard him angrily tell them to get lost. Their front door was heavy and white. Cooper knew all too well how heavy. It had broken his fingers when it slammed on them when he was little.

Or, more accurately, when his dad had slammed it. An accident. A drunken accident. Cooper had learned the hard way. He was more careful around him now.

It had been his left hand and one of the fingers had never quite got perfectly straight again. As the house shook with the door banging shut, he jumped with fright, and cracked the knuckle.

Nerves. He did it every time that door slammed.

Still, it didn't stop him from going to the window and drawing back the heavy curtains.

They were walking away. In their highly polished shoes. Cooper always noticed their shoes. When they came to the school and watched him, he would see their shoes. Polished and shining. Seemingly impervious to the dirt and dust around them.

Even their car was polished. And very cool. Black, old school Jeep. They could keep the shoes, but Cooper thought he would very much like the car.

One of them paused now to look back at him before he got in to it. Straight back and up like he knew exactly where his bedroom was.

He smiled at Cooper and raised his hand in salute and Cooper responded in turn.

"Get away from there! What the fuck are you doing! Get away from there!"

The stench of stale alcohol hit him as his dad pulled him roughly away from the window.

He hated that smell. He screwed up his nose at it, and pulled away from his father just as roughly.

He was just coming into the first hint of his strength. His dad tottered and Cooper looked away from him in disgust.

The hurt lanced through his father. At what had become of him. And the look in his son's eyes.

He had so much to tell him. So much to warn him about. They did this to him. They did this. But he was not allowed to say anything about any of it to anyone.

Well fuck them. They could not have his son.

"You're not going with them!" He yelled at Cooper. "You're never fucking going with them! You hear me?"

He lunged for him, but Cooper evaded him easily. Well-practiced. His poor, tired mother was suddenly there. Gently, expertly, also well practiced, she led his father away.

Later that night, when he got up to use the bathroom, he heard his father crying in the spare bedroom. Not crying like his mom cried. These were silent tears. Still, he heard him.

If it was his mom crying Cooper would hug her until she stopped. He had tried to do the same for his dad once and got a beating he would not soon forget.

He passed by the room and did not try to enter.

The next day, his dad swore off the drink again and started going back to his AA meetings. The recruiters came again a few weeks later.

When they were gone his dad stormed out of the house.

He came back with a bottle but didn't open it. Outstared it from the opposite end of the dining room table.

Cooper loved that table. Red wood colonial. Happy memories of homework and model planes, helping his not so tired mom prepare dinner. Afternoon treats. Stories. Milk and cookies.

They rarely used it now. His mom worked two jobs, sometimes three. There was no more time to prepare dinner.

The recruiters watched him at school still. He began to see their polished, gleaming shoes often.

The next time they came to the house, their timing was perfect.

A freak work accident. The machine had come down cruelly on her right hand, crushing bone and tendon. She was home alone. And a world away from the beautiful girl who had married the handsome soldier.

Broke, worn out, worn down, physically and emotionally exhausted.

It was a special program they said. For boys Cooper's age, conducted at a new state of the art facility at a base in California.

It would be a fully paid scholarship. Secondary and post. Cooper would come out of it with a college degree. He would enter the military as an Officer.

No, they only required her signature.

And that was the last of AA and the end of a marriage.

Cooper didn't see the worst of it. He was gone not long after the ink dried on his scholarship.

They collected him in the black Jeep.

They drove through desert.

Before they passed through the checkpoint to their highest level of their security clearance designations, they showed him the special center where parents could come to visit with their children.

His father came once. Outside of the designated time. Drunk and threatening lawyers.

His mother came separately. She was no longer in their family home and had moved back in with her mother.

She flirted with the guards who had forcibly removed his father. And embarrassed Cooper equally.

His father emailed him constantly. But it was edited almost to the point of being illegible.

His mother. Well, that was the last of it. He never heard from her.

Cooper threw himself into the rigorous schedule of the academy. From 5am to 10pm, six days a week, every hour was decided for him.

There were only thirty odd other boys and girls with him there at the start.

Each of them underwent the same surgery.

The surgery was a necessity for the military operations for which they were being groomed.

These were the third generation of Earth's Off-World Black Operations. Off-World-Black-Ops. OBO.

And it was hoped that with this generation, they had the surgery perfected.

Like the ones before them, all of these boys and girls had been chosen for a specific brain pattern configuration. Less than .05% of the human Earth population were likely to have it.

The military knew. They scanned for it regularly.

And of that .05% who scanned true, still only a percentage of them were detected young enough, and with the physical attributes and potential necessary to become Off-World Agents. Running solo missions on the numerous worlds the good people of Earth had no knowledge of.

Over time, the best of the best of these young recruits would be briefed on another mission. SIREN5. No matter where they were and what they were doing, SIREN5 immediately became Priority One, should it come into play.

Cooper was the best. Without question.

"Well done son."

Cooper saluted smartly. "Thank you, Sir."

The Commanding Officer before him meant the world to him. Had become like a father to him. He would follow this man into war. Go to battle. Would do anything for him.

The Commander looked as if he was about to say more.

It was a subtle eye movement from his own Superior, but enough. And he moved on without speaking, to the next specially chosen soldier.

It was a damn shame. He felt incredibly close to this young man. This star cadet. He was going to make an outstanding Agent.

Like his father. Before everything had gone to hell, and taken him with it.

One day, hopefully his boy here would get to know just what his father had done before that happened.

And he hoped the worlds young Cooper was going to see, and the adventures he was going to go on, were compensation enough for a long life lived well, and unknowing, here on Earth.

But what choice did they have?

Yes, the surgery was a ticking time bomb. But their own unique brain maps alone ensured that none of these young men or women would ever sit on a porch with their grandchildren.

But the worlds they would see. And the greater cause they would be part of. These young soldiers would bring back the keys to release Earth from its Old Ones prison. The Old Ones who left Earth stuck in an endless Forgetting Game. Their chains and their webs wrapped tightly around us while they terrorized the cosmos and prepared for the day they would win the final war and rule it completely.

These recruits would be the ones who stopped that happening. They would be the ones who brought back the weapons to free our allies behind the Veil. Those who had the power to fight the Old Ones. Break the game. Free Earth. Save the cosmos.

They would ensure the grandchildren of other men sat on porches truly real, truly free. Not on the porches they sat on now, which were illusion.

Moethiica. All the signs were pointing to Moethiica. So far it had been an impossible destination. An impossible mission. But Cooper would get there. He was sure of it.

CHAPTER TWENTY-EIGHT

While Rise showered in the tiny flyer bathroom, Cooper plotted their course to Earth.

They were not far away now. The Star and the jumps it had opened after the first drop would serve them well. If the disperser the mothership had laid over the initial drop held, there was no way anyone could catch them.

There were other ways to Earth. Other jumps. But they had a decent twenty-four hours on any of those options now. It was enough. It would have to be. He would take it.

The next jump was longer. They would be in stasis for the equivalent of just over three days. Horizontal this time. The chamber had already rotated itself in readiness for it.

It lay parallel to the floor, the padded cushioned side now the base on which they would lie. The domed cover was pushed back and would automatically close over them.

There was a longer process to going in. A calmer and diagnostics the chamber would run. The gas would contain everything they needed to survive in terms of nutrients. The diagnostics the chamber took for an hour or so prior to them going under would tailor the cocktail for them to perfection.

And shortly after that they would be at the outer webs.

OBO had a transitioning station there. He needed to explain that to her before they got there.

Earth.

Cooper steepled his hands and gazed out into deep space. Not really seeing any of it.

It felt like an age since he'd been there.

He'd seen some things, felt some things, done some things.

His mind drifted to the last woman he'd been with on Moethiica. Well the last woman he'd been with by choice anyway. He pushed the images of the women he'd been with as an Echelon far from his mind. Off-World there was no-one coming to lift you out of your Cover if things got too heavy. You rolled with it. Or died. That simple.

He wondered where he was going next. And then chided himself for getting ahead of himself. Was he really so keen to leave it again?

Rise emerged in one of the black flight suits the Confederation mothership, Savana9, had supplied them with. Almost identical to his own. They were light but tough. And this one she couldn't rip open with her fingernail. Unlike his completely ruined shirt.

Well it was not like it had been his to start with anyway. Part of the bundle of clean clothes CM Gemini had secured for him. He was half sorry to see her out of it. She wore it rather well.

She had used a small knife from one of the supply kits to cut two expert holes in the flight suit. He had hesitated only an instant before handing her the small knife and remained ready for anything while it was in her possession.

As he'd watched her carefully he'd wondered how many times she'd had to do that as a winged female growing up on Moethiica. It was forbidden to sell clothing especially made to accommodate them. Another subtle way to keep them downtrodden.

He had tensed again when it came time for her to hand back the knife. She had met his eyes, sensing his discomfort and instantly realizing the cause of it. "Relax, Cooper Pierce. I need you to fly the ship."

And she had turned on her heel and gone to take her shower.

She was holding her wings against her now, unbound. It always marveled him how they could fold in like that so compactly. The tips of them rose up high above her shoulders. But aside from those, her wings were invisible.

"I found these," he handed her the self-adjusting wing bindings he had found amongst their supplies. Most craft carried at least two of them. She could loosen them and take them off and on as she pleased. Rise looked at them and at him in astonishment.

"I've heard of these but never seen them." There were no wealthy or free winged on Moethiica who she would ever have seen sporting them. She examined them carefully and then fitted them over herself, struggling a little with the exact mechanics of their workings.

Cooper rose to help her. Tying them just underneath her breasts and showing them how to work them. An image of her from the Echelon room rose in his mind and he stepped carefully back and away from her.

Rise was delighted with the new bindings and surprised he had given her some which she could control herself. She looked at him with the beginnings of trust in her eyes.

"I wanted to thank you," she said, almost shyly.

"For what?" he asked, surprised and a little dumbfounded.

"For standing with me. For standing me up in front of the Star. Thank you." She reached out to touch his arm.

But he pulled sharply back from her and turned away to the control panel

"Rise, there are things I need to tell you about Earth before we get there." He changed the subject abruptly. "And we do not have a great deal of time before we need to be in stasis for the next jump."

"Will the others meet us there?" she asked him. Hurt by his reaction but determined not to show it.

"Perhaps," he said noncommittally. "Probably not until after you open the Veil Portal."

"Oh," she responded and re-took her seat in the co-pilot's chair, looking at him a little sadly.

Cooper remained standing. He was not looking forward to this. Not one little bit at all.

"Rise, when we get to Earth's outer webs we're going to land at a Transitioning Station. You've heard of these?"

Rise nodded. She knew that you couldn't just land on some worlds and jump off your ship like you could on others. You had to go through a transitioning process so you could be there, exist there. She didn't understand all the science behind it but she got the basics.

"We'll both need to transition there and go through that process. Earth is a Forgetting Game world. There's no way around it. We won't forget though," he added hastily. "We'll remember everything."

Cooper ran his hand through his hair nervously, looking decidedly uncomfortable.

"Cooper Pierce," Rise said, eyeing him suspiciously. "What aren't you telling me?"

He sighed heavily.

"On a Forgetting Game world, people don't remember anything. Who they truly are. All that's truly possible. Hell, they don't even remember there are other worlds out there. It's a very limited concept of reality. And whatever it doesn't include, can't actually exist there. So, the transitioning has to put us both in a form that the majority of Earth believes is actually possible."

He took a deep breath and then plunged on with it.

"Rise, there's no delicate way to put this. You won't have your wings there."

She just stared at him open mouthed, convinced she must have misheard him.

He said nothing further.

"What do you mean?" she asked, gripping the chair arms, wide eyed and horror stricken.

"No-one on earth has wings, Rise. So, if we put you on Earth without transitioning you, your wings wouldn't survive. Most likely, you wouldn't survive. At all."

"It's not as bad as it sounds," he reassured her earnestly. "Your wings are kept safe this way, out of Earth's atmosphere. And you walk Earth as one of us. As a human."

This was not going well. He could tell by the look in her eyes. But he didn't know what else to say. He'd explained it as well as he'd been trained to do so. Maybe she was just taking a little while to warm up to it.

"Well I'm not going. You can just take me back to Moethiica right now and I'll take my chances there. Because I'm not going!" Rise screamed the last at him and rose from her chair.

Or maybe not.

She seemed to be getting a little hysterical.

"Rise, Rise! Listen to me." He grabbed both her hands and held them tight. "Look at me. We've got this covered. It's what the Transitioner does. Your wings will be safe. Held in the station. In a sort of virtual stasis almost. You'll get them back Rise. You just won't have them on the ground."

"When will I get them back?" she demanded suspiciously.

"When you leave." Fark. Just the thought of her leaving evoked something in him. And he could feel her anger through her hands. It rolled over him. Not entirely unpleasant. He wanted to take that anger and roll it into something else entirely.

Almost like she sensed where his thoughts had taken him, she wrenched her hands away from him.

"Oh, so someone will just fly me back up to this transitioning station to get my wings reattached after I open the Veil portal, and send me on my way!"

She glared at him fiercely

"And what would you have me do then? Fly home?"

Cooper felt his own anger rise then. His brain to mouth filter deserted him. He said the first thing that came into his head.

"Rise, now you're just being silly."

She gasped at him, not believing the words that had just come out of his mouth.

She was so angry she wanted to kill him. But she really did need him to fly the ship. So, she yelled at him instead.

"No, Cooper. Do you know what silly is? Silly is expecting the winged person you believe to be a winged Siren no less, to be able to open a Veil Portal for you after you've taken her freaking wings away and turned her into an earthbound human! That's silly!"

She turned to storm off to the bathroom, but he swung her round, grabbing both her wrists and dragging her into him. Forcing her to look up at him.

"Listen to me. No listen to me!" He tightened his grip on her wrists until she stopped her furious struggling. "When that Veil Portal is ready for you, you're going to transition into whatever form you need to be in. And once the Forgetting Game is over you can take whatever form you goddam well please."

He released her wrists and pushed her away from him.

"And don't worry about getting home to your precious Moethiica. If you're so keen to get back there so a dozen Echelon can do you every which way and back again, it will be my pleasure to fly you straight back there personally, once you're done."

Where had those words even come from? He would have given anything to be able to take them back again.

"Rise, I'm sorry." He stepped forward and reached out to her.

She stepped in close, closing the rest of the distance and slapped him hard across the face. Then burst into tears and made a beeline for the bathroom door.

As the door slid shut behind her, Cooper heard the sounds of things thrown and breaking.

With a smarting cheek, he settled himself back at the controls and busied himself with the task of flying again.

He was so not looking forward to being on Earth with this woman when she discovered the slam-ability of its doors.

CHAPTER TWENTY-NINE

It was sometime later when Rise exited the bathroom. He hoped she had cooled off.

He had. He knew he probably could have handled the whole thing better. But, fark, it's not like he'd had much practice at telling Sirens coming to earth they were about to disconnect with their wings. Albeit temporarily.

"You Ok?" He didn't look at her, he needed to concentrate on his flying at this particular junction, but he asked the question. As gently as he could, he asked it.

She sat down beside him but said nothing, arms folded over her chest, and stared straight ahead.

He spared a quick glance at her face.

Her face was calmer. But sulky. He knew that face. He had seen it on women cosmos wide. It didn't matter what he would say now, it would be interpreted wrongly and go down badly.

He was learning.

He said nothing.

Wisely.

Instead, as soon as he was able to, he took one hand off the controls of the ship and put his arm around her shoulders, giving her a gentle squeeze and rubbing her upper arm in a soothing up and down motion.

It took her by surprise. She looked up at his face, but he said nothing and did not turn to her, just kept it calm and focused forward.

Which was fortunately necessary, as it was taking all of his concentration to maneuver the ship one handed.

She sighed and huffed, but the initial tension was broken and Cooper smiled to himself. Say nothing. Show no fear. Calm with touch. Give physical comfort.

The man who had unveiled that mystery of the cosmos to him should be knighted. Of course, it wasn't a man, but a sort of friendlier looking version of the creature from the old Alien films.

Apparently, this approach worked not only across worlds but across species.

There were a few clumsy moments in maneuvering the ship, and he had a wry thought that if they impaled themselves on a piece of space junk because he was too reluctant to remove his arm from her shoulders it was going to look very bad on his report.

Eventually it got to the stage where he had it. They were at the second jump. They needed to get into that stasis chamber.

"Rise, we're at the second jump. I need you to move into the stasis chamber now."

She nodded and got up slowly, seemingly only noticing it was horizontal rather than vertical for the first time.

"It's a much longer one this time round." He turned his head to look at her and then quickly back to the control panel. "Just go back there and lie down in it."

"Ok." What else was she going to do? Rise sighed heavily and settled herself into the chamber, lying back against the side closest to the wall.

Cooper activated the sequence for the chamber from the deck and moved back to join her.

He pierced her finger with the tiny diagnostics needle and then did the same with a second one in his own.

"How long do we need to keep these in," Rise asked frowning.

"Not long. Another minute," Cooper replied. "They go in there." He indicted a small pod on the side of the chamber.

They waited in silence until the pod sounded. Carefully he removed the needle from her finger and ripped a whole lot less carefully at his own, making Rise wince at the motion.

Turning to her he surveyed their lack of space and considered how much more restricted they would be when the dome closed over. The least space would be at Rise's back now where it curved. Which wouldn't do for her wings.

"Move forward," he said. " Let me get in behind you."

"But my wings," she protested. She had wanted to keep them out of the way of him.

"There won't be any room for your wings where you are when that dome closes." He said pragmatically. Which was true.

She shifted forward and he moved into the space behind her.

They were still bound of course, but loose enough that they could be parted. There is an art to it with bound wings. Parting them just so.

Cooper did it expertly, slipping an arm around her stomach and drawing her close back against him. Her wings spread perfectly for the comfort of both of them.

He had slept with a winged before. The realization struck her.

She swallowed hard, wondering why it meant so much to her. He had been off his own world on many different worlds. No doubt he had slept with many a different woman.

But a winged. And one had he had slept with carefully. Gently.

Somehow it changed everything.

The dome began to close over them, the first gases of the chamber activating.

Rise relaxed. For the first time enough that Cooper's energy hit her. Waves of it. Warm, male, thundering.

Cautiously she opened herself up to him a little further.

Heat, throbbing, rippling, seeking purchase, pushed into her. She felt the tingle at the base of her skull as they connected.

Possession. She knew it instantly. Whatever ebbed from him, engulfing her in its waves, sought not only purchase in her but possession.

She struggled just a little against it.

And just that slight struggle was enough to send the man who would possess her over the edge.

Cooper groaned. Drawing her even closer to him with the arm wrapped tight and hard around her waist.

It was like the Sirens in the Echelon courtyard all over again. Ripples of pure pleasure washed over him. She was the promise of the most exquisite ecstasy he had ever known. And there was no cold statue here to reach out a hand to and steady himself on.

There was just her. And she was his. And the struggle was exquisite. Because he wanted her to struggle just a little bit, didn't he?

Yes, he did. He wanted that. He wanted all manner of things. Some of them unspeakable. Some of them undoable here in this flyer. But he would start with her writhing underneath him, enfolded in her wings.

He knew wings. Knew the sensations that ran through them. And he traced the parting on them now, his hand moving up to come to close around her neck. Rise moaned and he drew her underneath him with an easy, well-practiced movement.

He kissed her. Hard and probing and deep.

And the kiss changed everything.

The Veil over Earth shimmered visibly and the Star began to sing.

And Rise felt her own song begin in response to it.

And it was the song of the cosmos, the song of worlds, and stars and rebirth. It was the song of creation as only a Siren knows how to sing it.

Cooper heard but a note of it. But that note was his note. And in that one note he realized why the Sirens had been given this power.

And he realized that the way through her was the way to himself, and something much bigger than himself. Much bigger than her. Much bigger than everything.

He saw then how worlds were made. How portals and bridges and gateways were shut and open.

And as he saw it, Rise saw it, and she saw how and what she must do. And she came to know herself.

Rise's eyes flew open, a deep awareness on the edge of her vision.

Cooper, knew at last what had always nagged at him, ever since he was a child, and for the first time felt at peace with it.

He raised his lips from hers, their eyes locked, and they knew each other, really knew each other.

And they knew there was another secret which would be unlocked once he was inside of her.

But in the world of the ship, the stasis sequence kicked in to its final shut down, the domed roof closing gently over them, the thick white gas encasing them.

And in the dreamless world of stasis, they felt nothing, knew nothing, saw nothing.

And in three days' time, when the stasis lifted, and the roof of the stasis chamber opened slowly over them, they remembered nothing of this.

They returned to the former versions of themselves. The whole experience, forgotten.

<u>CHAPTER THIRTY</u>

The creature looked like a man. But it had glittery eyes.

Not shining with health glittery, but glittery like they had sharp edges. Like a cut diamond.

The creature reading these thoughts from the General's mind smiled to himself. It had cost him a lot of energy concealing his eyes. He was glad to have no further need of it.

He stood. His suit had cost forty-eight thousand dollars. The product of Behemoths, goats and white gold. It was impeccably tailored and required no smoothing. He smoothed it anyway.

The man behind the desk did not rise. His suit had not cost forty-eight thousand dollars. But it did contain gold. Four stars worth of gold. Each and every one of them earned. He was not going to stand for one of these bastards.

The creature looked at the General. Disguising nothing. Letting the full glint on the outer retina shine. He leaned over the desk and let his full power wash over him. The General was a proud man but not too proud to admit it chilled him to the bone.

And they had done it to him too many times of late. His heart began to tap irregularly as the shaking started. He felt the sweat trickle down his back. But he held his eyes. Goddamn it! He was a General of the US Army and he would hold this bastard's eyes.

"The Veil Portal has become visible," the creature, the Old One, Rend, it called itself, said.

The General shook his head in confusion. The creature was back in his chair, like he'd never risen. His heart slowed but the dread rose.

"We've had no reports of any sightings." His voice disgusted him after they'd worked him over with their energy. And that was just the two of them. There were only two of them here now. Only two of them that could land. This one and the other one. He hated to think what power they would wield when there was more of them.

The creature ignored him. "Who is he General? Who exactly is the Cooper Pierce who is having such an effect on her?"

The General stared at him coldly. He had still been Lt General when Cooper Pierce left on this mission. The star cadet, the star recruit. He had been like a son to him. "He is an Agent. An OBO Agent. One of many. That's all I can tell you."

The creature sighed. "Don't play me for the fool General. He is more to you than that." He studied the General intently like he was scanning him. "No matter. We will know exactly what he is, as soon as he lands. If I find that you have with-held anything of significance at that point General…Well let's just say, things will be unpleasant for you."

He was at the door, another one of those sudden movements. The General tensed but continued to stare at him coldly as if it had not affected him.

The creature looked around the room as if taking it in for the last time. And he smiled.

The door clicked shut behind him.

And then his real power washed over the General. The shaking took a long time to subside. He clutched at his heart as the pain shot through it. The bleeds again. He could feel it come from his ears and nose.

A lifetime of memories flashed through his mind. All the way back. Back to when he'd first joined the army. Young, proud, patriotic. A family man and a country man and proud of it.

He would fight on the side of righteousness. Fight and change the world. Make it a better place. Leave it a better place than he'd found it.

These were the thoughts and memories of a dying man. He knew it. Had known it for a while now. And known the creature that had just walked out the door had done it to him.

Him and the other. God, how long had they been here. Working them over. Unbeknownst to all of them.

Cooper Pierce. He would see the boy safely back to Earth and away from these bastards. He could last that long. It was the least he could do for him.

CHAPTER THIRTY-ONE

Cooper woke first.

There was still an hour left of stasis. The activation sequence had only just started, but it was enough to bring him to consciousness. It was often like this for him.

But best for her to come out of it gently.

He keyed in the commands to pop the dome open, closing it quickly back over her once he was up and out of it.

Cooper checked the readouts. Perfect. They had come out exactly where he wanted them to. The autopilot was good to handle things for another couple of hours.

He flipped on the coffee maker, stretched big, and headed for the shower. It was good. Long and hot. Bliss after coming out of stasis.

He let the hot water pound on his neck, rotating it this way and that. As he moved it he felt a flicker, a remnant of the waves between them.

There was a slight thread which connected them now. Golden, glimmering, gossamer. It existed beyond sight. But could it have been seen this is closest to how it would have chosen to reveal itself.

Cooper steeled himself. Shaking his head. Trying to rid himself of the sensations and the connection.

That's what they did, didn't they, Sirens?

They had warned him about this. Trained him in it.

It wasn't him feeling anything for her. It was just the pull. The pull of the Siren.

"You need to get yourself together soldier," he said sternly to himself in the mirror.

They were almost there. Mission complete. He would hand her over to the powers that be and be done with it.

He had been in close quarters with her for too long was all.

He needed to get some distance.

When he exited the bathroom, he felt more himself and better.

He opened the shields on the windows and looked out on their location.

So close. So close to Earth now.

He could fell the pull of it already. The heaviness, that vague sense of sorrow. And the fear. It was almost like you could taste it. The fear that ran the game of the Forgetting Worlds.

Fark. Where had all of that come from?

He shook his head again. And poured himself a coffee.

Once he'd had a second cup he took the ship off auto-flight and busied himself with flying.

Eventually he heard the dome on the stasis chamber open. He did not turn around, but stayed staring resolutely ahead of him.

Rise sat up, stretching and yawning. She felt groggy and out of sorts. She felt a sadness come over her, like she had lost something exquisitely precious.

She hesitated, about to say something to him, but then changed her mind, and said nothing.

When Cooper heard the bathroom door close and the shower start, he felt an unexplainable disappointment. He let out the breath he hadn't realized he'd been holding and set his jaw. Hard, cold, shields up. Pleased with himself. He couldn't feel her anymore. She was an Asset.

They barely spoke in the hours that followed. An uncomfortable silence stretching between them.

Hurt. Confusion. Anger. Ice.

Neither of them had any clue where any of these things had come from, but they believed firmly in their validity none-the-less.

Welcome to the Old One worlds of the Forgetting Games.

CHAPTER THIRTY-TWO

"We're here," Cooper said.

Breaking the silence.

They were at Earth's outer webs.

Rise sat up straighter in her chair and surveyed the scene before her. They were in close. The webs were thick. Thick and awful. Rise sank back in her chair glumly. None of this looked particularly inviting.

Pain, panic, fear. They all struck her at once. It was all about to happen. She was about to lose her wings. She was about to transition to Earth.

But she would get them back. He had said so. But the Cooper who sat before her now seemed very different to the one who had said those things to her earlier.

She looked at him. His face was total concentration. Intent on the task now before him.

And they were here. What other choice did she have but to trust him?

Trust comes hard to many. And Rise was no exception.

But when you grow up denied, bound, segregated and promised to people who will rape you, beat you, rip out your wings, and eventually kill you, there are many things which come hard. Trust is just one of them.

And hope is its companion. How ironic, that she was now the hope of others. That they were counting on her to succeed where others had failed. Because they had all failed. The last one an age ago.

It was a long time between drinks for the Veil Sirens.

Far from Moethiica. They had all been far from Moethiica. It was a helluva place to hide a Siren, intended for such a task at hand. In the midst of the enemy.

She reached out, trying to sense the Veil Portal, and felt nothing.

She probed deep in her mind for the diamond, and it was silent, heavy and still. Like a big lump of dead, black rock.

Wow, she thought. That's just awesome. Go silent on me now. Desert me here.

She sat for a time, and got a little angry, with every damn thing about the whole freaking scenario.

Screw it thought Rise. I'll give it a red hot go. I'll give it everything I'm capable of. And that's the best I can do.

And something clicked into place. That was all that was ever that was required of her. And, unbeknownst to Rise, the Veil Portal shimmered even more visibly to those awake enough to register and discern such things.

Cooper, meanwhile, frowned. He had never seen the webs this thick before this far out. He had not been away *that* long. They had gotten awfully thick. Awfully fast.

It wasn't good to approach where the webs were too thick. Better to come in where they were sparse and transparent.

Where they were thick and almost opaque like this, they could hide all manner of things.

He thought about circling out and coming in a different way. But a look at their read outs told him otherwise. This craft was magnificent but not limitless.

They had come a long, long way, and the ship was waning.

Besides, if the webs were this thick here, chances they were this thick everywhere. Better to come in close to the station.

He stopped the ship, hovering before the first of the thick strands and reconfigured the controls to enter them.

They seemed deserted enough here. He froze. Rise froze. Both their senses crawling.

Both peered intently into the webs but could see nothing.

Cooper flicked more of the controls. Before he flicked the last of them he reached across and checked her restraints were good and tight. Their eyes met while he was close to her, locking briefly.

Godds she was radiating that same intensity she had back on the rebel ship. He drew back from her and his voice when he spoke was a little hoarse.

" We'll be at the station shortly. Hold on. Here we go."

And he banked them sharply into the webs, turning the ship expertly between the strands.

It was back to that truly sucky part of space travel Rise thought as they weaved and turned.

And then the motion of the ship began to even out. Rise peered keenly out of the cockpit window but there was nothing to see. Grey strands. Grey mists. Nothingness.

But there. She saw it now. A shape began to materialize out of the mists. Like a tiny space station.

Except this one was well out of use. It stood half demolished, debris floating all around it. Rise frowned, tilted her head. It looked almost like it had been attacked. That someone had blown it open.

When the first body bumped the window of the ship they both jumped in unison and swore. It looked in at them with unseeing eyes, its forehead pulpous and bloody.

They both reeled back from it, but then it was gone, as quickly as it came, back into the endless strands and mists. And now they could see the shadows of more floating bodies out there.

"Fark!" Cooper hit the flight deck violently in frustration. Making Rise jump even harder.

"What has happened here?" She said, begging every godd she vaguely knew of for this not to be their intended transitioning station.

"Someone's taken us out. That was our transitioning station."

Ok, damn.

"What do we do now?" Rise felt sick to her stomach.

"Fuck. Fuck. Fuck!" Cooper banged the flight desk in frustration with his fists. He tried the comms, but he was still coded out. He could not get through.

When it came down to it, he needed that transitioning as much as Rise. He could not land anywhere on Earth. Could not even get much closer to Earth in the webs without it.

He put his heads in his hands and tried to think of another option.

The silence stretched. And Rise grew more and more nervous. It felt vulnerable sitting here like this, doing nothing, in front of the destroyed station.

"Cooper, what do we do?" She asked again, grimacing as another body floated close by past them.

Cooper sighed and straightened in his chair. He ran a hand through his hair and cracked a knuckle on his left hand before he grabbed the controls again.

"We're going to have to take our chances with the Pirates," he replied grimly. And abruptly spun the ship around in the opposite direction.

"The Pirates? What about my wings?" It suddenly hit Rise that without the transitioning station she would have no safe place for her wings.

"The Pirates," Cooper muttered. As if that explained everything. And set them grimly on their way.

CHAPTER THIRTY-THREE

They flew deeper and deeper into the webs. Cooper seemed to know where he was going. How, though, Rise had no idea.

Out of the mists, the webs grabbed at the ships, sticky, distended and disgusting. There were things held in some of those webs. Long dead, and rotting.

Rise was glad they couldn't smell them and shuddered as one distorted, suspended corpse smacked unexpectedly against the glass as Cooper pushed relentless through a thick knot of webs. Some of the strands broke against the ship on impact. Others were so thick and strong they held against it, quivering back into place after they pushed past them.

Rise was sure she saw a creature scuttle hurriedly towards them as one of the quivers reached it. But they were through, before it could get close enough to her to discern anything but shadow.

Not long past this they stopped. Cooper kept the ship hovering and carefully took some readouts from the flight deck. He checked them carefully a couple of times before coming to a decision.

He looked about to key something in to the wrist communicator they had given him on the mothership, Savana9, when a sharp movement in the radar, sent him frantically reversing the ship backwards into a thick cluster of webs.

Rise gasped as the other ship came suddenly into view. It was smaller even than their own. Almost ball like. She caught a quick glimpse of the creature at the controls manning it and wished she hadn't.

Snub nosed, the eyes were black, opaque, red rimmed. Pale, withered lips drew back on sharp, pointed, teeth. The head was huge. Strands of lank hair hung from the bulging forehead.

Human ears. Human body. Pale skin. Muscles and big bones. The dirty, yellow claws on its hands at the controls were hideous. It had what looked like a long string of small, wooden beads around its neck.

"Weeza Gremlin," Cooper hissed between clenched teeth.

He had not expected one of them here.

"Is that an Earth creature?" Rise whispered nervously. "Are there things down there that look like that?"

"Only on the inside," Cooper muttered drily. Which was far from reassuring to her, but she let it go, as he gestured her to silence. He keyed in something on the wrist communicator and elevated the ship into a dive position.

The Weeza Gremlin nudged his ship forward into the thick knot of webs before him. As he did so, Rise saw they had a slightly different color and consistency. A glow and health to them that was different to the others.

Nothing happened. Cooper remained tensed at the controls.

The Weeza Gremlin grew brave, nudging his ship more aggressively into the strands before him.

Still nothing.

But Cooper patted the flight deck of their own ship and said, "Sorry baby."

The Weeza Gremlin's ship exploded in a flash of bright red and orange fire. And in the light of that fire, the other creatures concealed carefully in the webs close to them were illuminated.

And then the titanium shields closed in place all around them, obscuring her vision. Rise screamed as Cooper dove. He hurtled their ship through the flying shards of the Weeza Gremlin vessel, through the red-hot fire itself.

The heat, even through the ship's shielding, was unbearable. The cockpit shield and the glass underneath it buckled and morphed but held.

And then they were through.

And the ones waiting behind this section of the webs, descended.

Rise jumped as loud metallic suckers clanked onto position on their ship.

The ship swung violently in their grasp and Rise gripped her chair looking frantically at Cooper for an explanation.

Cooper sighed, flicking off various controls on the deck, releasing their restraints, unlocking their chairs and turning them so they faced inside to the ship. "Follow my lead and don't say anything," he advised her. "Don't react to anything they say or do. Keep your hands on your head and do exactly as they tell you. Say. Nothing." He emphasized the point again. And then clasped his hands on top of his head, indicating Rise should do the same.

She did, after only a moment's hesitation and watched nervously as the hatch lid of their ship cluttered loudly to the floor with a resounding metal clang.

Lights then. Smoke. Tracer beams.

The pirates were in and quickly.

Rise and Cooper were dragged roughly from their chairs on to their knees. Guns pressed to their heads as well as leveled in front of them.

There were six of them. The leader said nothing. Just looked at them appraisingly, a reader in hand. It was a 5-Element, like the ones the Confederation used. An expensive toy and not easily acquired.

Two behind and two in front with guns. The fifth man searched the ship.

It was a small ship. It was a quick search. He found nothing. "Lots of broken shit in the bathroom," he reported back to the leader in an odd accent.

"Lover's tiff?" the leader smirked at them. He shut down the reader and communicated his findings over a wrist comms in a language Rise had never heard before.

He made a sharp gesture with his hands and the men stationed behind them moved instantly.

The blindfold took her by surprise. The gag was in her mouth before she could even cry out. Both were pulled tight and hard. Wince worthy.

Her hands were brought down quickly behind her back and cuffed in one fluid motion. Rise was dragged roughly to her feet by multiple hands. She felt the point of the gun pressed hard against her.

And then she heard a hit on Cooper and his answering muffled grunt. It infuriated her and she struggled furiously, kicking out at whoever might be in front of her and swinging her head back at the one behind her.

"Steady little girl, steady." She was gripped even tighter, and she heard the gun humming off its safety as it was moved from the small of her back to the side of her head.

That was probably enough to quiet her on its own, but the next words uttered brought her to complete stillness.

You, valuable cargo little girl. Perhaps. But your boyfriend here is not so valuable. You try anything like that again and we kill him. You understand me?"

Rise nodded.

"Excellent." Anger shot through her as the speaker gently slapped her cheek. It was more playful than hard, but still held plenty of warning.

They moved them roughly out of the ship and into their own craft positioned directly above it.

And a labyrinth of a journey, for what seemed like hours, of twists, dives and turns, began.

Fortunately, Cooper, knew enough to follow and make more sense of them. And he did so, using the time wisely.

When they eventually docked, his own blindfold and gag hid a small, surprised but knowing smile.

The leader of the group watched him carefully, sensing some awareness there behind the blindfold. Before they exited the ship, he punched Cooper hard in the stomach again. This time the grunt he drew from him was louder, and he smiled, satisfied.

Rise, propelled forward in front of them, heard it and tensed, willing her anger under control.

The leader noticed her minute reaction and was tempted to hit Cooper again for the sport of it.

But an urgent transmission over his comms stopped him. They needed to deposit the prisoners and destroy the entrance.

The three ships which had managed to tail Rise and Cooper through The Star jumps had just arrived in the outer webs. Unheeded, it would seem by the disperser, and merely a few hours behind them.

CHAPTER THIRTY-FOUR

The space station they were on was vast. Enormous. A rabbit's warren of dark, metal corridors and small rooms.

There were outside areas as well. Balconies encased in blast proof glass. Oxygen pumped hard into these areas giving the illusion of being outside.

Up in the webs, the pirates, like the other communities who lived up here now, did their best with what was available to them.

Most of them could not land on Earth at this time. None of them would leave before the Veil attempt. And even the hardiest of space travelers will crave a cool breeze ruffling their hair eventually.

And so, they created it. And made their own mini oases in the webs.

They passed these balconies on the way to Psy, the Pirate Leader.

But all Rise felt on her face was the still air of the space station. All was quiet. Apart from their boots on the metal floor beneath them, the only sound was the soft hum of the station systems working in the background. Keeping them floating and alive.

In the den of Psy, they were kept kneeling with their wrists bound. They were on carpet. Rise felt the softness of it beneath her knees as they pushed her down.

She heard murmurs and conferring and then sharp commands in that strange language. The blindfolds and gags came off as quickly and efficiently as they had gone on, and Rise blinked her eyes and worked her mouth, glad to be free of them.

The room was longish and narrow. Dimly lit. Atmospheric. The walls were bookshelves, top to bottom. And lined with books of all manner and description. Only the occasional object or trinket interrupting them.

The carpet they were on stretched out before her. It was thick and lush and its colors exquisite. She followed the intricate patterns in it until they came to rest on the boots of the one who has acquired it.

His boots were high, black and polished. He leant against an ornately carved desk. The wood was dark and beautiful. The carvings in it like the carpet, intricate.

"You like what you see, Siren?" The leader raised an eyebrow at her, drawing her attention away from the desk to him.

He was tall, lean, dark. Fathomless eyes. Almost black, but not quite. Bright eyes. Dancing with hidden lights. Almost starlit.

Sensual lips in an aquiline, masculine face. The long dark hair which framed it fell perfectly, straight and thick, almost to his waist.

Rise said nothing, just stared at him levelly, looking deep into his eyes and trying to get a gauge on him.

He laughed at that. "I like your eyes Siren. Maybe they look at me a little differently before your time is up here."

Cooper struggled against the two men who held him at that. His eyes glaring. A third stepped forward, gun held like he was going to hit Cooper in the head with its butt.

And it was Rise who struggled then. "No!" She commanded, her voice ringing through the room. "Stop this! You disgusting cowards! Stop this!" Desperately, she fought to position herself in front of Cooper and the coming blow.

But there was no blow coming. The room had frozen. Its occupants frozen in place by the power of her voice.

Even Cooper was still, but he stole a sideways look at her. How could he have forgotten? This was the voice she had used amongst the Echelon. The voice which had drawn the Diamond to her.

At the memory, he recovered completely. He shot a warning look at her with his eyes, and she moved back into her place. But her lips trembled and her eyes were blue violet fire.

The pirates were longer to recover. A fact that was not lost on either them or Cooper. It was Psy, the leader, who recovered first amongst them and he glared at Cooper. "Stand down!" He commanded his men. "Stand down you fools. Stand down."

Shaking their heads as if to clear a ringing in their ears, his rather dazed and confused men, lowered their weapons and stood back against the book lined walls.

Psy fixed them both with a hard stare.

"You have a lot of nerve bringing this unchecked to me, Cooper Pierce," he said eventually.

Cooper said nothing, just stared resolutely ahead of him.

The pirate leader turned to Rise.

"And you, will hold your Siren voice in check here, little girl. You are guest, huh? You show better manners."

Rise opened her mouth to retort but Cooper spoke before she could.

"You are not showing a lot of manners yourself, friend."

Psy grunted. "Troubled times, Cooper Pierce, troubled times. With so many changing, last minute sides, one must be careful."

He moved suddenly. A large knife at Cooper's throat, he gripped his hair and wrenched his head back suddenly with his other hand.

"Have you perhaps changed sides also, Cooper Pierce?"

"No. I have not changed side, Psy," Cooper hissed between clenched teeth. "Now get your filthy hands and your filthy blade off of me."

Psy growled at him and threw him back roughly as he moved away. Cooper sprawled, but righted himself quickly enough, no mean feat which his hands still tied behind his back.

Rise looked to him to make sure he was alright. He looked furious, and the cut on his neck dripped slowly. Rise glared daggers at Psy who ignored her, concentrating all of his attention on Cooper.

"You seek a landing," the leader said.

Talking calmly as if nothing had transpired between them.

"And a Transition," Cooper replied, just as calmly. "For us both. Virtual. One that will preserve her wings."

Psy, looked steadily at them both, considering. Rise looked from one to the other between them.

"There are no landings on Earth, at this time, Cooper Pierce. And as for Transitioners, well, they are expensive. Especially the kind you seek.

"You know who pays my wages Psy. And you know you will be paid handsomely. And there are landings. There are always landings. We both know that," Cooper replied evenly.

"I know who used to pay your wages Cooper Pierce. I am not sure even you know who pays them now."

He looked at Rise.

"Many people in these webs, pay handsomely for this little girl never to see a real Earth sunset. They don't want her little cosmic door opened."

Cooper glared at him but stayed silent.

The pirate stared thoughtfully at them both and then smiled. "Lucky for you, the people who want to see her little cosmic door opened pay more."

"Un-cuff them," he gestured to his men. "If either of them step out of line, shoot *him*."

The men un-cuffed Rise and Cooper, dragging them both up to stand on their feet. Both of them rubbed feeling back into their wrists.

The wrist comms on Cooper's left wrist, glinted out from under the sleeve of his space suit.

"Cooper Pierce. What is this that you are hiding from me?" Psy had him by the arm. He pulled at the comms unit and Cooper drew in a sharp breath. Rise gasped in horror when she saw the thing was embedded deep into him.

Where Psy raised it, the flesh piercers he exposed were red with Cooper's blood.

"I will have this," he said to Cooper. "In addition to other payments."

"It is not mine to give," Cooper replied calmly, keeping a perfect poker face. "It is hers. And she will not complete her task on Earth without it."

Psy stared into his eyes but let his arm go. "You are bluffing Cooper Pierce. And I will call you on it. If it is hers, put it on her now."

"I cannot put it on her until after she transitions," Cooper replied, sounding almost bored and like Psy should know this. "It is why I wear it for her now."

The Pirate grunted, but relented. "Fine. As you say. But if the pretty bracelet doesn't fit her perfectly, after she transitions, I kill you."

Cooper shrugged. "I have no doubt you will try, Psy. I have no doubt you will try."

It drew a laugh from the Pirate. "I like your spirit Cooper Pierce. I like your spirit. But not enough to keep you alive if I don't need to. You understand me?"

"I understand you."

The Pirate looked at him pointedly, before gesturing to his guards to take them away. "I hope you do, Cooper Pierce. I hope you do."

CHAPTER THIRTY-FIVE

They were held in a small dark waiting room while Psy prepared the Transitioner. Several of his men waited with them. Crowding the tiny room with their guns and mutterings.

A couple of them goaded Cooper a few times, but he said nothing, did nothing, staring straight ahead and not reacting to them.

A few of them leered at Rise and she followed his lead.

Eventually the word came, and they were led down a level to the waiting Transitioner. The Med-Bays were down here also, and their clinical brightness contrasted strongly with the round, stone cave like room which held the Transitioner.

Cooper stopped and stared at it, disbelief in his eyes.

He looked at Psy. "You've got to be kidding me."

Ancient. Medieval. *Round.* It looked like a somewhat gaudily adorned sputnik. Like what a sputnik would look like if you let a rabid hippy loose on one with craft crystals.

The Pirate slapped the machine heartily. "Good as gold. Best ever. They never make another one as good as this again."

"When did they make it?" Rise asked suspiciously. There were rabid hippies with craft crystals on Moethiica too. This did not look like anything one would trust to anything too technical.

"Ah, a few years back now." Psy was evasive. "It no matter. Get in the machine little girl."

Rise was looking at it stubbornly and shaking her head. "I'm not getting in there and letting that thing take my wings."

The pirate spread his arms. "Ok! Well that settled then. You keep your pretty little wings and no Earth landing for your You want quick passage back to your bitch ruler and those lovely Echelons. We can arrange. Plenty of money on that one too."

He bowed to her sardonically.

"I just want my wings back in working order when this is over," Rise said icily.

"You get your wings back. Now get in the machine."

"Let me go," Rise demanded, kicking and struggling furiously as two of the pirates began to drag her towards the machine.

Two others had grabbed hold of Cooper to make sure he didn't interfere.

Psy checked the settings on the control desk and motioned his men to get her in the machine quickly.

"No more delays. We all counting on you now. You get your pretty little butt to Earth and open cosmic door." They gave her a final push in the door, locked it, and Psy hit the button.

She put up a fight even in the machine. She kicked and pounded and screamed. But Transitioners are designed to accommodate people reluctant to surrender their body parts, even if it is temporary.

And after a few minutes there was silence.

"She out." Psy nodded round at them in satisfaction and then looked at Cooper. "She a little HellCat. You going to have your hands full with that one."

"I'd happily have a handful of her," one of his men guffawed. "I like my women spirited."

All the men laughed but Psy silenced them. "Shoosh now. You going to upset lover boy over there."

Cooper said nothing, just kept his eyes on the machine, his face dark.

When the Transitioner began to rattle and smoke, he lost it. "What the fuck! Get her out! Get her out of there now!" He strained against them so violently he almost broke their hold. But they got him back under control quickly enough.

"Is all good!" Psy reassured him expansively. "Always does this. No harm. No bother."

The machine quieted somewhat but continued to smoke and Cooper struggled again and looked at him furiously.

The pirate held up his hand. "Uh! You control yourself Cooper Pierce. Two more minutes and you see."

Cooper hung his head, shaking it slowly. A transition shouldn't take this long. It just shouldn't. The minutes ticked over. They took forever.

"Good as gold," the pirate pronounced, looking at the read outs on the desk and sounding very pleased with himself.

He unlocked the over-ride lock and gestured to his men to open the doors.

They peeled them back carefully, coughing and holding their hands over their eyes to stop the smoke from the inside of the machine bellowing into them.

Cooper held his breath as they all waited for Rise to emerge.

But there was just smoke and silence. No movement. Nothing.

"Fuck! What have you done to her?" Cooper yelled at him. And this time he did break the hold of both men. He rushed to the machine and jumped into it.

At first the smoke was too thick and he couldn't see anything.

And then his heart sank as he saw her unconscious form, lying sprawled against the far wall of the transitioner.

He lifted her. Fark she was wingless. He stepped back out into the room where Medics were there, ready and waiting for her.

"Here, here, lay her down over there. On her stomach." One of the Medics gestured to a black leather cot against the right-side wall.

Cooper swiftly moved to the cot and lowered Rise.

The back of her flight suit was in ruins. Cooper could see the torn edges of it flapping around her sides. It was impossible to tell the true state of her back as there was still smoke coming from it.

He glared at Psy, but the pirate dismissed his look with a wave of his hand, and a smug, confident look on his face.

The Medic checked her pulse, and waved over a floating, hovering MedBot. "Scan and medicate," he ordered it.

The small, floating, round bot, scanned Rise quickly and expertly, immediately extending one of its surprisingly long arms and injecting a glowing pink liquid into the side of her neck.

"What the hell!" Cooper lunged forward again, but this time it was Psy himself who held him back. "She fine. The pink liquid is good. If it green liquid, then we worry."

The Medic still had a hold of her wrist and was still monitoring her pulse. "She's fine," he smiled at Cooper. "But we need to bring her tattoos up to the surface."

"Her *what*?" Cooper stared at him in disbelief.

The Medic raised his eyebrows at Psy and turned his full attention back to Rise. "I'll let Psy explain this one."

"What?" Psy spluttered as Cooper turned to glare at him. "You think this is coat check system? I write you out receipt for wings?"

The pirate pointed to Rise's back. "Tattoo!" He pronounced proudly. "Impossible to lose, no matter what shit she gets up to on Earth."

"Unless they skin her or set fire to her," he added thoughtfully. "They barbaric idiots still a lot of them so this possible. But hey, I can only do what I can do."

"They're coming through nicely," the Medic remarked, sounding genuinely happy.

Still trying to get an understanding on what was actually happening, Cooper blinked furiously and turned to look where they were all staring.

The smoke had cleared. Rise's back looked smooth and healthy.

But where her wing joints had been, two vertical lines of tiny, exquisitely crafted black rune symbols marked her back.

It looked amazing.

And then Cooper looked closer. These weren't just any runes. There was something familiar about them.

He bent over her back, studying the runes carefully.

He looked back at Psy in astonishment. "These are Cirillean runes."

The pirate nodded at him. "Impressive Cooper Pierce. Yes, these are Cirillean runes. This is a Cirillean machine. Not looking so shabby now, is it?"

Cooper straightened, stared at him mouth open. "That is a Cirillean Transitioner?" He pointed back to the now non-smoking and quiet machine.

"One of only four outside of Cirillea itself," Psy replied smugly.

Cooper said nothing, but Psy spoke for him.

"Apology accepted," the pirate said, waving off his potential next words.

"Want to know how I got it?" He winked at him conspiratorially.

"No." It was Cooper's turn to wave him off. "No, I really don't."

"Fine!" the pirate huffed. "We save that story for another time. It is a grand tale. A very grand tale."

He looked at Cooper thoughtfully.

"Now your little station out there gone, maybe your people need to use my machine. Maybe we strike a deal on it, eh?"

"What do you know about what happened to the station?" Cooper asked, ignoring Psy's other question.

Psy sighed. "I don't know who blew up your little station. But one who wants to stop her or one who doesn't want you to control her, eh? Could be many, many people out there who do this."

Cooper nodded and ran a hand through his hair.

The runes on Rise's back were fully formed now. The skin around them perfect.

"Can you read these?" He asked Psy.

"Not me, Cooper Pierce." The pirate shook his head. "But have no fear, we have some here who can. We get your little HellCat to the Med-Bay now. We read her runes later."

Cooper nodded, staying close by Rise's side as the Medic prepared the cot so it could be wheeled without the need to move Rise off of it, to the Med-Bay.

As they left the room, Cooper cast one look back at the legendary Cirillean Transitioner. Be damned, these pirates had actually impressed him.

CHAPTER THIRTY-SIX

Rise eased herself carefully back against the pillows. Her back was perfectly healed. There was no tenderness. But it was the oddest sensation.

She had never felt her entire bare upper back against anything. Always there had been the beautiful, sweet cushioning of her wings.

She was excruciatingly aware of the bareness of her back. And at the same time of the fact that she could still feel them. She felt like she had her wings, and didn't have them, all at once.

The Medic had showed her an image of them in Virtual Stasis. He had tried to explain exactly how it worked to her but stopped when he realized that was doing more harm than good.

"They're safe and you're well That's all that matters," he said kindly, patting her arm. "Would you like to keep looking at them."

Rise took a last lingering look at her slowly spinning virtual wings and handed the screen back to him. "No. That's enough. Thank you. The next time I look at them I would like to see them on me."

"Fair enough," he smiled and closed down the image.

Rise tensed as it disappeared but forced herself to remain calm. It would all be Ok. It had to be.

"What did you mean it's good that I'm well?" She asked suddenly as the Medic fussed with some equipment. "Do some people come out of it badly?"

"Some, yes," the Medic replied. "Not often. But it happens." He patted her arm again. "Don't you worry about Cooper Pierce though. That Cirillean machine's going to do a better job for him than that piece of junk his old transitioning station had going."

"Why would I worry about Cooper?" Rise asked. Suddenly worried.

The Medic shrugged. "The brain's always the tricky one. And he's got a bit of a cocktail in him at the moment, that boy. His pre-scans turned up all kinds of interesting things. He was posing as an Echelon when he found you, eh?"

"Yes," Rise replied, deep concern in her eyes.

"Scary. "The Medic shivered and then began to protest loudly as Rise climbed from the bed.

"Woah. Hold on there. Where do you think you're going?"

"To see Cooper," she replied. "He shouldn't do this alone. He was there for me. I want to be there for him."

"Rise you can't walk yet. You won't have your......."

"Ow!"

"Balance," he finished as she fell flat on her ass. Completely uncoordinated without the weight and balance of her wings.

~ ~ ~ ~ ~

"Now. Cooper Pierce. No more delays. We need get you in machine," Psy shook his head, staring at the read-outs. "You got quite a little cocktail in your system. You sure you want to do this?"

Cooper smiled wryly. "Do I have a choice?"

Psy shrugged. "You could always choose to forget."

Cooper shook his head. "I'll take my chances. I'd rather remember."

"Ok," Psy shrugged again. "Is your brain cells."

"You're not going to tattoo my head, are you?" Cooper asked suddenly.

"No!" Psy said expansively. "You I give coat check ticket to. Of course, it tattoo your head. Is how machine works!"

He stopped shaking his head at Cooper to nod at the cleverness of the Cirilleans. "They smart those Cirilleans. Pity those stories with the cows. Your people." He pointed a finger accusingly at Cooper. "Your people did that."

Cooper grunted. What could he say. Psy was right. It was true.

"Makes you wonder what lies they spread about your little Siren lover as well, eh?"

"She's not my Siren lover," Cooper replied pointedly.

"Maybe not yet. But you and the little girl got quite the googley eyes for each other. You going to be able to hand her over to your goons Cooper Pierce?"

"They are not goons and there are no googley eyes."

"Whatever you say, Cooper Pierce, whatever you say. Now get in there."

Cooper grunted at him, shaking his head, noting carefully what settings Psy keyed into the Transitioner before getting into the machine.

The inside of it was smooth. Golden. It was like being in the middle of a big golden egg.

In a traditional Transitioner you were upright and held in place. Here there was nothing. It was not high enough for him to stand in.

Not seeing any other alternative, he sunk down on the smooth golden floor and rested his back against the curving wall, legs outstretched before him.

The smooth surface was surprisingly comfortable, cocooning almost. He felt his body relax and his mind slow down.

A fine golden gas began to mist through the egg. Those Cirilleans. So graceful.

The golden mist began to have its way with him, leading him gently into a peaceful state of receptive unconsciousness.

Before it took him completely, he saw an internal panel emerge from the back of the machine. A part of the smooth golden surface slid back to reveal it. But there had been no joins there before to indicate its presence, no telltale markings.

When he opened his eyes again, it felt like only seconds had passed. He was propped up against the wall at the side of the room near the control desk. He had no memory of getting there.

Psy handed him a flask of water. "Drink, Cooper Pierce. All good. You Ok now."

"How long was I out?" Cooper asked. "I don't even remember getting out of there."

"A few minutes tops you been out here. My men get you out." Psy gestured to two men now carefully and almost reverently wiping down the machine.

Psy finished powering down the control desk and handed him a read out.

"All good. Your tattoo not as pretty as hers though."

"Where are they?" Cooper asked curiously.

"Back of your head. Just one. Underneath skullcap."

Cooper prodded the area cautiously but it felt fine, not tender. But he could feel the raised surface of it on his scalp and began to trace the pattern of it.

"Leave it Cooper Pierce," Psy commanded him. "Let it settle. We show you in mirror."

He grinned at him.

"You be pleased that the part of your brain you need to remove for Earth not affect your googley eyes for pretty little Siren. I am also pleased with this. I like to see how this play out on Earth. Could be more entertaining than Veil opening."

"Nothing is happening and nothing is going to happen," Cooper replied abruptly, studying the read out. "She's an asset. A valuable asset. My mission is to get her safely to my people. That's it Psy, so give it a rest. I don't feel anything for her."

The Medic cleared his throat uncomfortably.

Cooper looked up in surprise, he hadn't heard anyone approaching.

Rise stood there. Wobbly, not able to balance properly yet without her wings.

"I just wanted to see how you were," she said quietly. "To make sure you were Ok."

She turned from the room without saying another word and gripping the wall, made her way slowly and determinedly back to the Med-Bay.

The Medic hurried after her, after throwing a look back at Cooper that made him feel helplessly and confusedly, lower than low.

CHAPTER THIRTY-SEVEN

An hour later, Rise was walking Ok. Cooper was ready to leave.

He had tried to talk to her about what she'd overheard him say, but she had shushed him with a raised hand.

"It doesn't matter Cooper Pierce. I am a job to you. I get this."

"Rise, it's not that. It's…." He ran a hand through his hair, unsure of what to say.

"Yes, it is that," she replied. "Maybe you should just own it."

"Rise." He reached for her.

And she slapped his arm away.

"Don't touch me. Please don't touch me." She kept her voice remarkably calm, but her blue violet eyes flared a little.

Cooper dropped his arm. So be it. She was right. He should just suck it up and own it.

Psy appeared at the doorway.

"Come, you." He gestured to Rise. "Rune Teller ready. She see you now."

Rise looked confused.

Cooper did too until he remembered. "No," he said, shaking his head. "No Rune Teller. We need to leave. Now. We don't have time for this."

Psy shrugged. It was no skin off of his nose.

"What?" Rise asked, her interest piqued. "What is this Rune Teller?"

Psy grinned at her. "She read runes on your back, Siren. Maybe tell you secret message in them." He grinned at her.

Rise's eyes lit just a little and Cooper groaned.

"No," he said in a tone that brooked no argument. "You're not doing this."

"Excuse me?" The look that Rise threw at him should have been enough.

Psy chuckled. "Oh, this going to be good," he muttered to himself.

"Oh, Rise, come on," Cooper said in exasperation. "You know this is bullshit, right? These people are fakes. Charlatans. All they do is play with people's heads. They cause more trouble than they're worth." He looked pointedly at Psy.

"Hey. I thought you want to read her runes," the pirate said defensively.

"Read, legitimately, yes. Not have some quack fill her head with all kinds of made-up bullshit." He gestured vaguely in the direction of Rise.

Rise shot more daggers at him and then turned to Psy. "Take me to the Rune Teller," she said to him imperiously. The good people of Earth can wait a little longer for their 'asset.'" And she marched as swiftly as she could on still slightly coltish legs from the room.

"Or they can open the damn Portal themselves," she threw back over her shoulder, causing Psy to double over in fits of laughter.

"Oh, Cooper Pierce, none for you tonight. You in all sorts of trouble."

"Shut it," Cooper snapped at him as he strode hurriedly past him after Rise. "You've caused enough problems already."

~ ~ ~ ~ ~

When he entered the room, he was struck by how odd it seemed for something like this.

Glass, half walls, cheap plastic chairs and tables. It looked like one of those cheap meeting rooms you find in dodgy office blocks and public hospitals.

Rise was already seated before the Rune Teller. She had shrewd, dark eyes and long, thin fingers. She took the last image she needed and told Rise she could cover herself.

Rise pulled her top back up over her shoulders from where she had let it fall down her back to expose the tattoos, and turned in her seat to face her.

The Rune Teller was staring intently at Cooper. She smiled a wry smile when he raised a pointed eyebrow at her and began enhancing the tiny markings forming the tattoos on the screen before them.

She inspected the images before her carefully with the magnifying glass for several minutes. She sat back in her chair for several more, tapping the magnifying glass slowly and rhythmically against her chin, considering.

She looked at Rise and then at Cooper.

"These are not Cirillean Runes," she said, leaning back in her chair.

"It is Cirillean Transitioner," Psy protested. "How it not throw Cirillean runes."

The Rune Teller shrugged. "I know not the workings of this machine. I only know the runes. And these are not Cirillean."

"What then?" Psy demanded.

"Nothing," the Rune Teller shrugged. "Pretty markings. A nice receipt for Moethiican beggar wings. A pretty girl. A pretty picture. Nothing."

She looked at Rise when she said it and her eyes were cool and appraising.

"I was not a beggar," Rise responded coolly. Fark, she had worked hard to pay for what she had on Moethiica. Worked two or three jobs at a time to scratch out an existence and pay for the privilege of racing Junar Run.

"Nor were you a Siren. Or one destined to be one. Nothing," the Rune Teller repeated.

She looked coldly at Rise and then nastily at Cooper.

"You have brought the wrong one Cooper Pierce. You have brought the wrong one."

Rise stared at her open mouthed. Her whole world shattering.

Psy gasped.

Only Cooper spoke. And his voice was strong and confident. "No, I haven't."

"Oh, but you have," she replied. "Your people are going to be very disappointed.'

"No." Cooper replied. Arms folded over his chest and legs parted. Cool. Calm. Unwavering. "They won't."

Rise looked up at him, wishing she shared his confidence. But her stomach was doing somersaults. Her mind a shambles. She could not comprehend that everything she'd truly started to believe about herself was a lie.

"I was not a beggar," she whispered quietly. Almost to herself. She could hold on to that. She knew that much.

The Rune Teller smiled at her condescendingly.

"Soar," Rise said to her, her voice unsure of itself and shaking. "It was Soar all along."

"Perhaps," the Rune Teller smirked, reveling in her own power.

"No," Cooper said emphatically. 'It wasn't."

"You're very sure of this," the Rune Teller snapped at him, her dark eyes flashing angrily.

"Yes," he smiled at her then. And it was a smile of supreme confidence. "Come on Rise. Like I said. This woman is a fraud. We're going."

"How dare you," the Rune Teller hissed at him.

"No," Cooper replied, moving one menacing step towards her. "How dare *you,* charlatan?*"*

"Psy, my friend. You should choose your friends more wisely," Cooper said to him, and held out his hand to Rise.

"Come on Rise. We're out of here."

Rise hesitated. Glancing at the Teller, the image of the markings on her back, and back to Cooper.

Part of her had thought this all along. Had believed that she was here by accident. That the mind-diamond Soar had passed to her was the only reason she had felt any of what she was feeling.

And exactly what had she been feeling?

Doubt began to play across her mind.

Had she imagined it. Had she imagined all of it?

But the others had been sure of her. And Cooper now. So sure of her. Why? What gave him this confidence in her.

She looked into his unwavering eyes and remembered the Nephliim Blade. It was funny, it was not the first time she had looked into his eyes and been reminded of it.

The mind-diamond in her stirred at her memory of it.

The Rune Teller's eyes widened slightly. She had sensed its movement and something about it had surprised her. She looked less sure of herself now. Slightly worried even?

Rise narrowed her eyes, assessing her carefully. Yes, the Teller was worried. There was something here now that her carefully controlled performance had not accounted for.

"Look at the runes, little one," said the voice. It was the male voice inside her head from that night. From the night of the Echelon. Cool. Calm. Amused. "And please don't give your power away quite so easily to morons," it added.

The Rune Teller flinched visibly and looked about her nervously.

"Look," the voice continued. "She has put a hole in your awareness so she can dig a hook into you."

Rise felt a warm rush of energy undulate through and over her.

"Remove the hook. Close the hole. Give the hook back to her," the voice intoned. Like it was bored with the whole thing.

The mind-diamond stirred again and Rise suddenly knew exactly what to do.

She gave the Rune Teller back her psychic hook.

The Rune Teller stared at her evenly. It was not the first time one she preyed upon had given back her first hook to her. It was closing the hole that was difficult. And once that hole was open it would let in all manner of things. Her hooks would be the least of this pretty little girl's worries.

Rise closed the hole effortlessly and looked down at the Runes.

She could feel the Teller's fury.

She ignored her.

"You are wrong Cooper Pierce," she said eventually, raising her head to him. Her voice was strong again and her eyes were shining.

The Rune Teller was momentarily shocked. But recovered herself quickly from her fury to smirk in triumph.

But the smirk faded quickly when Rise turned the full weight of her gaze on her, and spoke with the full power of the Siren.

"And you are more than wrong, *rune teller.*" She said the title mockingly and with a flick of her hand, cleared the screen of the image before her.

The Rune Teller howled and lunged for the screen to capture the image but Rise was already out of her chair with her head in a lock before she could do it.

"Fark me," Psy swore under his breath, surprised at the speed of her movement.

He drew his knife and called for his men. Cooper was ready to move if he had to. He looked at Rise, his eyes still confident and unwavering.

Rise smiled at him and tightened her grip on the Rune Teller's neck making her gasp. "The runes on my back are Nephliim ones, matching the Blade. And this woman is an Old One's spy."

She pulled her hold tighter with brutal efficiency. The Rune Teller passed out of consciousness and Rise let her head drop hard on the blank image screen in front of her.

CHAPTER THIRTY-EIGHT

After that, it was a flurry of activity.

Psy stepped forward without hesitation. Lifting the Rune Teller's head up by the hair and slicing her throat open.

The pale blue blood of an Old One gushed on to the image screen before her.

He threw her head back hard on to the screen and spat on her, muttering a curse in his own language. He turned to his men and barked orders.

Cooper strode up to Rise and grabbed her by the arm, pulling her from the room.

The space station was in pandemonium.

"We need to leave now," he told her.

"This way!" Psy was suddenly running before them.

"Ship ready?" He barked into his comms.

"It's ready but we got incoming," came the response.

"Fuck," Cooper swore. "Go with him," he ordered Rise. "I'll get the packs. I'll be right behind you." She nodded sharply and took off at a run behind Psy.

Cooper retrieved two packs now topped with a goodly supply of guns, ammo, food, water, clothing.

He caught up with Psy and Rise in short order.

"You'll move the station after this." It was statement not question.

"You bet your pretty little Siren's butt we will Cooper Pierce." Psy's tone was light but his face was grim.

"Maybe this last move though." He stopped and looked at Cooper intently as they reached the dock's doors. "Next time, no move. Just fight."

"You get this little Siren of yours where she need to be quickly. Sooner she open that cosmic door, the better."

He grabbed him suddenly by the collar. "And you keep her safe Cooper Pierce. You keep her safe. Otherwise I lose that little part of your head I got and put a nice juicy price on the rest of it. You understand me?"

"I understand you. Now get your freaking hands off of me."

Psy let him go, raising his hands mockingly. Cooper eyeballed him as he re-shouldered both packs, but it appeared the pirate had had his say and was done.

They moved into the dock where the pirate ship waited.

The ship was long and cylindrical, like a cigar. A single file row of seats stretched down it's center. Psy and three of his men were making the trip with them. Psy and his co-pilot moved swiftly to the cockpit. They would reconnect with the space station after this, in its new position in the webs.

Rise could not see the faces of the other men, they were hidden behind the seat backs in front of her.

Cooper checked her restraints. "Hold on," was all he said as he took the seat behind her.

And then the Pirate ship lurched and suddenly sped out of the dock. Careening over the edge at breakneck speed and nose diving straight down into the webs.

Rise opened her mouth to scream with everyone else. It had all obviously gone horribly wrong. But the scream died in her throat as she realized no-one else was actually screaming. Which meant the ship was probably supposed to move like this.

Space travel, she thought to herself, again. Absolute suckiest thing ever.

The ship gained speed, hurtling straight down and ridiculously faster. Rise held on and prayed to godds not yet even willed into existence.

Cooper reached a hand forward and laid it on her shoulder, squeezing gently.

She raised her own hand to cover his and squeezed back. I'm Ok.

Their hands lingered for just a little time longer than they should. And parted.

He would have warned her if he'd had a chance that they would fly the ley lines.

There were only a few still open. Sometimes they are impossible to capture. But most times the pirates position themselves and time it beautifully.

This time was no exception.

Back in the webs, Psy's men fought valiantly against the space station's attackers, and prepared it to move in the webs.

By the time Psy had them landed on the outskirts of Harriman, New York it was dark on Earth. The air was cold. The sky overcast.

As Rise took her first steps on Earth, she could see little of it. But she was aware of trees. Forest.

"Thank you," she said to Psy.

"I think it is I who should thank you little Siren HellCat. You keep Cooper Pierce safe now, Ok." He winked at her. Drawing a smile from Rise and a disgusted look from Cooper.

The two men shook hands though. "See you on the other side Cooper Pierce."

"On the other side, Psy."

And then they were gone. The ley lines do not stay stable long for return journeys. And the space station had now moved significantly.

It was, as Psy had predicted, their last move. They were now in the thick of the web community in the northern webs. A community so large there was barely room to contain them.

Still more came. They were pouring in, according to the reports from the station. Pouring in and waiting for the Siren to do her thing and open the Veil Portal. Waiting for landings on Earth, and all manner of things to become possible.

On the ground, Cooper instructed Rise quietly they would be making their way on foot to a Safe-House.

She was to move as quietly as possible. Speak, only if absolutely necessary, and then, only in the lightest of whispers.

He showed her a small number of hand signals he would use to communicate with her and made her memorize them.

And they set off.

As they walked, the weight of the Forgetting Game reminded Rise of a shield grip. She was glad Cooper had warned her how, and she steeled her mind against it as best she could.

Still, the night was eerie, and Cooper seemed as edgy as she'd ever seen him. She would be glad when they reached his Safe-House.

CHAPTER THIRTY-NINE

They walked for a good hour.

The night remained black as pitch. All Rise could do was follow closely in Cooper's footsteps and try to make her own as quiet as possible.

They had not spoken, and she could sense his tension growing. Every little sound made her jump.

He had stopped them more than once, turning to her and signaling to her to be quieter.

Easier said than done. Not being trained in such things like him.

He stopped again suddenly and she ran into him clumsily. He didn't look but reached back with a steadying hand.

A cloud shifted and the first light glinted on glass, revealing the window of a house. It was so unexpected it almost made Rise gasp out loud. She had thought they were still deep in the woods. But that glimmer of light had revealed them just in their perimeter.

The house itself, was perhaps thirty feet back, across a horribly looking open and unprotected clearing of mown grass.

The trees surrounded it in a standoff. Almost like they were closing in on it. And when its occupants were distracted, would shuffle forward, one tiny inch at a time.

There was not a good feeling about that house.

The cloud passed and the woods were plunged back into darkness. Rise held up her hand and could not see it in front of her face. You would never have known the house was there without the stars of the night sky revealing it.

Silent. The woods were so silent now. Not even the hum of insects intruded. Cooper put his finger to his lips and motioned down to Rise with the other.

Get down. Stay silent. He wanted to see what would be revealed in the next cloud parting.

They waited some time for it.

Crouched there in the pitch black. Rise felt something large and unpleasant crawl over her. She bit her lip to stop from screaming or swatting at it.

And as they waited there in the dark, and Cooper's ears attuned, he felt the others coming towards them.

They were good. They were very good. Just the occasional rustle of a branch. The soft cracking of a twig.

The light hit the house almost like someone had turned it on by a switch.

But it was another movement of cloud. And this time it was the full reveal of a huge, low hanging yellow moon.

It lit the single window in the upper level A-Frame of the house.

Showed the face in it. Staring straight down back at them.

And then Rise did gasp, and tumbled backwards on her butt.

The face moved from the window and the sounds coming towards them in the woods became louder.

And closer.

One forward scout closer than Cooper had even realized.

He whirled and took him out with a single shot to the chest. The silencer was impressive. The man looked almost surprised that he'd been hit.

Cooper grabbed Rise and they ran. Backwards to the house. Cooper had a different gun in hand now. No more silencer. He sprayed a round of covering fire into the woods on either side of them.

Only when they reached the porch did he cease his reign of fire. He pushed Rise down low and kicked the door in.

And then they were through, Cooper propelling her through at speed. "Stay down!" He yelled at her. She needed little encouragement as a couple of bullets sailed over her through the still open door.

Cooper kicked it back closed and shoved a heavy hall side table up against it. Rise stared at the staircase in front of her, waiting for the face from the window upstairs to emerge. But the stairs remained empty.

"Basement," Cooper commanded, lifting her up and pushing her in the direction of the kitchen at the back of the house.

Basement sounded like a very bad idea to Rise. But Cooper knew that in this basement there was a tunnel that led to all kinds of interesting places.

They made the trapdoor in the basement as the first bullets exploded past their heads.

Cooper hit the code into the door unit. It sprung open at the same time Rise saw the face from the upstairs window emerge from the shadows.

It looked like a woman, but its red eyes glittered strangely, even in the dark.

The power coming off of it was awful, rolling over her in hideous, nauseating waves. She felt chilled to the bone and paralyzed with fear. She thought at first it was a Cybriid and then with horror realized it was worse.

Old Family Hunter. Cooper didn't hesitate. Pumping shots in it until his gun clicked empty.

The shots had moved it violently back against the wall. Each one distorting its face and throwing its limbs akimbo.

But it did not bleed. It did not go down. It smiled at them.

And launched itself.

Cooper pushed her through the trapdoor, at the same time spinning and catching the launching Hunter with an upward kick from the ground. It caught it squarely on the chin and the creature flew hard into the wall.

Cooper didn't wait to see it relaunch itself.

He threw himself down the trapdoor and felt the impact of the creature hit it as it closed above him.

It was a nasty drop. He'd had no time to tell Rise to roll when she landed and hoped she was Ok.

He landed. Rolled. Crashed into her. Good she was on this side of the wall.

Jumping to his feet he ran for the stone wall and punched in the code that activated the titanium steel blast wall.

It came down beautifully and then stuck two thirds of the way down.

He hit it in frustration, but it was jammed good and proper.

He had no choice though. He could hear them coming through.

"Run!" He screamed at Rise as he dragged her to her feet and pushed her roughly into the tunnel. "Run!"

She looked at him and the look in his eyes was enough. She ran.

He lingered at the wall. He activated a different code and ran after her.

The sound of the blast when it came was horrific.

A whoosh of air and smoke and rubble knocked Rise senseless, bellowing down the tunnel and taking all in its path.

She lost consciousness for a second and then came to, coughing.

The tunnel was a dust chamber. She could hear after blasts and aftershocks and the tunnel shook with them.

She could not see Cooper.

And then the glittering red eyes of the Hunter were on her and she felt her brain rattle and her skin split open as it landed the first blow.

CHAPTER FORTY

Rise got her arms in front of her face and bucked her hips, trying to throw the hunter off and move her body out from directly underneath it.

It readjusted itself effortlessly and came down with a nasty elbow. Rise took the best defensive position she could and braced for the impact on her forearms.

It never came. The thing went flying off of her. She heard it thud against the tunnel wall, and then nothing.

She edged cautiously towards it. A small dart protruded from its neck. It appeared to be alive but going nowhere.

Still, it was hard to tell with these creatures. They needed to move quickly.

Frantically she scrambled to her feet. "Cooper!" She called into the darkness. "Cooper!"

Silence.

But surely it was Cooper who had shot the hunter? Something glinted in the darkness, catching her eye. And she moved towards it. It was Cooper's gun. The light on it was catching the metal on the side.

But Cooper was out cold. He didn't even look as if he was breathing. And the light. Where was the light coming from?

Rise whirled.

A pair of small black eyes, leaned forward over the flashlight to peer out of the darkness at her.

She screamed.

And was met with a chuckle.

It was a good chuckle. Deep, heartfelt and bellyful.

The creature stepped forward, light in hand.

He was small and upright. Perhaps four feet tall. The small, gleaming black eyes belonged to a face with a pointed snout, covered in short, hard, fur. The fur was black with two large white stripes running down his face. His ears were small and triangular, sitting on the very top outer edges of his head.

The nails on his hands were long and pointed. The hands rested comfortably on his belly and he seemed completely at ease.

He cocked his head at her and said, "I can help you, if you wish."

Rise scrambled desperately away from him, but stayed close to Cooper, protective.

"Who are you?" she demanded, desperately trying to get Cooper's gun from his hands.

But even in a state of complete unconsciousness, he had something like a death grip on it.

The creature watched Rise curiously as she struggled unsuccessfully with the gun.

"Who are you?" demanded Rise again.

"I am the one who shot the dart in your hunter friend," the creature replied. "And I would imagine, your only way out of here."

He looked up the tunnel in the direction they'd come and Rise jumped as she heard the first thud, thud, thuds of their attackers trying to break through.

Boom! Boom! Boom!

They were using some sort of blaster to come through the rubble.

Rise bit her lip, looking from the sound of the blasters to the creature and back to Cooper.

He was still out cold.

What choice did she have?

"How?" She nodded her acquiescence to the creature. "How do we get out of here?"

"Do you wish to save him?" the creature, gestured to Cooper, regarding her curiously.

"Yes of course," she responded, horrified that the creature would even ask.

The creature visibly relaxed at her answer. "Take his pack." He directed. "I will put him in a sling."

He pulled what looked like a small leather stretcher type contraption from the shadows.

He was agile and graceful when he moved. And when he handled the bulk of Cooper with relative ease, his obvious strength unnerved Rise even more.

"It will suffice," he said, almost to himself, happy with his work of securing Cooper to the seemingly undersized contraption. "And now through."

His voice was so calm and normal, almost melodious, Rise didn't even register it was him who had pushed her into the wall when she hit it.

There was the initial slam, a small resistance, like walking into a bubble, and then she was through.

She emerged, shaken, but intact, in a low, narrow passage with light sandy floors and walls of the same rough grey rock.

She scrambled away from the entrance and had enough seconds of being there alone to feel her heart pound, before the creature came sliding through behind her.

He had his hands on the top part of the sling and when he dragged the rest of it through, Rise was relieved to see the still unconscious form of Cooper, equally intact, atop of it.

"You should warn people when you do that," she scolded.

The creature shrugged, repositioning Cooper to his satisfaction and setting off at a steady trot.

'Wouldn't work if I did," he shot back over his shoulder. "You wouldn't believe you could do it."

They walked for a long time and Rise began to tire.

When they came to a little rounded out area, Rise thought she heard the sound of running water and a thirst hit her deep and furious.

"Please," she gasped. "I need to stop."

"Of course," the creature replied, and Rise sank gratefully to the ground and retrieved a water flask from one of the packs. She drank deep, finishing it easily.

"You should refill all your flasks here," the creature advised. "It is a natural mineral spring and most delicious." He gestured in the direction of the sound of it, as he checked on Cooper. "Please. Help yourself."

"Thank you," Rise said and went to investigate.

The stream was exposed in a small crevice. She cupped her hands and drank some more. It was indeed delicious.

She filled both flasks from it and when she was done, the creature did the same.

While he did, she crept over to Cooper. He looked a little better. There was color in his cheeks and his pulse was steady. Still, he had not given up the gun. It made her smile.

She felt eyes on her and looked up sharply. The creature was watching her intently. "Get some rest," he instructed her. You are still acclimatizing. I will place a medi-patch on him."

"You have those here?" Rise asked curiously.

"Some of us do," the creature replied with a small smile. He wet Cooper's lips with some drops of water from the spring and then opened his shirt, placing a small medi-patch near his heart.

It eased some of the tension in Rise to see the creature do this. Surely, if he meant them harm, he wouldn't do this.

"What is your name?" Rise asked him.

"My name is Badger," he replied with a wry smile.

"I'm Rise," she said and felt odd saying it because he had never asked her.

"Why are you helping us?' she asked.

"Why would I not help you?" the creature replied enigmatically and settled back against the wall and closed his eyes.

Rise opened her mouth to press further, but then thought better of it. He had been nothing but kind. More than kind really. He deserved to be left to rest while he could.

So instead she followed his lead and did the same.

The creature counted patiently to ten before opening his eyes again. He looked steadily at Cooper's pack and at Cooper. Carefully and silently he laid a hand on the sand floor and began to ease himself upright. But a mumble from Cooper stopped him in mid track.

He looked thoughtful for a moment, almost indecisive, and then, some decision reached, he settled back down to the sand, and closed his eyes again.

~ ~ ~ ~ ~

"What..." Rise drew in her breath sharply and sat up too quickly. She didn't remember falling asleep. "Ow!" Way too quickly. Her head throbbed and she saw spots in front of her eyes for several seconds.

She blinked rapidly, taking in the scene around her, coming to focus on the creature.

He was regarding her dispassionately, head cocked to the side.

"How long was I asleep? How is Cooper?" she demanded.

"Not long," the creature replied. "And Cooper is fine. You needed the rest. We will make faster time for your brief nap. And I think you will find you move much easier now."

"Sleep, on this world, is essential," he continued. "It integrates, heals, realigns. It allows you to tap in to the larger part of yourself which exists outside their carefully controlled webs. Consciously, you may not feel this. But the body knows. The brain knows. They work it out. They remember."

"Is that not the nature of sleep on all worlds?" said Rise.

Badger nodded. "Yes. But only part of it. On this world, at this time, only the smallest and most basic connection is let through. What is necessary to survive, work, function."

"The Forgetting Game," Rise said quietly. "How do you bear it? It's so awful."

Badger said nothing to that, just gave her a small smile and turned away to busy himself with Cooper and the sling.

Satisfied, he turned to her, "Ready?"

Rise shook her head and headed after him. She did feel better and their pace was significantly quicker now, just like he'd said.

But she still had no idea where they were going, or who was taking them there. She didn't like it. She didn't like it one bit.

And when Cooper came to, he would kill her.

CHAPTER FORTY-ONE

They were an hour closer to their destination when Cooper did come to.

And Rise, having grown more anxious by the minute, let out a long deep breath of relief. She moved quickly to help Badger get Cooper out of the cocoon sling and propped up against the wall.

Cooper spluttered and coughed and choked for several minutes. "Give him some water as soon as he is able," Badger said softly and retreated into the shadows.

"Where are you going?" she asked.

"Nowhere. Attend to him." Badger's voice came softly from the darkness. "It is for the best that he does not see me straight away. Familiar faces are best when one is coming out of deep unconsciousness."

One of his flasks slithered across the sand to her. "And he will be thirsty."

Rise laid what she hoped was a comforting hand on Cooper's back where he was bent forward over himself coughing and positioned the water flask in easy reach. "Cooper, it's Rise. Drink. It's wa......Oh!"

Cooper lunged at the flask, snatching it out of her hands and drinking like a man possessed.

When he was done, he tossed the flask aside. "Is there more? Give me more. I need more."

"Sure," Rise said cautiously, proffering him the other flask. She kept a good grip on it before he could snatch it this time. But he was more in control now. His eyes stared intently at her. They were glittery and bright, staring out strikingly from his dirt smeared face and hair. "It is the last we have," she said as he drank, a little more slowly now. "You need to leave some."

He nodded slowly, his eyes never leaving hers, boring into her own.

When the attack came, it was like nothing Rise had ever experienced.

One-minute Cooper was propped against the wall in front of her. The next he was roughly dragging the inert form of Badger out of the shadows.

He had known exactly where the small creature was and had launched himself at the small creature with considerable instant affect.

For a horrible moment Rise thought he had killed him.

"What have you done!" She exclaimed. Bending over Badger and gently tapping his face. "Badger. Badger. Can you hear me?"

"Ow!" Cooper pulled her roughly back from the little creature by the shoulder, unceremoniously sending her hurtling backwards along the sand. He had his gun cocked at Badger's head in an instant.

"Who the fuck are you?" He asked roughly, his voice gruff and still raw.

Badger stirred, coming to a little and Cooper shoved the point of the gun more forcibly into his head. "I said, who the fuck you are?" He repeated. This time a little louder.

"He's the only reason we're alive!" Rise scrambled back beside him. "Leave him alone!" She tried to pull Cooper back from him, but he was immovable. Like rock.

Now it was Badger's turn to cough. "It is alright Rise," he wheezed, rubbing the side of his head that didn't have a gun imbedded in it. "He is right to respond in this manner. It is I who should have been more careful." He opened his eyes then, his own small black eyes boring up into Cooper's.

They stared at each other a long time. Nothing was said, but something passed between them. In that silent manner that men have of communicating with each other at times. Where much is said with no words needed.

Eventually Cooper simply nodded once and eased his gun back a little. Badger pushed it gently to one side with his hand, and scuttled backwards on his hands to ease himself into a sitting position against the wall.

Rise half expected him to disappear again. But the rock walls of the tunnel remained shadow free. Light enough that she could see the cut on his forehead above his right eye.

"You're bleeding," she said to Badger. She glared at Cooper as she moved past him to tend to the little creature. Tearing a strip off her shirt, she poured a tiny drop of water on it. There were protests from both Cooper and Badger at that. But she ignored them both and dabbed at the cut, cleaning it as best she could.

When she was satisfied, she tore another strip from her shirt and wrapped it tightly around the creature's head. "It is the best I can do for now, but I think you will need lasering."

It was a nasty cut. The kind you got from particularly vicious elbows. The fact that Badger's forehead was covered in coarse hair meant this elbow was even more vicious than the usually vicious ones.

And Cooper was weak and half unconscious when he landed it. How did he even know that Badger was there? How could he pinpoint him so easily in the shadows?

She moved back against the wall and regarded them both steadily.

Cooper had settled back onto his heels and was still staring at Badger intently. One hand crossed over his wrist. The gun seeming to dangle casually from that hand.

Not so much.

"Stitches," he said, to no-one in particular.

"I'm sorry?" Rise asked.

"There's no lasering cuts closed here. He'll need stitches. My pack?" He said curtly to her. Glancing at her for only a second before turning his focus back to Badger.

Rise fumed at his rudeness, but handed the pack to him.

He did not open it. Just ensured it was securely fastened and placed it beside him.

"Where are you taking us?" He demanded of Badger.

"The city. Across the harbor. We have a residence there," Badger replied. "It is an easy walk from here."

"The city?" Cooper clarified incredulously. "The city is an easy walk from here? How long have I been out? And why did we ditch the transport?"

"No transport," Badger replied. "You have been out a few hours at most."

Cooper raised a very skeptical eyebrow at him. "We landed just outside of Harriman. That's a 52-mile, 17-hour walk. Not exactly easy."

"On the contrary. We are already under Battery Park," Badger replied. "It is just a short walk now across the harbor."

"These tunnels are not what they seem," he added. Quite unnecessarily.

"Underneath," Cooper clarified. "We're going to stay in this tunnel and cross underneath the harbor."

"That is correct," Badger nodded.

"How far down are we?" Cooper asked him.

The creature smiled at that. "Further than you want to know."

"Where I take you is safe. You will have everything you need. Food. Beds. Communications. You will be able to make contact with whomever you wish. Securely."

"Why?" Cooper asked him. "Why would you help us? Who the fuck are you?" he asked again pointedly.

"I am aligned with the Resistance." Badger replied. "Resistance1." He clarified before Cooper could ask.

The original Resistance. Thousands of years old. Perhaps tens of thousands. Perhaps more. Who really knows the true date of the First Awareness. Old school.

"How are you maintaining form?" Cooper asked him curiously.

"With great difficulty," the creature replied wearily. He rose to his feet as though it pained him. "We must keep going."

"Why were you in the tunnel?" Cooper persisted, not budging.

"I have been in the tunnel the last three nights. We have been expecting you."

"You knew we had left Moethiica then."

"Even your own people saw that," Badger responded. He glanced at Cooper's pack as if something had suddenly drawn his attention there, but said nothing.

"Do you know who attacked us?" Cooper asked him.

Badger shook his head. "I could guess, but I would be guessing. I would rather wait until we get to the residence. We have the means to make more educated guesses there," he smiled.

"Must be quite the set up," Cooper said warily.

Badger nodded. "Everything you need Cooper Pierce. Everything you need and more."

Badger looked again at his pack and then back at Cooper. He waited patiently as if expecting more questions. But there were none.

"We should leave now," he said then.

Cooper grunted and nodded curtly, rising to his feet, surprising Rise by extending a hand to the little fellow to help him up.

"Let's do it then," Cooper said. Badger nodded and gathering the sling, set off at a steady pace down the sandy tunnel. Cooper, seemingly now fully recovered, with only a cursory glance at Rise, fell in easily behind him.

Oh yeah, great I'm fine, thanks for asking, and totally clued up on everything going on now, thought Rise drily.

She scrambled to her own feet and trotted after them down the rocky passageway, shaking her head at the pair of them.

CHAPTER FORTY-TWO

The tunnel grew cold under the harbor. Rise began to shiver, in spite of the pace they were maintaining.

Cooper looked back at her as if he'd sensed her discomfort. Wordlessly, he handed her a spare shirt from his pack and she slipped it on gratefully.

Glad for the extra warmth, and the fact he'd remembered she was alive and sort of important to this whole business.

Of course, he'd remembered. He just didn't want her in close range of the Badger. They had no choice but to follow the creature now. But once they were out and above ground, he would reassess the situation accordingly.

And he could not wait to be out and above ground. Enough of these tunnels. He could feel the weight of the water over them, pressing down on them.

His pack moved a little oddly on his back and he readjusted it. He must have dislodged something and thrown the balance around.

The tunnel began to edge ever so slightly upwards.

It turned as well, veering sharper and sharper up towards the left. When they rounded suddenly on the spotlit piece of tunnel floor indicating their exit was above them, it was almost too quick and too final.

And both Rise and Cooper had a sense of other tunnels stretching out into the unseen.

Badger secured the sling on his back around his shoulders and began to climb.

The ladder was metal and black, barely visible against the dark rock wall.

It was a long ladder and they climbed for a long time.

Rise's legs and arms were burning by the time they reached the top. Even Cooper was feeling it.

"When you exit at street level, proceed immediately straight until you reach the end of the alley," Badger directed them. "Do not deviate from this. Wait for my call."

And then he was up and out and gone, leaving Cooper cursing.

He climbed cautiously out of the manhole. They were in the middle of a crossroads. Cooper swore profusely but silently. Two streets. Two alleys. They were smack bang in the center of all of them.

Close to the action but lost in ghost like industrial silence. He could see the lights of the Brooklyn Bridge in the distance. He could smell whiskey.

He remained in a crouch and gestured Rise out of the manhole, covering it quickly as soon as she was out,

As Rise straightened and looked about headlights swam over her, blinding her.

Cooper cursed some more and grabbed her by the arm, propelling her straight ahead and into the alley proper.

The buildings were two and three stories at most. The building on the corner looked to be a shop front. An old NY Lotto sign still lit neon in its window. But the shop itself looked vacant and long deserted.

The car moved on.

Cooper considered their options.

He knew where they were now. And he knew of Resistance1. Better still he was about to learn the exact location of one of their residences. The military had guessed at something close to here for them. But to have an actual address was going to be valuable information.

He knew another thing too. Resistance1 had been waiting eagerly as long as any of them for the coming of the 5th Siren. They wanted her here. Wanted her safe. Wanted her to succeed.

And they had some might behind them. They had survived a long time. Which meant they had not only might, but street smarts.

Until he had a better option this was as good as it was going to get. He needed information. He needed the lay of the land. He really, really, really needed to know who had attacked them.

They kept walking.

They continued down the alley for only seventy feet or so when they came to another tight alley dissecting theirs. So narrow, it was little more than a corridor between the buildings.

There was no light here and the shadows closest to the building walls were dark.

Badger emerged from them suddenly, on their left. He gestured them down the narrow corridor.

It was shorter in distance than one would have imagined and they emerged into a wider laneway.

Badger produced a set of keys and used a large one to open a nondescript looking metal door just a little ways down from them.

He beckoned to them and they followed him in. Cooper had his gun drawn and shielded Rise with his body, keeping her behind him.

Badger moved quickly to secure the door once they were in. They had emerged into a small underground garage. There were three cars in there. Cooper hoped they would have use of at least one of them.

Well no, he corrected himself. They would have use of at least one of them. It was just a matter of if it was willingly lent or surreptitiously borrowed.

It was a typical garage with both stairs and elevator exit. For some reason the elevator reminded Cooper of the elevator to the prison hold on Incandesca3, and he wondered if the others were close to Earth yet.

All elevator resemblance faded however when they got inside and it began to move with rattily, jolting twentieth century Earth elevator slowness.

"Is this safe to travel in?" Rise asked him quietly, clutching the strange wooden railing on the wall of it with both hands.

"Quite safe," Cooper replied, not sounding overly convincing. "Technology here is a little different to what you're used to."

"This counts as technology," Rise muttered under her breath.

"This is a very old Elevator," Badger reassured her. "The newer ones are much better."

Rise nodded and kept a good tight grip on the railing.

They arrived at their floor, the top floor, and were announced with a solid rickety rumble.

Rise exited the contraption gladly, feeling very much safer out of it.

The hallway they exited into was dimly lit. The elevator opened facing down the length of it. Facing them at the opposite end was a solitary window. Through it, a neon sign from the wall of a neighboring building shone through.

It was the light from the sign that was illuminating the hallway. The naked globes resting peaceably in its low ceiling were long since gone.

The carpet was green to match the walls. A sort of muted olive. Down each side of the hallway were several dark brown doors.

"For show only," Badger assured Cooper. "The entire floor is completely our own.

He produced another key for the fourth door on the right.

The sound of the elevator jumping into action made Rise jump.

Cooper cursed as Badger fussed with the key. "Relax Cooper Pierce. Only friends in this building."

After a little more fussing and jangling he opened the door.

The elevator had halted on a floor below them. They heard its doors noisily open.

Badger entered the apartment and performed a cursory check, beckoning them in, in short order.

Cooper was keen to be out of sight and moved in quickly, gun raised, to perform a cursory check of his own.

Stunned but satisfied he turned to Rise and swore in exasperation when she wasn't right beside him.

She seemed lost almost, still out in the hallway, staring at the neon sign lighting it.

It just seemed so incongruous with its bleak, barren surroundings.

Rise couldn't put her finger on it but something disturbed her about that sign.

Cooper moved swiftly back to the doorway and yanked her forcibly into the apartment. Though apartment was an exceedingly poor word for the surroundings before them.

CHAPTER FORTY-THREE

The space was a large rectangle of a space like a warehouse. But there was nothing warehouse about it.

Black and white squared tiles, a foot square in size, covered the floor like a massive chess board.

Large, round pillars dotted the space with color.

The flat ceiling was thirty feet high. Large chandeliers hung in the spaces between the pillars.

There were several doors set into the opposite wall, one of the long sides of the rectangle. A small balcony ran the length of the wall above them.

A black, curving wrought iron stair in the center of the room led up to it. Its landing faced what looked to be a tiny outside balcony. Barely big enough to stand on. Double French doors were protected by heavy wrought iron bars.

They made a pretty framework for the staircase and broke the monotony of the plain dark walls. Which were painted deepest, darkest indigo.

Sheer white drapes hung in front of the doors and Cooper frowned at their transparency.

"One-way glass," Badger said, guessing his thoughts. "Shatter proof. Bullet proof. Blast proof. Like the walls." He gestured around him. "We are quite safe. Quite private. Quite protected."

"Won't you please sit." He gestured for them to proceed down the length of the room. I will bring us some refreshments." He took off at a trot towards the far end of the room.

About half way down, behind closer spaced pillars and large potted plants, was a cleverly concealed lounge area.

And beyond, separated by an island bench top, a modern kitchen. Professional. Stainless steel. Gleaming. Functional.

Large, leather chairs and couches surrounded a huge heavy wooden coffee table. A large flat screen was suspended from the roof.

Rise flopped into a large leather chair, dropping her pack at her feet and Cooper frowned at her. He did not want her getting too comfortable.

But the chair was comfortable and Rise was exhausted. She did her best to pretend she hadn't noticed him.

Besides she trusted their host. He had done them right so far. And there was a goodness and familiarity about him. For some reason she could sense it.

When he emerged from the kitchen with fresh water, steaming bowls of delicious food, followed by a pot of divine smelling coffee and fresh cream, she trusted him even better.

Even Cooper relented at that stage. Taking a seat near her, but keeping his gun out.

"Eat. Drink. Refresh yourselves," Badger gestured, losing no time in hoeing in himself.

They did. At the end of it, all three of them sat back in contented silence.

Only then did Rise notice how exhausted the little creature looked. What he had done had taken a lot out of him.

"Thank you," she said. "For everything."

He smiled at her. "It is my honor and my pleasure. My friends and I have waited your arrival with much anticipation. However, I am sorry I was vague in answering you when you first arrived. But I needed to be sure of your intentions."

He turned to Cooper. "You must have many questions Cooper Pierce. There are secure systems here I can give you access to. But I must tell you one thing first up and straight up."

Badger sighed, looking like it was the last thing he wanted to do, but squared himself.

"There are two Old Ones here. Somehow, they have discovered a way to walk the earth before the Veil opens. Their power is much diminished and they use much of their energy to conceal themselves. But still they are here, and even diminished, they are formidable."

"Where?" Cooper asked intently, leaning forward.

Badger looked at him with sad eyes. "One in the Military. Your Old Unit. OBO. It has been compromised. One is around your General now. I am sorry Cooper Pierce. Your General is a good man. He has put up a good fight, but they are. They are too powerful for him."

Cooper's face was white. "I need to meet with him."

Badger nodded. "He wants that also."

Cooper looked at him sharply. "How do you know that?"

"It is he who sent us to collect you." Badger looked at Cooper and said something. It was not a word that Rise had heard before or meant anything to her, but her mind was reeling from the knowledge that Old Ones were already here, walking the Earth.

The word meant a lot to Cooper though. The subtle sign the creature had made with his hand even more so. Neither were things said or signed lightly. And neither were known outside of a very select group of people.

Cooper nodded to Badger. "You will arrange it?"

Badger nodded. "I will arrange it."

"When?" Cooper asked.

"Twenty-four hours from now," Badger replied.

Cooper nodded. "Ok."

"I suggest you both get some sleep before then. There are bathrooms adjoining your bedrooms and spare clothes."

Cooper shook his head. "One room." He looked at Rise. She didn't argue. She looked worried and frightened.

"If there are Old Ones here, she is not going out of my sight. No offense to your security systems."

"None taken. I understand," Badger nodded. "We will accommodate whatever requests you ask of us. Within reason of course," he added, smiling, but it was a tired smile. Wan and almost painful.

"Are we truly safe here for this moment?" Rise asked, looking form one to the other.

"Yes," Badger reassured her. "As safe as you can be for this moment."

Cooper nodded. "Where is the other?" he said suddenly.

"High up," Badger replied. "High up and hidden. He is cloaking heavily. All we know is that he is in the government, or is wealthy enough and close enough to the government to influence some of their decisions."

Cooper hit the arm rest of the chair in frustration. "How long have they been here?"

"Not long," Badger replied. "But they are Old Ones. They do not need a long time to work their influence."

He was being deliberately evasive but he wanted Cooper Pierce to rest and regain his strength before he heard the worst about his General.

"How long?" Cooper repeated grimly.

"Eight months," Badger replied.

Cooper put his head in his hands. Eight months. It was too long. Too long to have been in their presence and held against them. He would kill the bastards if they'd hurt him beyond repair. He would kill them. But eight months. Was there any hope? Yes. There was always hope. He pushed any thoughts to the contrary from his mind.

"Ok. Twenty-four hours," Cooper said. Running his fingers through his hair and standing suddenly. Rise stood as well and Badger followed. He did not get easily to his feet and Rise's heart went out to him.

"You will rest too?" she said. Laying a hand on the creature's shoulder and squeezing gently.

"I will," he said. Putting his small, furred, clawed hand over hers. "Come. I will show you to a room."

It was the third door along the far wall he took them to.

There were two King Single beds, a built-in robe, a large chest of drawers, two small bed side tables, and a sizable adjoining bathroom.

Rise used it first, luxuriating in a blissfully hot shower. Badger had brought in a stack of fresh clothes, including some for sleeping.

Rise pulled on the soft, warm PJs and moved back out into the bedroom.

Cooper had placed both their packs on the chest of drawers.

He indicated the bed furthest from the door for her and took his own shower.

By the time he returned to the bedroom, Rise was sound asleep, exhausted.

Which was a shame, because he had wanted to say something to her. But it would have to wait until morning. As sleep took him too, quickly and deep, he reconsidered.

Considering the circumstances, it was probably better to say nothing at all.

CHAPTER FORTY-FOUR

While Rise was in the shower, Cooper and Badger had talked.

"How long can you sustain this?" said Cooper.

Since Rise had left the main room, the creature had waned noticeably.

"Not long," the small creature admitted wearily.

"Where will you go when...." Cooper left it hanging.

"I will retreat to our mountain hold. I can sustain there indefinitely until the veil opens," Badger replied, wiping a weary hand across his brow.

"You do not think you will last here until she opens the Veil," Cooper said with genuine concern.

"I am sorry my friend, no," Badger replied.

They both stood in silence for a time, lost in their own thoughts.

Cooper raised his wrist and showed Badger the comms unit. "Best I give this to you now then." There was no point in handing it over to his compromised unit.

They were standing in the kitchen and Cooper turned to the sink. As he began to peel the unit out of his wrist, the bloodied flesh piercers and the wounds they left behind dripped dark red blood into the large, square, sunken surface.

He turned on the water and rinsed both unit and his bleeding wrist under it.

Badger had retrieved a first aid kit and two soft, clean hand towels from one of the cupboards. He laid out antiseptic wash and bandages for Cooper to use on his wrist.

Cooper handed him the now blood free comms unit and Badger took it reverently in one of the soft towels. He wiped it carefully dry and then wrapped carefully in a piece of black cloth he retrieved from one of his pockets.

"Who brought you through?" Badger asked him curiously.

"The pirate, Psy," Cooper grunted.

"How did you ever get it passed him?" Badger asked curiously.

Cooper smiled. "He did not realize exactly what it was. I told him it was hers to use here. "

Badger smiled at that.

"And then all hell broke loose," Cooper continued. "And it was forgotten in our rather hastily forced exit." He looked intently at Badger. "There was an Old One spy amongst them too."

"Then to have it here is even more of a priceless win." Badger lifted the black clothed bracelet in salute. "To the war ahead my friend."

Cooper nodded. "To the war ahead."

CHAPTER FORTY-FIVE

Rise awoke with a start, instantly knowing she had slept long and late.

Godds she felt the better for it. But she wondered what she had missed. Cooper's bed was already empty. She had not even heard him come in last night.

The bedroom was toasty but when she peaked her head cautiously out of the door the chill of the main area hit her like a blast. She could see Cooper and Badger sitting together in the lounge area they had been in last night.

Large heaters burned all around them, wrapping the space in warmth. They were both staring intently at a small screen on the coffee table before them.

Badger looked up and smiled at her. "Rise, come over here and join us. It is unseasonably cold. And the rest of this space, though impressive, is impossible to heat."

Rise squealed as the cold of the tiles hit her bare feet and she hightailed it on tippy toes to the lounges. It was indeed toasty and she sank gratefully into one of the large armchairs, tucking her feet up under her.

"I'll fix you some breakfast," Badger said kindly and rising.

"Thank you. I will help," Rise made to get up after him.

"Nonsense. Sit. Get warm. I will bring it to you."

"Ok. Thank you," Rise settled back into the chair. Cooper was still focused on the information in front of him, swiping between screens and keying in commands and queries. Rise thought he had not even looked at her, and wondered if he even knew she was there.

An uncomfortable silence stretched between them. Uncomfortable for Rise anyway.

It was almost odd to sit with him like this. All the time they had been together it had been one thing after another. On the run, always moving. This stillness was almost more unnerving than the chaos.

Rise wondered how far they were from their final destination. And how they would get there.

"The Veil." Cooper turned the screen to her so she could look at it.

She raised her eyebrows at him and he gestured to the screen. "There. You can see it."

Rise looked. It was some sort of radar system. Green on black. A misty golden line, appeared and disappeared amongst the other green images.

Rise felt a catch in her throat. The shimmering, elusive golden line pulled at her. The mind-diamond deep within her mind came to life and began to turn.

The brilliant white gold light within it glinted as it spun. The pressure on her head was too much and she grew dizzy with it. She pressed the heel of her hands to her head, willing it to stop.

Cooper was looking at her with concern. "Rise, what's wrong?”

"It makes the diamond spin," she said between clenched teeth. "It feels like my head will split open. Please, take it away from me. Please."

"Ok. No more looking then." Cooper put the screen away carefully.

She began to feel better after a few minutes and dropped her hands.

"Is it far from us?" She asked Cooper, grimacing at the pain still shooting through her head.

"A hundred miles or so," Cooper replied. "North east."

Rise nodded, and remembered another thing she had noticed on the screen. A red dot blinking steadily. "What was the red dot?" She asked.

"It's woodland. Close to the Safe-House where we landed," he replied. "Psy gave me a clone tracker. It will deceive them for a little while."

"They'll think it's me. Us," he responded to her questioning look. "Even after they pick it up it will take them a while to unscramble it." He looked around. "And the walls here are heavily scrambled. It will bide us some time. They won't be able to see us properly for a little while yet."

"They track you?" Rise asked him.

"Yeah," Cooper replied. Pointing to the area just below his ribs. They implant it when we're young. Part of the cloaking implant."

"Perhaps CM Gemini removed it when she fixed you," Rise said hopefully.

"No," Cooper said. "She already told me. She tried. Couldn't do it without killing me. It um, it gets in and wraps around things. Very crude CyTech. Anyway." He ran a hand through his hair. "Doesn't matter. We're safe here for the moment. That's the main thing. Eat your breakfast."

He turned the screen back to him and studied it intently again as Badger placed steaming hot pancakes, juice and coffee before her.

She had a million questions but he had said they were safe for the moment.

The questions could wait. Rise tucked in heartily. Like the meal the previous night it was delicious.

While she ate, Cooper and Badger excused themselves to retire to a small study.

The study was warm. Centrally heated like the bedrooms. A large L shaped desk configuration dominated the small space. Computers, screens and systems dominated the desk. Rising in two tiers above each of its lengths.

Rise finished her breakfast. Showered. Dressed. In warm black leggings and layers. She found some thick warm socks and a pair of boots that fit her perfectly. She slipped on the socks and left the boots aside. Not much point until they went outside anyway.

She sat with Cooper and Badger for a time. But they were engrossed in whatever they were doing and most of it was meaningless to her.

Restless, she wandered out of the room. She grabbed a warm wrap from the bedroom and explored the space around her.

She started with the pillars. Colorful images snaked up around them. The undulating serpent energies of the cosmos. The ancient goddess temples where the sacred snakes and all they represented were revered. There were Pann too. Planets, stars, Makers, Nephliim, Sirens, Cirilleans, Old Ones.

Rise went from Pillar to Pillar and there were more worlds and more races. More tales and stories. Close to the curving black, wrought iron stair case, she found the first Diamonds.

They lit the path of the free until the Old Ones shut down all true light of the worlds with darkness.

But it was false darkness. And they matched it with false light. The light was pale and insipid next to the blinding light of the Diamonds.

But all reach for the light. It is an innate element of creation. And the light the Old Ones dangled was easier to attain than the light of the Diamonds. The worlds chose freely. And they chose the easier illusion.

They had handed their freedom over, oh, so willingly, on a platter.

The Veil. The Sirens and Nephliim retreating behind it. Old Ones too. More powerful, and more terrifying than any currently walking the cosmos.

The Cirilleans staying on this side of it.

The Veil closing.

There were images of the Rebels now as at least some of the Beings awoke. The Cirilleans played their part. Breaking through enough on even the Forgetting Worlds, to be seen and recorded.

To get people wondering and talking no matter what their governments told them.

And on the Pillar closest to the staircase was Earth. Thickly coated with webs. The golden Veil Portal shimmering above it.

Rise peered closer. The paintings on the murals were intricate and detailed. And here was depicted much more than the thin gold line on the radar. But she felt Ok here. The diamond was pleasantly tingling. Not spinning like it would burst out of her.

Ah. She thought, drawing back. Suddenly recognizing the patterns on the golden line. Honeycomb. The Veil here looked like a golden rope of honeycomb. And the skilled artist had given it movement. It looked like it was undulating across the indigo sky.

Undulating.

Rise peered back in close again.

And there they were. In the honeycomb. Two white gold diamonds as large as small eggs.

Rise clutched the pillar as the diamond inside of her stopped tingling and began to spin and pulse with hot, white fire.

It was not honeycomb. It was scales. The scales of one of the Golden Cosmic Serpents.

Could it be? No. Surely not.

Desperately she clutched the pillar and moved cautiously to the next image.

Earth. The Veil. The Golden Serpent. Separate now. She could see the distinct golden line of the Veil. And the body of the Serpent above it.

The body was empty now. And there were no white diamond eggs within it.

And she realized she had seen this image before. Depicted in gemstones on the walls of the sprite cave in the depths of Junar.

One of the Golden Serpents birthed two eggs. Two diamonds of pure light. To be used to wrest control of the cosmos back from the Old Ones. And their false light and their false darkness.

And one was hidden deep in the bowels of Earth by an Original Maker. Because the Original Makers walked Earth many years ago. Nephliim and Sirens too. They left many clues they had been here and many unexplained mysteries.

But the Old Ones spun the Forgetting Game in motion and set the endless players of the game on Earth to mining for it. And they set the players to worshipping fear instead of mystery. And it did not take much. It was surprisingly easy.

And the other diamond was hidden deep on a world at the far ends of the cosmos, away from Earth.

And of all the lies the Old Ones spun, perhaps the most hateful to the Cosmic Golden Serpents and the Original Makers, was the lies they spun about the Sirens.

And so, this other diamond they fused with a Siren's song. And only a Siren could sing to it.

And it was the Siren of the Veil who would carry this diamond in the end. Until then, it would be hidden and passed carefully amongst many chosen to help conceal it.

But when the time came it would be the diamond, lodged deep in her mind, that would guide the Veil Siren in exactly what she must do to open the Portal.

CHAPTER FORTY-SIX

Rise steadied herself against the pillar as the mind-diamond within her sent out delighted sparkles of white fire at her new awareness.

Well at least she wasn't cold anymore.

She loosened the wrap down around her shoulders.

"Rise." Cooper's voice was sharp and he was looking at her strangely. "Come and have something to eat."

"Ok." She pushed off of the pillar and moved towards where Cooper stood, just outside the study room door, waiting for her.

A flash of yellow caught her eye. Not on the pillar, but above it, in the French doors on the balcony. Two eyes. Glinting.

Rise gasped and staggered back.

"What. What is it?" Cooper demanded, rushing forward.

"Eyes. There's someone out there," Rise pointed to the balcony.

Cooper was up there in three bounds, gun drawn. He moved to the side and peered out. Badger moved Rise quickly behind the cover of a pillar and took the one next to her.

He put his finger to his lips and cautioned her to silence.

She waited patiently but after several moments could not resist a peek.

Cooper was already making his way back down the stairs, putting the gun back in his belt, his back to the windows.

"It's Ok. There's nothing out there," he said.

"Are you sure?" Rise said doubtfully.

"I'm sure." He touched her upper arm reassuringly. "Probably just a reflection. Come on. Come have something to eat."

"Yes, food," Badger declared and marched to the kitchen. "Our dinner. Your lunch, Rise," he called after him.

In the kitchen he glanced at the time. "Cooper, you'll have to leave soon," he called out to him.

"I know. I know," Cooper responded. Checking the time on a watch Badger had supplied him. He had it on his right hand. His left wrist was still heavily bandaged.

"Sorry," she mumbled. "I've been staring at these murals for so long I must be seeing things."

Cooper gave her a penetrating look and lifted her chin in his hands, staring at her eyes and turning her head this way and that.

"You feeling alright?" he asked. "More headaches?"

At his touch, the mind-diamond spun wildly, and warm, undulating waves washed over her.

"No. Not a headache. I feel…." she broke off, unable to finish her sentence as a particularly strong wave broke over her. Her voice came out husky. She put her hand on Cooper's, trying to move it gently away from her. Conscious, that his touch was making the waves stronger.

But at *her* touch, something flared equally in Cooper. His eyes dilated and his hand moved, tightened, almost unbearably, around her own.

"Ow," Rise said, but it was a whisper.

Cooper stepped in even closer to her. The mind-diamond began to spin and somersault madly.

He dragged her roughly into him. And she felt instantly, how much he wanted her.

He bent his head to hers and rubbed his stubble against her cheek. His lips brushed hers. The diamond stopped spinning. And surged.

Cooper pushed her back against the pillar and kissed her madly, deeply, exquisitely, hard.

And the diamond exploded into shards of white golden light. Rise not only felt them. She saw them.

And they travelled, madly, blindly, ridiculously fast, up out of her, and into Cooper.

CHAPTER FORTY-SEVEN

Cooper saw nothing, but he felt a white heat sear through him.

Up out of Rise and deep into his mind. The diamond shards settled, reformed themselves and began to spin. He was rock hard for her already. But whatever she'd done to him was pushing him over the edge.

He pushed himself even harder into her. "Rise, what have you done to me?" He whispered hoarsely against her ear, nuzzling against her.

Rise was reeling from the sense of the diamond lost to her. The diamond crucial to her. Crucial to what she had to do. She must have it. Panic began to flood her senses. He had taken it from her. He had taken it so easily.

He had taken it just like an Echelon.

Rise froze in terror.

She struggled furiously. "Give it back to me!" she screamed. "Give it back to me!"

Badger came running out of the kitchen and stopped short at the sight of them.

"Rise. Cooper. What on earth is going on? Cooper Pierce, perhaps it would be best to step away from Rise."

Cooper pushed roughly away from her and there was anger in his eyes now. "What have you done to me?" he yelled angrily at her.

"You have taken it!" she screamed at him. "Just like an Echelon! Give it back to me!" She stepped forward. Her eyes were blazing in anger and her voice began to ring with the power of the Siren.

Badger's eyes grew wild at the power of it. He quailed visibly and covered his ears.

Cooper stood unmoved by it. Legs apart. Arms folded across his chest. He regarded her icily.

"Give it back to me!" Rise stepped closer and although her voice was quiet. It shook the walls.

Cooper didn't flinch. Badger did. But he used every last bit of strength to move himself over to them.

"Please." He took one hand off of his ears to touch Cooper's arm. "Please. Whatever it is, give it back to her."

"I didn't take anything. She did something to me." His voice held accusation.

Rise was shaking with anger. "He stole the diamond. Just like the Echelon do." She spat the words out and looked like she would lunge at Cooper at any moment.

"Oh no," Badger said at the mention of the diamond. "Oh no. This is not good. This is not good at all. Cooper, you must give it back to her."

"I didn't take anything from her," Cooper retorted. "If I've got it, it's because she shoved it into me. I saw you with the Echelon Rise. Don't forget that. You took it as easily from Soar as they did. Whatever you shoved into me, take it back now."

"I did not shove it at you. You stole it!" This time Rise did lunge but Cooper caught her easily, capturing both wrists in his hands and holding her still.

The energy that flared between them was so intense it was visible to the naked eye.

Badger winced. "What were you doing?" He cried, trying to break them apart.

"Rise! Cooper! What were you doing?"

Cooper broke the steely eyed standoff. "Kissing her," he spat. "I was kissing her."

"Kiss her again," Badger sighed. "And give it back to her, or you take it back from him. However, you do it, just make sure it is done."

Rise and Cooper stood glaring at each other.

"Please," Badger implored them. "I beg of you, please."

"Fine." Cooper threw Rise against the pillar so hard that Badger winced. And then he was on her. Forcing her wrists up above her head and grinding into her. He kissed her roughly and thrust his tongue deep into her mouth.

He willed whatever she'd put in him back into her and felt a white heat turn in his mind. But it would not budge. It stayed there. It would not go back into her.

As soon as he knew it would not go back in her for sure he cut off the kiss abruptly and pushed himself away from her.

He looked at her in disgust. "What's the matter? Not Echelon enough for you, Siren?"

Rise stepped forward and slapped him hard across the face.

"You have ruined everything!" she screamed at him. "Don't you understand? You have ruined everything!" Then she burst into tears and ran straight to their bedroom.

She had discovered the slam-ability of Earth doors. And the entire space shook with this one.

CHAPTER FORTY-EIGHT

Cooper tended to Badger as best he could. What had transpired had taken the last out of him.

But in the end, he had to go. He had a meeting with his General.

"You need to get to the mountain, my friend," Cooper said to him.

He laid a furred, clawed hand on Cooper's arm. "Don't go," He implored him. "Stay here with her. With the diamond jumping like that I have a bad feeling about this."

"I've knocked. She won't open the door. Don't you worry about that. I'll fix it. We'll fix it. We'll work out how to do it when I get back. No kissing," he added grimly.

Badger smiled weakly at that. "Now that I would not be so sure about Cooper Pierce." He coughed uncontrollably then and Cooper raised a glass of water to his lips and helped him ease back against the tunnel wall. The little creature was wheezing terribly now.

"Thank you, Cooper Pierce. You are a good man," he gripped his arm tightly. "I feel my people coming for me. "Godspeed. Cooper Pierce. Godspeed."

His eyes grew distant and Cooper hoped he heard him say, "You too, friend." Before the tunnel went black and he felt Badger's weight move away from him.

The tunnel came back to normal light. A dim, luminous grey. It was empty. No trace of Badger or those who had come to collect him.

They would see him right and get him to the mountain.

Cooper stood and shut the door quietly, locking it with the key Badger had given him.

He looked at the time. "Fark." He had to go.

He paused at the door to the bedroom and knocked softly. He didn't know what had happened before but he felt like an asshole. And it would be scary and odd for her here with both of them gone.

He tried the door knob. It was still locked. And then he heard the shower running.

He scrawled a note and left it with the key to the tunnel door on the kitchen bench top for her. *How domestic.* He thought ironically. He checked he had the key to the front door and the garage in his pocket.

Cooper Pierce took a lingering look around Resistance1 before he left. At the sea of pillars. Blocks of solid color. No patterns or images, that he could see, on them.

He shook his head and waited for just a second. Would she come out the door. But no, there was nothing. And there was no more time.

He shut the door quietly behind him and exited.

~ ~ ~ ~ ~

The cold air sliced through him. Moethiica was warm and desert. It would take him a while to get used to this again. He pulled up the collar on his jacket so it covered the lower part of his face. Dark sunglasses and a baseball cap hid the rest of him.

He meandered a little at first, doubling back now and then, stopping suddenly and checking for tails.

But it looked like he was clean. From the best he could tell, no-one was following him.

He thought he would devour every sight and sound of Earth once he was back here. But now he was here it was the opposite. It was all too familiar. And cutting through it all was the gut wrenching feeling of taking steps away from her. With anger between them and hurtful words unresolved.

He stopped. Almost wanting to turn back to her.

But, no. He was already here. The bar was as seedy as he remembered it.

The doors flew open and a couple of loud drunks poured belligerently out into the night.

Cooper stepped well aside, but one of them still managed to knock into him. Probably on purpose. The guy was clearly looking for a fight.

Cooper left him disappointed. Moving unobtrusively into the dim, dark quiet of the bar.

He slid into a booth near the door. The table was filthy. The General was at the bar.

Cooper's heart sank. He had barely recognized him.

The man's hand shook as he downed his shot glass and called for another.

He downed that one and signaled another again.

And then he ordered two scotches. The best they had. Neat.

It broke Cooper's heart to see him limp over to the table. He would kill the Old One bastards who'd done this to them. He would kill them.

The General placed the glassed shakily down on the table and slid into the booth.

"Cooper Pierce. It's good to see you son. I'm sorry it has to be like this."

"And you Sir," Cooper replied. "And you."

They lifted their scotch glasses to each other, took a sip, and laid them down on the table.

"How long?" Cooper said. Godds, he was so pale, this close up. His eyes were ruined. Bloodshot.

"Right after you left. Just two of them," the General replied. "Not that we knew for a time. And then eight months ago they didn't bother to pretend anymore." He looked at Cooper and his eyes were watery. "I fought them as long as I could. But eight months. Eight months and they did this to me."

He took a huge gulp of his scotch and set the glass down clumsily.

"It's all lies, you know, son," he said, his eyes darting to the other side of the bar and back to Cooper. "They've inverted everything. All the religions, all the meanings, all the symbols. Upside down. What's bad is good and what's good is bad, and it's all they had to do. Flip it upside down. And we swallowed it."

"They don't need to do it. We do it for them."

"And if more of *them* come through that Veil, we're done for."

"They're mining us Cooper." The General leaned across the table and gripped his hand. "They're mining us. Do you understand. Mining *us*."

He hissed the last bit, and then looked to the door and smiled.

Cooper turned in time to see the hit's face before the door closed behind him.

He felt sick to the stomach and angry. So farking angry. But when he looked back to the General it was as if a peace had settled over the man.

"Is she pretty?" The General asked him, leaning forward eagerly.

"General?" Cooper felt a chill as he realized what the General had sensed awaited him on the other side of the door.

"The Siren. Is she pretty?"

"Stunning," Cooper replied.

The General smiled. "Well pretty is as pretty does and it's a dime a dozen when it all comes down to it. No shortage of pretty girls on the horizon. But if she's pretty on the inside, take her and walk away."

"I'll see if I can talk her into that right after she opens it," Cooper tried to say light heartedly but his voice was catching.

"Don't open it," the General smiled at him. "Leave the damn thing closed and walk away with her. Get off-world. Get anywhere. Just get away."

"But if you don't, remember this." He said a word. A word that Cooper had never heard before. He repeated it. "Have you got that?"

Cooper repeated it perfectly. He had learnt many words like this from the General. Just like the word Badger had used to communicate with him earlier.

But he had known what that word meant in that context. He had none for this one.

He looked at the General questioningly.

"You'll know," the General replied to his unspoken question. "You'll know better than me when the time comes. Just remember it."

Cooper nodded and the General drowned the last of his scotch.

"Your father was a good man, Cooper. I wanted you to hear that from me."

The change in subject and the tense threw him. "Was?" he said quietly.

"He tried to take them," the General smiled, remembering. "He could sense them. He could sense them before any of us did. Wounded one. Wounded one real bad. Your father was a good man, son. He tried to take them out to save you."

"Save me?" Cooper began.

But the General was already standing.

Cooper stood too.

"I'm sorry Son."

"We'll walk out together," Cooper said to him.

"No. You will save yourself. And that's an order. My final order. Understood?"

Cooper opened his mouth but the General cut him off sharply.

"Understood, Soldier?" he barked.

"Understood, Sir," Cooper said quietly.

He took Cooper's hand. "It's been an honor Cooper Pierce."

"You too Sir." To hell with it. Cooper saluted him smartly. The General saluted him back, tears pricking his bloodshot eyes.

And then he was gone, out the door before Cooper could stop him.

The General walked two blocks. He had left his coat at the bar and the wind went right through him. But he savored it. Savored how alive it made him feel. He looked about him, taking it all in.

He had done all he could. He had done all he could. He looked up at the stars and said a prayer of thanks to the God he'd thought he'd known.

They used a silencer. Pain. For just an instant. And then he was free of them. Free of everything. The chill wind blew uncaring over his body on the pavement. And that was the end of it.

~ ~ ~ ~ ~

Cooper stayed in the booth until he felt it. And then he went to the bar and drank heavily for the dad he'd never truly known, and the one he'd been so keen to replace him with.

The one whose death he'd felt. He had not felt his childhood's dad's death. But how was he supposed to feel his death if he didn't even fucking know anything about him.

He squashed that thought. Washed it down and away from him. He needed, very much needed, to be numb.

Would he feel his own death? Because surely, they were going to be outside waiting for him. Just like they'd been waiting for the General.

Well fuck it. If these were to be his last few hours, he wanted to sit at an American bar. Watch sport, drink beer. Maybe even indulge in idle chit chat.

Well maybe not the idle chit chat.

He wished he could have taken Rise to a bar. Ideally not this one. But a nicer one. One where they could just sit and talk. Relax. Put his arm around her.

He wished.... he pushed it out of his mind. Never going to happen.

He got so hammered, but they didn't throw him out.

He left the bar at closing time and waited.

The street was quiet. Surely, they would take him. Nothing.

So be it. Cooper turned and began to make his way unsteadily home.

He stopped every few blocks, to check for tails, but couldn't see anyone.

He shrugged. Perhaps a sniper then?

He walked more blocks. And nothing came.

When he made it to the alley, a rush of exhilaration shot through him. He had made it. They hadn't taken him. He would see Rise. And he would make everything right between them.

And the General was right. Fuck this. Fuck all of it. He would get them off-world somehow. They would. They would. He lost the thought. Got the key out of his pocket. Reached for the door.

They came from nowhere. Everywhere. His innate, finely honed, superbly trained senses kicked in only a fraction of a second too late.

But a fraction of a second too late with these people is more than enough. A fraction of a second is all they need.

The pain hit him as hard as the realization that of all the worlds he'd travelled, all the things he'd seen, it had come to this. A hit, alone and drunk, in a stinking alley next to a dumpster.

He was caught suddenly. In limbo. And in that limbo, he heard a voice. It was a good voice. Steady. Calm. Almost amused. It was directing him without directing him. Guiding him effortlessly. Giving him the facts of the situation. Telling him exactly what to do. And what it was telling him to do contradicted every bit of Earth "logic" that had ever been instilled in to him.

But who had instilled that Earth logic?

Ah, these people, killing him. How interesting.

And as the blackness took him, he thought of Rise, so close, just above him. And for an instant, he felt the truth and weight of the connection between them. And it was magnificent. More magnificent than he ever could have imagined or known.

And then the voice stopped. The blackness took him.

And everything was gone.

CHAPTER FORTY-NINE

Black sorrow engulfed her. Twisting the images of her dreams into nightmares and driving a knife deep into her stomach.

It woke her with a start. The bedroom was in darkness. No Cooper.

She thought she heard a movement out in the space beyond though and bolted for the door.

The main space was only dimly lit and in silence. Rise hesitated, but then steeled herself. Cooper had said she was safe here.

But something was terribly wrong. And it was not just the fact that she no longer had the diamond. Screw the diamond. She would have swapped it for Cooper Pierce in a heartbeat.

She checked the study, the lounge area, the kitchen. Deserted.

Rise stayed in the kitchen, not sure what to do.

She saw the note and the key then. It was a business-like note, brisk and efficient. But it was from him. And that was enough.

Her heart skipped a little beat as she sank to the floor, holding it to her. As she sank, her eyes took in the reality of the time on the wall.

No. It couldn't be that time. Too many hours had passed. It couldn't be that time and he not be back here.

They had gotten to him. She knew without a doubt then they had gotten to him.

There was a thread between Rise and Cooper. Pulled tight.

It had been a golden thread. But it was blackened and bloody now. Almost lifeless. Almost broken.

Funny to notice it now, when it was almost broken, rather than when it was whole.

But she did notice it.

And was overwhelmed by its sorrow.

And he had left, thinking she thought he was an Echelon monster. Left, thinking that she hated him.

Her heart constricted at that. And then her anger flared.

Rise angrily wiped the tears away from her face.

How dare they. How dare they take him from her.

Think. The voice came to her. Male. Sardonic. Amused.

An image of Soar flooded her mind.

Soar with the Echelon. Rise recoiled from it.

But it was like someone was forcing her to watch. Except she was not seeing it as frightened, naked, Rise. She was seeing it from another perspective.

She saw Soar, in the midst of all of it, become aware of Rise's presence in the room.

She saw Soar recognize the marking of the Pann on her. Deep in her mind he had lodged it. Lodged it and hidden it well.

She saw Soar frantically work to free the Diamond from herself. She saw her throw out the golden thread to Rise that the Diamond would travel upon.

And she saw the dark magic of the Echelon Mage, Arc, slice through that thread like it was nothing.

The Diamond changed course from Soar and moved towards him.

And now she could see into Soar and she saw that she had space for two mind-diamonds. And she still had one. Her own was still lodged deep within her.

Rise suddenly became aware of Cooper in the vision.

And she could see his diamond.

But no, wait. She looked again. Oh, Cooper had space for two diamonds too. She could see one there already. So big. As big as the one Soar had tried to throw to her.

But his second one was oddly placed. It has been removed from his mind and placed beneath his ribs.

His cloaking implant, Rise realized with horror. Whoever had operated on him had put it in his cloaking implant.

Her vision shot back up to his face. And through the visor she knew he was deeply aware of her. Cooper was aware of her. He was about to save her. And the Echelon around him were becoming aware that he was not one of their own. He was about to blow his cover.

And Soar saw this too.

Using her last remaining strength, Soar shielded Cooper from the surrounding Echelon and pushed the mind-diamond closer to Arc, so intent on taking it from her. Distracting him with false triumph.

It worked.

And Rise felt the power of the Siren swell in her. She commanded the diamond to her, and together she and Soar broke the dark magic's hold on it.

But I do not have it anymore! Rise felt the panic rise in her.

You have your own. Surely that is enough. The calm, amused voice answered in reply.

And Rise saw her own mind then in the vision. And she had space for two diamonds as well. And one already lodged deep and secure within her, before the one from Soar lodged on top of it.

Cooper has three diamonds in him now. Rise thought suddenly to herself.

Yes. Said the voice, ridiculously cheerful now about the whole thing.

"This is terrible," she whispered out loud.

Nonsense said the voice. This is actually all working out rather well. But you should probably find him and get the big one back from him before you try any Veil opening.

"*I* should find *him*?" Rise whispered aloud again, with great uncertainty.

Excellent. Glad that's all sorted. The voice replied. Once you've got the diamond back you should spend some time worrying about the Big Blade, it continued. On a roll now. I bet you haven't given a lick of thought to how you're going to get that off of them, or what you'll need to do with it. It's quite crucial you know. It added helpfully.

"He's alive." Rise struggled to her feet. "If you're telling me to find him he's alive," she said. Hope flaring in her.

Silence.

"Thank you," she said uncertainly to the air in the kitchen, once she was up. Not really knowing what else to say or do.

More silence.

But warm, undulating waves broke over her, willing her to certainty and action.

"Hold on Cooper Pierce," Rise whispered.

"*I* am coming to rescue *you*." she added determinedly. And hoped if he could hear her, she sounded more confident than she felt.

CHAPTER FIFTY

Rise took the kitchen wall corner at a run, headed for the study. Badger had a mixture of Earth and Off-World systems in there. She would figure them out. All they needed to tell her was the location.

And Cooper had already shown her what it looked like on their radar systems. They would realize what was inside of him. They had to realize what was inside of him. And then they would know they had to keep him close by the Veil.

A hundred miles or so, north east. That's what he had said. She just needed to find someone to take her there.

The study door was still open from when she'd been in there earlier. She made towards it and stopped dead in her tracks. On the balcony level, above the winding black wrought iron staircase the heavily barred French doors stood wide open. The thin gauze drapes which covered them blew gently in the night breeze.

Rise saw the same glint of eyes she had seen hours earlier.

They were outside and then they were in. Leaping effortlessly from the first level to the level on which she stood.

They bounded towards her on a body of sleek black shadow.

Rise flew into the study, slammed the door and threw the lock. The creature hissed loudly. And Rise jumped back into the room. By the sound of that hiss the creature was right outside the door.

The creature scratched long claws down the length of the door, over and over and over again. Rise threw her hands over her ears. Godds it was awful. She looked desperately around the room for a weapon.

And had to settle for an ancient looking keyboard. Bless Earth and its old tech. She grabbed it and held it ready to do maximum damage.

"Materialize," hissed a strangely familiar voice. "You scare her half to death like that."

Rise heard a plaintive growling meowy sort of sound.

"Yes. Yes. Ok. I gets. Is her. Relax. Rise. Is Balia. Is Ok. Just HellCat Kitten. You come out now."

"Balia?" Rise moved closer to the door.

"Yes. Yes. Great. Is Me. Now you come out. No more waste time here hiding from Kitten." The creeping irritation in Balia's voice was growing more and more evident. The sardonic, "Big brave Siren," she muttered under her breath made Rise smile for the first time in hours.

She unlocked the door and burst through it. "Balia. Thanks the godds. I'm so glad it's you." The Minx Fae was close enough for Rise to plant a kiss on her cheek and she did so.

Balia screwed up her face in distaste and wiped at her cheek disgustedly.

At the same time, the now fully materialized HellCat Kitten began rubbing itself insistently against Rise's legs, purring loudly.

"Yes. Yes. Is her," Balia said impatiently to it.

She fixed Rise with a meaningful stare. "You want kiss things. Kiss the HellCat Kitten. Not me. It like that shit."

The HellCat Kitten purred loudly and rubbed itself even harder against Rise's legs. She bent down to scratch its ears and plant a kiss on its head. It purred so loud, the vibrations almost shook the room. Rise laughed delightedly and sank down on the floor to sit with her back against the wall.

The Kitten was beautiful. All sleek black fur over hard, graceful muscle. It had foreboding claws, and fangs to match. It's head already reached to Rise's mid-thigh. Its weight, when it sprang into her lap knocked the breath out of her.

"This is a Kitten?" she gasped at Balia, struggling for breath.

"Yes. Yes. Hellcat Kitten. She Damask. Youngest of Scion. Queen of all HellCats. Big Sook." Balia looked at the Kitten disgustedly.

"She's adorable," Rise said.

"Yes. Yes. All HellCats very cute. Wait till see adults," Balia said dismissively. "Now what mess has been made while I sleep and transition to this shit hole? What have you done with Hot Delicious?"

Rise sobered at that. "Oh Balia, he's been taken. We need to get to him." She tried to rise, but the weighty HellCat Kitten was having none of it.

"Balia." She pushed frantically at the big HellCat Kitten. "We have to get to him, now. They're killing him. It's where I was going when I saw the window open. Please, you must help me find him."

Damask, the HellCat Kitten, sensed her distress and sat up to run a big lick up her cheek in reassurance. It was like a normal cat tongue exfoliation times one thousand. As good as the slap Balia was planning on giving her to end her hysteria.

Rise quietened and Damask settled back in her lap comfortably.

She jumped when she realized how close Balia had flown into her face. Balia sniffed at her head suspiciously. She held Rise's face in her small hands and peered closely into her eyes.

She flew back and regarded Rise steadily. "You no have it anymore?" she said sharply.

"No. Cooper has it. Balia, we really do have to get to him."

"How?" Balia demanded. "How it end up in Hot Delicious?"

"I don't know," Rise wailed. "We were kissing. And it flew into him. And then he kissed me again to give it back to me. But it didn't work."

Balia frowned at her. "All this swappy diamond business no good." She waggled a finger at Rise. "Maybe Hot Delicious take that one because you take his other one!"

"No!" Rise fought the urge to cover her face with arms lest the Fae attack her while she was pinned to the wall by the HellCat Kitten. "He was never missing one!" she added hastily as the Minx Fae angled her horns dangerously. "It was here." She pressed her finger into the space below her ribs. "In his cloaking implant thing."

Balia paused in mid-air, her wings beating slowly and rhythmically behind her. Like their own little war drum.

Eventually she relaxed her body back out of attack mode. "You tell truth I think," she relented eventually.

Balia tilted her head, considering. "More I think though, this make Cooper Pierce not who he appear to be. You are right Siren. We need get to him ASAP."

CHAPTER FIFTY-ONE

Close to death, his face beaten to a bloody pulp, too many bones in his body broken to keep track of, Cooper felt Rise fade from him and was glad of it.

He prayed she had gotten there. Prayed that Badger's people could sense enough about what was going on to get her from that tunnel.

Because that's what his note had said. If he did not come back, she was to use that key and take the tunnel to the mountain. Get as far as she could down it and wait until Badger's people came and got her from it.

He had given none of that to these bastards. They had got nothing from him.

The Old One with glittery eyes stood just a foot back from where they had him strung and appraised him curiously.

"Did we read him?" He asked the leader of the three henchmen gathered behind him. Crude Earth humans, enslaved to a crude control system that forced them to do virtually anything for money. Even this, what they had done to one of their own, before him.

Money. It was the best control game the Old Ones had ever invented. The slaves created all manner of their own nonsense around it. Glittery eyes stood lost in contemplation of the simplistic sweetness of it all, waiting for an answer his paid humans were too scared to give him.

Not that he could blame them. He was down to three after all. He had started with double that close to him. But wrong answers. Grave consequences. Literally. He smiled at the inner joke only he had been privy to.

"Well?"

"Ah, yes boss. A couple of times now."

"And?"

"Three." the henchman choked.

"You're sure of this?" The Old One's eyes had never left Cooper's.

Cooper's mind ran in circles but his swollen eyes revealed nothing. Three? What the fuck were they talking about?

"Yes boss," the henchman laughed nervously. "Three."

"And what exactly are these *three*?" The Old One whirled on him, and all of the henchman stepped back nervously.

"We can't tell. They keep morphing and changing in him," the henchman replied nervously. "It doesn't look healthy. Whatever he's got in there. And none of them match the pattern you gave us. They're all different. Here."

He stepped forward bravely and handed the Old One the readout.

The Old One, Rend, looked at it.

He looked at it for a long time and his face grew mottled with rage. His eyes glittered even more dangerously. If Arc were here perhaps he could interpret this mess.

But no, he could not trust Arc around this one.

They could not risk killing him now. And Arc would most certainly kill him. The Echelon lacked a modicum of control when he became overly excited.

But now, with this new discovery, they must keep him alive enough to survive the Veil opening.

He looked up at Cooper. And the raw hatred in his eyes was like nothing Cooper had ever seen on another living creature before.

It was a long time before Rend spoke. And when he did, his voice was quiet and deadly. Cutting. Cooper could feel it bite through his already torn and ruptured flesh.

"Well played *Cooper Pierce*. Well played. It seems I must keep you alive for a little while longer than anticipated. But know this."

He stepped forward and grabbed Cooper's broken jaw in a vice like grip, turning him head this way and that, reveling in the pain it was causing him.

"Both you and your bitch whore siren will pay for this dearly before you die."

He released his hand from Cooper's jaw and plunged it deep into the flesh beneath the center of his ribs.

As the cold, sharp fingers dug and tore inside of him, Cooper did howl then.

The fingers found what they sought and ripped it cruelly from him. Cooper sagged in the chains, nearly passing out from the invasion and the pain.

"Get him down and get him healed. Stasis. Whatever. No expense spared. I expect him presentable to me within 12 hours."

"Boss he's almost dead," his chief henchman said doubtfully.

"Fix it. 12 hours. All of your own lives, and your families lives now depend on it."

He flicked the bloodied cloaking implant and tracker from his fingers in disgust. And crushed them both to smithereens under his expensive shoe.

In the Array Room, Tilds, Nate and Jonassen saw Cooper Pierce R9's signal on Deep Space Debbie flicker and go out. Just three seconds too early for them to have an accurate read on him.

The large mind-diamond carefully morphing and concealing both itself and the other two, slowed and faltered wearily.

It had been on such a long journey to make it here before the Portal, once again.

But it had taken everything it had to save Cooper Pierce.

The Siren, Rise, would need to open the Veil without it.

CHAPTER FIFTY-TWO

"Is Safe-House," Balia explained to Rise. As they exited via the French balcony doors and the fire escape.

There were bodies down below them and in the Alley. Balia and Damask had been busy before they got to her. Some of the other HellCats had helped, Balia had told her. But they had left to reconvene with the others close to the Portal.

"How did you get here? And how did you stay in form?" Rise had asked her as she dressed quickly.

"In Hot Delicious pack!" Balia had exclaimed as if that was perfectly obvious. "I shrink-invisible. Sleep. Transition. Wake up. Sprite medicine," she shrugged. "Take bit longer. But let me keep my wings."

"There is time limit though," she had chided and stamped a midair foot impatiently at Rise. "Like Badger. I only keep this up for so long in forgetting shit hole. Hurry!"

"Wait!" Rise fingered the lucky charm from the Savana9, now secured around her neck on a chain Badger had given her. She held it up to Balia. "If you wear this, will it dematerialize with you?"

Balia had flown forward and examined it curiously. "Yes," she sniffed. "But not easy. Use up more energy."

"Please." Rise had removed it from her neck and pressed it in to her hands.

"Fine!" The Minx Fae had rolled her eyes and secured the chain around one of her horns, hiding the charm in her hair. "Now we go!"

They had gone. And now here they were, stepping over the bodies of the humans who had known exactly where she was. She shivered. She had been oblivious to all of it. Even their deaths at the hands of Balia and the HellCats.

When she'd asked how Damask was also keeping her form, both the Minx Fae and the HellCat Kitten had looked at her like she was mad. "She HellCat," Balia spluttered. "They keep form wherever in cosmos they like." And she had rolled her eyes like Rise was a prime idiot.

Rise had kept her other hundred questions to herself.

They stopped before they reached the main street proper. Damask rubbed herself against Rise's legs and dematerialized to a vague black shadow. Balia had scolded her about not dematerializing her eyes properly before, and Rise could not see them at all now.

Balia had dematerialized immediately after her.

Rise could hear her though. Her sardonic voice whispered impatient directions in her ears as she moved down the unfamiliar streets towards their destination.

A Safe-House. Right here in the city. An Off-World one. Not run by Earth. But by Off-Worlders. Aliens. That's what they called us here, she thought. Aliens.

It was ridiculously close to Resistance1. They were there in no time.

A small singularly uninviting cafe. Dark. Serving only coffee, white or black. And the white only came from cows. Full strength. No variations above, below or in between.

It was a very effective door policy.

She pushed open the door and went in. A bell over the door heralded her arrival.

A couple of crusty old men played checkers at one of the small tables against the wall closest to the entrance.

They glared at Rise like they glared at anyone who dared push open the grimy door.

It was a most unwelcoming place. It was meant to be.

This was no place for the natives, restless or otherwise.

Rise ignored their glares and took a table over the other side of the room from them, as per Balia's instructions.

She felt a weight against her legs as she sat, and started in surprise before she realized it was Damask.

The bell rang again and the crusty old men turned their glowers on the new customer.

It was a native. It was most definitely a native. And a very restless one.

The man was young. Maybe early thirties. Sweaty and jumpy. His shirt was askew and his shirt and pants were cheap, synthetic, crumpled.

A woman emerged from the back room behind the counter. Striking. Red lipstick standing out against ivory skin and platinum blonde hair pulled back in a tight bun.

She cast a sweeping glance in Rise's direction but gave no indication of seeing her or knowing who she was.

"Mr. Evans," she addressed the man before her in dry tones. "I have told you before we cannot help you. We do not carry the answers you are seeking here."

"You know! I know you do! You have to tell me!" He was almost sobbing.

"Mr. Evans, I am going to ask you to please calm down and to remove yourself from the premises. Again." She looked at him pointedly. Her eyes were a very rich dark brown.

The young man looked from her to the men. "Why won't you help me?" He implored them. "Why won't you help me to remember?"

The men at the checker table were not looking so crusty anymore. They were ready to make a move as soon as the woman gave the signal.

The woman did not wait for the Earth human to do anything stupid. She gave the signal.

It was over in a flash.

He would have a nasty headache in the morning. But he would not remember this interaction for quite some time. When bits of it began to float back into his memory, it would be as if he had dreamt it. Or imagined it.

If he found his way to this place again, he would perhaps have a powerful sense of Deja-vu.

Or, he would remember everything. Some did. No matter what measures were taken with them.

Mr. Evans had proved most resilient. But still, it had been two years since he'd last found his way here. Perhaps this time would be the last.

"Lock it," the woman ordered the checker man after he pushed Mr. Evans roughly out of the door. The other was meticulously wiping the checker piece clean he'd used on him. Satisfied, he retracted the needle probe back into it.

He grinned at Rise, flipping the checker like a coin. "Nifty no? They making them this small now. Perfect dose."

"Wouldn't a chess piece be easier?" Rise asked. Wondering that she cared about such things, but knowing what handy little doses of things were held in chess pieces with retractable needles all over Moethiica.

"Bah!" Scoffed the checker man. "If they make us sit here and play chess we both quit!" He spat.

"So fucking cliched," grunted his partner.

The woman behind the counter beckoned to Rise, "Come Off-Worlder. We will talk out the back."

"Hey, come back! Why you have to take our new friend away so soon? We can teach her Dhrezt checkers," they called after her good-naturedly as she made her to the woman at the counter.

The platinum haired woman shook her head, raising her eyebrows at their banter as she closed the door on them and ushered Rise into the tiny office beyond.

It was messy and cluttered. Exactly the sort of office you would expect to find in a place like this.

She turned to Rise, taking her in from top to toe with a practiced eye.

"You cannot stay here Off-Worlder," the woman said without preamble.

"I do not wish to stay," Rise replied. "But I need transport."

"To where?" the woman replied noncommittally.

"One hundred miles, north-east of here," Rise replied. "The site of the Veil Portal."

The woman gave a short bark of laughter. "And I cannot help you with that either. None can help you with that. It is a little bit late to want to get to the Portal."

"Why?" Rise asked in horror

"Because the Old Ones have sealed every way there. War is coming Off-Worlder. And the Old Ones will win. The Old Ones always win. The final plays are in motion," the woman replied.

Then she cocked her head to the side, and gazed into space past Rise, listening to something only she could hear.

"Those who hunt you draw near to us. I will not have your shit brought here. Move."

Rise was momentarily disorientated, like the world had shifted all of a sudden. And perhaps it had because the blonde woman was suddenly beside her. Hand gripped firmly on her arm, and a gun digging deep into her head.

The woman shook her head at her like she pitied her. "I am sorry Siren. But I do not believe in your little fairy tale. What I do believe is that all you bring is trouble to me. But this. This chance to get away. This I will do for you."

She marched her then.

Stairs. Many stairs. And a cold metal door which opened up onto another dank alley. The woman pushed Rise out into it.

It smelled disgusting.

She stood in framed in the light from the doorway. Balia and Damask were silent and invisible, but present and reassuring beside her.

The armed woman, watched her. Gun pointed. Making sure she would leave.

Rise stood there staring at her though, wanting to remember the bitch's face, unmoving.

"Begone," the woman hissed eventually and slammed the door in her face.

Night was well and truly falling now. The alley was cold and freezing. Rise drew her jacket around her more closely.

"What now?" she said out loud, breaking the string of curses and colorful names Balia was now hurling at the woman who had turned them away.

"I would say cab, but we are too late. They are already waiting for you."

Rise turned then and saw the sleek black car at the only exit from the alley. Its windows heavily tinted. The back door already open waiting for her.

She stood and stared at it. "So be it. Let our enemies give us the ride there. Stay close," she whispered to her two invisible companions and made her way towards it.

CHAPTER FIFTY-THREE

As Rise drew closer, the chill emanating from the limo, made the cold night air seem positively tropic.

She stopped. Just out of reach of the door. Not wanting to get any closer. Her heart pounding in her chest. Damask rubbed reassuringly against her leg. Balia's weight came to rest on her shoulder.

She needed to get there. She needed to rescue Cooper.

And they needed her to open the Portal.

They would not kill her before that.

Cooper. They might well kill him before that, if they didn't realize he had the diamond.

She felt eyes on her at the thought. Not from the car but across the street. She looked up. Jackdaw? Was it Jackdaw from the rebels?

She felt Balia and Damask both stiffen, both hiss quietly.

It must not be Jackdaw. They would not hiss at him.

Whoever it was, the face was gone, melting back into the darkness.

She got in.

Complete blackness.

But whoever waited for her within was ready for her. Several pairs of hands were all over her instantly. She was cuffed and blindfolded before the car even sped away from the curb.

Her arms hurt in the tight cuffs shoved back hard against the seat. The restraint they clasped tight around her upper chest and shoulders made movement impossible. She could feel men on either side of her, their breathing hot and heavy on her cheeks.

They held her legs immobile and harmless while others secured the restraints around her ankles.

After that they sat in silence. The car started and stopped at endless traffic lights. Rise could no longer feel Balia and Damask beside her, and she prayed they had found space and safety in the car.

"Who can you no longer feel, Siren?" The power and chill of the voice reverberated through her as she gathered her wits enough to feel its mind trawling hers.

Old One.

Fark.

Rise schooled her mind to silence. And thought no more of anyone.

"Ah, see," the voice said approvingly. "The Siren is well schooled from her time as a winged whore on Moethiica. They teach them well to guard their thoughts there. Not like you." He seemed to be addressing someone else in the car now. "You, my pathetic little earth human, scream your inane thoughts so loudly, I am having to use all of my powers to block them out."

There was a snicker at that. Not a voice. But even in the snicker there was something familiar. Rise strained to hear it when it spoke again so she could identify it.

But he did not speak again.

He simply lunged at her from the limo seat across from her and nuzzled his helmeted, black visored face into hers.

The terror coursed through her and the Old One laughed at it, delighted.

It was Arc, the Echelon.

Arc rubbed his visor roughly against her and she felt it tear at her skin. Warm blood trickled down her cheek.

He placed his gloved hand tight around her throat and it took everything Rise had not to scream.

Do not scream for them. It was another lesson from Moethiica. One the winged women passed amongst themselves.

"Oh, you will scream Siren," the Old One said mockingly. "I promise you, you will scream a great deal before the end."

Fark. Her fear had opened her thoughts to him again. Breathing deep, she schooled herself to closing him out.

"I know what you have done. We have your little friend. Very clever, Siren. Very clever. But you know, Arc wanted to destroy you in front of him before he killed him, from the start. So, no matter. We will just make both your deaths a little more interesting to compensate."

Rise felt a tension ease out of her. They knew Cooper had the diamond. And they would not kill him before she got there.

Arc must have felt her reaction because he tightened the grip on throat and growled threateningly at her. He pushed his visored head roughly back into her face, tearing her skin again.

"Now, now Arc, move away from her. I told you she is yours to do with what you will after she opens the Veil Portal. We are all so looking forward to it, and I am counting on you, Arc, to make it a very long and very entertaining show. There. Move back now, Move back."

She felt his visored head still close to her. He did not move back. Echelon mind tricks. He pushed something into her. And in terror at it moving in at her, she dropped her shields again.

"Mmmm, Arc I can see why you favor her. Her essence is exquisite. "I look forward to tasting more of her. Until you rend her to a bloody, unidentifiable pulp of course," the Old One said urbanely.

Rise bit her lip, the fear rose in her. But she willed her mind to silence again, and did not rise to his bait.

"Perhaps the Siren would like a little demonstration of what is in store for her?" the Old One said brightly. "Yes. I think that is a splendid idea."

"Gentlemen. Remove her blindfold. Arc, would you be so kind as to demonstrate on the human just a little of what you have intended for our precious Siren here?"

The men beside her laughed at that and ripped the blindfold from her.

Rise blinked her eyes. Arc was opposite her. The Old One was next to him. Looking remarkably human except for the eyes. He held a terrified human woman almost casually by the throat beside him. Like Rise she was cuffed and bound. But she was also gagged.

Her eyes were wild. Too white. She was already damaged beyond repair by this, Rise thought and hoped the breaking of her mind would spare her the worst of it. She tried to feed the woman something, anything with her eyes, but then a flash of red to the left brought her own eyes around.

And Rise did scream then and began to struggle fiercely. The Old Family Hunter smirked at her and the Old One laughed delightedly again.

"Pierce her," he barked at Arc. He meant the human, who he thrust across his lap at Arc, but his eyes did not leave Rise.

Rise yelled "No! Leave her alone!" But at a gesture from one of the men beside her, she found herself also gagged.

Arc let just a little of his power wash over all of them and Rise felt the men beside her quake with fear.

The Old One turned his attention back to Rise.

"Do you remember the Nephliim Blade, Rise? Remember how it made you feel, pressed against your skin?" He purred at her. "Well imagine how it will feel tomorrow when Arc is wielding it on you like this. Arc if you please?"

"Make her watch. Keep her eyes open," he directed the Old Family Hunter. The Hunter moved delightedly in close to Rise. Her cold, CyTech hands splayed around her head, so strong they could crush it instantly.

They held her eyes open and her gaze pointed directly at the helpless human.

The cut with the blade was so small, she was momentarily confused by it. But then she felt

him draw on his magic and realized what he was truly after. And was even more confused. Why would they seek to take such a thing from an earth human?

It came out of her so easily.

Tiny. Barely the size of a pea. It was small and dull. But it was still hers. It was still her diamond. And she had only one. And only capacity for one. Rise saw and felt this instantly.

If she had not been gagged she would have screamed it at the woman. But all she could do was will it at her. Don't give it to him! Don't give it to him!

But the woman did. Not even knowing it had gone.

Arc held it aloft in his gloved hand, staring at it, almost curiously.

Rise tried to will the diamond away from him. Not to her. But back to the woman. Anything but letting him have it.

But she was powerless.

There was nothing.

And Rise watched in horror, as Arc crushed the woman's diamond to smithereens in his gloved fingers.

The woman stiffened and then lurched violently.

The Old One laughed triumphantly and threw the woman at Rise.

She landed in the Hunter's lap and Rise thought she must be dead.

But when the Hunter lifted the woman's head up by her hair, she was still alive. But her eyes were no longer the eyes of the living. They were vacant and dead. And she felt connectionless. Like she wasn't connected to anything. Just a body, breathing, independent.

Arc, leaned back in the seat and groaned as the power of the woman's immortality flooded over him.

For that is what he had taken from her. Her connection to creation. Her immortal awareness. Her everything.

Rise felt it and thought she would be sick.

The car stopped, a door was flung open, and the woman was flung viciously to the curb. It did not look like a nice neighborhood. Rise saw a group of youths approach her eagerly as the limo sped away.

She looked at the Old One and Arc, and realized she truly had no idea what depths these bastards were capable of.

"Oh, don't worry Rise," the Old One said to her. "Arc is far too possessive of you to throw you to a common street curb once he has your diamond. I'm sure he has far more interesting things planned for you than that."

He smirked at her fear. And the car sped on through the dark night.

CHAPTER FIFTY-FOUR

Rise had been blindfolded again at some point. As she could not remember when, she presumed they had drugged her.

Terror shot through her at the thought they could have read her mind while she slept.

Again, she schooled herself to calm. If they had, there was nothing she could do about it now anyway.

Enough. Enough of these assholes. Enough of them.

They were on an island. She knew that much at least. She had heard the shouts as the car was secured on something to take them over the water.

She felt the Old One brush against her mind. Almost cursory. She kept it still. And he passed over her again, bored.

She felt the car slow in a sweeping arc, tires crunching on gravel.

Several car doors opened and slammed. So, they had more than one car. A convoy.

As she was bundled from the car she wondered just how many humans he had enlisted in his service.

The Old One lifted her chin with his fingers and she tensed. She had had no idea he was before her. "Until tomorrow little Siren," he had whispered at her.

And then she felt his presence gone. They left her to the Old Family Hunter.

She was herded up a large flight of carpeted stairs. Her blindfold and cuffs were removed and the Hunter threw her roughly threw the open door in front of her.

She heard it locked from the outside and securely bolted.

When she turned there was no handle on this side of the door. Just a sheet of metal covering the entire length and width of it.

The room was opulent. The adjoining bathroom had no exit points. One window in the main room. Sealed shut. Heavily barred.

It was a pretty prison. But a prison none-the-less.

She wondered if Balia and Damask had made it safely. She worried lest the Old One hear her. But they had to be close to you to do that didn't they? She prayed to all the Godds and that other voice inside of her, to help her shut him out with everything they had and then some.

She was a long time in the shower. She threw the clothes she had been wearing in the small bathroom bin.

There were clothes laid out on the bed for her. She dressed in the track-pants, tank top and sweater they had left. They were army like. Some sort of militia uniform.

She looked at what they had laid out for her for the Veil Opening tomorrow and sighed. She would keep what she currently had on if she had any say in it.

Rise moved to the window and looked down at the space below her. There were spot lights here and there. It appeared to be some kind of drill yard.

It was. And she had guessed correct about her clothes. Like now, this house had been used at various times over the course of its history, to both base and train private troops and militia.

There were barracks, hidden from view, but not far from the house. Now that the time drew near, the private contractors in the employ of the Old One were using them. Here around the clock. For the last few weeks, security of the premises had been paramount.

Over the years the house had passed through a succession of owners. But outside of certain families, certain circles, you could bid as high as you wanted, and this house would never be sold to you.

When the house was first built, many hundreds of years ago, it was known it was the prime location for the viewing of the Veil Portal.

Just as this was known to the occupants of the land before that, who had little interest in houses at all.

A more recent owner, not the current one, had turned one end of the drill yard before Rise into a basketball court. Only one hoop remained, and some faint markings.

Rise sighed, and turned away from the window, and threw herself on the bed. She wondered where they had Cooper and if he was aware of her presence here.

In the yard below, the frayed netting on the lonely basketball hoop blew gently in the breeze.

Balia perched on the hoop and regarded the Echelon standing under Rise's window steadily.

He was looking straight up at it. He had been there for some time now.

Damask had made it in there just before the door closed.

She would stay with Rise. Balia would scout the area and search for Cooper.

She had done the first and was still on the latter when she had stopped to rest on the hoop. She was very tired now. Especially staying invisible. It was very draining on her.

If she did not find Cooper soon she would need to find somewhere safe and materialize for the night.

At the thought, her control lapsed only a little, but it was enough. One gossamer wing and the tip of one horn began to shimmer back into reality.

The Echelon whirled in her direction.

Balia dematerialized instantly.

But he had already raised his fingers and called his magic. He pulled her completely into the physical and to himself.

Balia struggled with all her might to fight him as he advanced steadily towards her across the yard.

In the bedroom, Rise jumped as Damask materialized suddenly by the window. She stood on her back legs, paws on the ledge to look out of it. Her yellow eyes glinted and she growled quietly.

Rise dashed to the window and looked where the Damask was staring intently, but could see nothing but the frayed net of the basketball hoop blowing gently in the breeze.

Damask pushed Rise away from the window and herded her back to the bed.

She was fretted deeply for her friend the Minx Fae, but her mother, the Queen had told her, her first charge was the Siren. She would be in big trouble with her mother if anything happened to Rise in her care.

She hoped her mother would be proud of how she had shielded the Siren's thoughts from the Echelon underneath her window.

He was very powerful and she was very tired now, but she had done the best she could.

And the Siren's mate was here. The one she searched for. And he was living.

She pushed her warm, comforting weight into Rise, settling against her. Rise held her close and scratched her deliciously behind the ears. She planted a kiss on the Kitten's head before she lay her own head down.

The HellCat Kitten licked Rise's nearest hand in gratitude and willed her to sleep. Damask was here. And she would keep her safe and sound until morning.

CHAPTER FIFTY-FIVE

In the morning, Damask was nowhere to be seen. Rise panicked that they had come in the night and taken her.

But if they had, they said nothing when they came. Two militia and The Hunter.

It watched her with its cold, red CyTech eyes as she showered. And made her dress in the thing they had selected for her.

Black and flowing. An Echelon robe. She felt sick as it settled on her naked skin. Evil emanated from it. It smelt of blood and fire and their sickening dark magics.

It weighed on her as heavy as a shield grip.

Rise felt the anger build in her. They were trying to mark her as their own.

The Hunter gripped her arm cruelly, but did not bind her. The militia settled in behind them. And she was marched briskly out of the room, down the carpeted stairs, and out a side door into the drill yard.

It was a cold, grey, blustery day.

And for such a big event, one that would change not only the path of Earth, but of all the worlds in the Cosmos, it was a small crowd that gathered.

The second Old One was there. That famous face. Trusted by so many. His true eyes no longer hidden. Multifaceted and glistening in the muted grey light.

There were a handful of other men and women there who Rise did not recognize. The rest were armed Militia.

They marched Rise to the middle of the yard. A wall of the Militia stood before her.

It was an imposing sight, but Rise barely glanced at them before she looked up and beheld it.

The golden line of the Veil Portal shimmering in the sky above her.

She felt its awareness of her pushing at her. And if not for the Hunter holding her, she would have fallen at the power of it. As it was, her knees buckled and she gasped loudly. The Hunter righted her roughly, and shook her.

Rise turned to glare at her and then looked at the small audience. All eyes were on the sky, on the Portal. All waited breathlessly for it to open.

But as it finished its probing of Rise's mind it flashed an angry red. It had not found what it was looking for. It began to close again.

"What is she doing? Make her open it!" one of the unknown women in the small audience screamed.

Her shrill shrieking tone shattered the silence.

The Old One, Rend, from the car was speaking. "Calm yourself. She has something to reclaim first, don't you Siren?"

He was dressed in an identical robe to her own. Fresh blood glinted on it. She could smell it sharply on him as he moved closer to her.

"Yes, the blood of the Minx Fae has quiet a tang to it, wouldn't you say?" he smirked at her. "But she will make a fine sacrifice for the ceremony. Guards."

The Militia before her parted as she took in the full horror of his words.

And there stood Arc. Balia, held upside down and bound in his hand. He had a knife to her throat now. But there were wounds all over her. She dripped blood from all of them on to the drill yard cement beneath them.

"You bastards. Let her go. There is no sacrifice required for this." Rise lunged at Arc madly, almost breaking free of The Hunter.

"Uh. Uh. Uh. Little Siren," the Old One chided her. "Our ceremony. Our rules. Now. I will perhaps spare the Fae creature. But it will be your choice. You can only have one. Now will it be her or your precious Cooper?"

He gestured and more of the militia stepped back. This time revealing Cooper. Alive. Back from the almost dead. And then freshly beaten this morning. Surface wounds. Ones that bleed a lot and bruise a lot and swell a lot. Enough to draw a sob from Rise as she again almost broke free of the Hunter as she lunged towards him.

Rise looked at the Old One in hatred. "You cannot kill Cooper and you know it. You know what resides inside of him," she gestured to the sky. "The Veil will not open without it."

She looked at Cooper and his eyes locked with hers.

Two of the Militia held him tightly. His wrists were clearly bound behind him.

"The Fae, then." The Old One turned to Arc, and Balia moaned as he dug the blade in deeper on her.

"You fools," Rise said. Her voice beginning to carry the weight of the Siren. "I need the Fae to get the diamond back from Cooper." She shook her head. "I fear I cannot even do this with what you have done to her. You have ruined everything."

"Arc. Hold." The Old One looked at her shrewdly. But there was just the smallest doubt in his eyes.

He stepped up close to her. "You lie."

"How dare you, Old One," Rise spat at him. "I am the 5th Siren of the Veil Portal and I do not lie."

The power of the Veil was coursing through her. The Siren in her was waking.

And twice now she had nearly broken the Hunter's hold.

Rise smiled at the Old One as she realized the true extent of the Power coursing through her.

His eyes widened and he took a nervous step back from her.

She broke free of the Hunter as if she was shrugging out of a cloak.

The Hunter looked at her empty hands as if she did not believe it.

She lunged madly at Rise and Rise turned back to her and punched her. The Hunter's face shattered into a hundred pieces. Its body flew back several meters along the cement yard ground.

The Old One retreated from her rapidly as she turned to him. Most of the Militia were on their knees, trembling.

"Cooper, The Minx Fae and the Nephliim Blade," Rise demanded. "Bring them to me now. Or I will do the same to all of you."

"I will not give her the Blade," Arc objected and the Veil thundered ominously.

Rise's eyes began to glow golden. The shadows of huge black wings shimmered behind her. On her head shimmered tiny horns.

"Bring me the Blade or die now Echelon scum," she commanded. And at the power in that voice, even Arc trembled.

"Give her the Blade you fool!" the Old One screamed at him. A mad wind was blowing through the Courtyard. Robes and clothes whipped their owners. One of the women's hats flew across the yard.

At the Old One's instruction, two of the Militia had dragged Cooper to her and left him there. He was so weak, he could barely stand. She held him upright. Like he weighed nothing at all.

He grunted and drew in close to whisper to her in her ear. "Rise, I'm so sorry. I don't have it." he sagged against her and she took his weight easily. "It has died in me Rise. I can feel it. I'm so sorry."

He moved his head back then to look deep into her eyes, begging her forgiveness. She smiled at him and the power of her attention on him almost dropped him to his knees.

"I know," she said. And she did know. She had known as soon as she'd laid eyes on him.

"But don't you worry, Cooper Pierce, I will save you." She smiled at him. "I will save you."

Unspeakable, what he felt and what he felt for her at that moment. Unspeakable. If this was to be the end of him, what an ending.

She turned her attention back to Arc.

"The Fae and the Blade. Now!" she commanded.

Arc staggered towards her and dropped both at her feet. "Get away from me Echelon scum," she hissed at him. And he flew backwards away from them as if he was carried by the wind."

Still holding Cooper with one hand she reached down and picked up Balia, handing her to him. "Can you hold her while I take the Blade?" She asked him. And he nodded and took the small, bleeding Fae in his arms. She was unconscious, barely breathing. But she came to enough to sigh "Hot Delicious," and then she sagged.

"Gently Rise, reached into the Fae's hair and retrieved the lucky charm from Savana9. The charm looked dead and she thought for an awful second, she had misjudged it. But then it began to slowly turn and glisten.

Rise smiled, steadying Cooper and picked up the Nephliim Blade.

The Veil Portal began to shimmer back to golden and prepared itself to open.

Rise did everything in her power to keep it closed as she wound the lucky charm around the handle of The Blade.

The Blade knew her as before, but it was calm in her hand. She felt the Nephliim runes on her back sing to it. She felt her own mind-diamond, the one she carried in her head always, begin to spin a little faster.

In her left hand she steadied Cooper Pierce. In her right hand she held the Blade.

She turned to him and smiled at him again. And as she turned, she saw Arc working his way back to them. He knew. He knew Cooper did not have the diamond and he would kill them.

"What is the word, Cooper?" she asked. Calm. Not rushed. Her glorious golden eyes blazing at him.

"What word? What do you mean?" he asked her frantically.

In the background she was aware of Arc screaming. "He does not have it! Neither of them have it! They do not have the diamond. They are charlatans! They Veil will not open! Stop this!"

All eyes turned to them and she felt the weight of both the Old Ones press against both her minds and Coopers.

"Arc speaks the truth!" the famous Old One in the audience shouted. "Stop them!"

"The word Cooper. You know it. It is a Nephliim word. I need you to tell it to me." Her voice was a little more urgent now.

"I don't know any Nephliim word!" he screamed at her. The wind was ferocious now and the Veil pulsed angrily.

Arc was almost upon them. The militia had raised their guns, but were struggling to hold their feet in the gale force winds.

"You do Cooper. You do know it. Tell it to me."

Not knowing what else to do, Rise pressed the Nephliim blade against him at the same time as Arc surged over the final feet towards them.

At the touch of the Nephliim Blade, Cooper's eyes flooded with awareness. And he remembered. The strange word his General had told him in the bar, made him repeat back to him. If they got to this point, he had told him to use it.

Cooper said it to her, staring at her in wonder.

"Thank you," Rise said to Cooper.

"Too late asshole, and we are not charlatans," she said to Arc. And the power of her voice and the power of her eyes stopped him cold.

And to the Portal she drew on every last ounce of the Siren power coursing through her and said a Nephliim word. She said a Nephliim word as only a Siren could say it. And she threw the Blade.

The Veil was impossibly high. Impossibly angled.

But she had practiced and hit impossibly high, angled targets before, back on Moethiica. It made her wonder all of a sudden, what she had been truly practicing for.

The word reverberated around them, the Blade turned over and over in the air, going impossibly higher.

At the very last instant it stopped, suspended. And looked like it would fall again. The reverberations of the word stopped.

Rise slumped. The power of the Siren was gone. There was nothing left in her, but her.

And that was enough. It was more than enough.

She whispered the word and then she blew it towards the Portal like she was blowing out a candle.

And with Nephliim Word and Nephliim Blade, she pierced the Veil.

CHAPTER FIFTY-SIX

The worlds on both sides of The Veil stood still, plunged in darkness.

The cosmos and its Veil made some slight configuration changes. Did some adjusting.

It seemed that the Siren of the 5ᵗʰ had decided to take matters into her own hands and change the rules ever so slightly.

"What have you done?" Cooper whispered to her in the darkness.

"Saved you Cooper Pierce," she responded. "And changed the rules a little bit."

She looked about her. Her power was spent but her eyes were still golden. She could see well in this light. She flexed her shadow wings and found them real enough for this purpose.

"Hold on." She picked Cooper and Balia up effortlessly and glided away from the center of the courtyard to the side of the building.

She settled them both against the wall. A small balcony covered them barely. She hoped it would be enough.

And then the darkness began to lift and the landscape began to light up around them.

She felt her shadow wings dissolve away from her and dashed away a tear at their passing.

The gold began to fade from her eyes as they melted back to violet blue.

And then the first of the Veil beings, giant and Nephliim came through.

*****

The flyer hurtled to Earth, shattering the concrete floor of the drill yard with the force of the impact.

The Nephliim within had emerged from it well before it landed. The reverberating impact and the flying debris from the landing gave him all the time he needed to roll and right himself.

He was seven foot tall at least. Heavily muscled. His hair was white and cropped close to his head. His eyes were large, vividly green. He had small, pointed ears, set close and flat to his head. Strong and proud. Strong hard bone. Strong hard muscle. Big. The force of his presence was huge. As mighty, if not more, than the muscle.

Still crouched, he beheld the scene around him and smiled.

He turned to Rise and Cooper and placed his fist over his heart. He bowed his head deeply to them.

They did not even give him time to rise from it. The first of the snipers shot true.

It was a shoulder wound. And it rocked him. But a tiny med-bot emerged from his armor and scurried towards the wound. It extended a needle arm and retrieved and discarded the bullet instantly.

It lasered the wound closed. And it looked like there was nothing there at all.

The militia who hadn't deserted at the first sight of Rise in full Siren glory, instantly began to regret their decision.

The Nephliim roared in anger and turning in the direction of the sniper, raised a gun of his own.

His aim was good. And there was possibly no med-bot in existence who could have repaired that damage.

A sniper on a different wall struck him in the leg. He staggered. But again, the med-bot was there.

And then more Nephliim were through. And these ones stayed in their small craft long enough to clear every high vantage point of snipers with the guns on their flyers.

When they abandoned them as the first Nephliim had done, the real fighting began. And it became a ground game and a bloody one.

For all the militia that had deserted, they still outnumbered the Nephliim three to one. Still the Nephliim were huge and powerful and spectacularly armored.

The white haired Nephliim barked instructions at the others. He had lost his gun at some stage in the close-knit fighting. But it did not seem to worry him. He stalked the Old One, Rend, having only eyes for him.

Rend looked frantically up at the shimmering, pierced Veil. He was close to Rise and Cooper now and he turned to hiss at her. "You will pay for this Siren bitch."

And then the Nephliim leader was on him.

They fought viciously and ferociously for a time, seemingly well matched despite the Nephilim's bigger size.

The Nephliim eventually got the better of him and rolled up to sit on top of him. He slammed his fist down into the Old One's face, one, two, three times.

And then Arc emerged from the thick of the fighting. And the blade he wielded struck the Nephliim hard and deep from behind.

It was the dagger he'd had in the car, Rise thought, sickened once again by it.

Arc twisted it cruelly in the Nephliim leader's head. He reached up, his hands grasping madly at it. But he could not dislodge it. And as he did this, Rend punched him hard in the stomach and wriggled free of him.

Arc kicked the Nephliim flat on his face as soon as the Old One was clear. The med-bot began to work feverishly at the Blade, but Arc smashed it away contemptuously. He bent down to twist the knife and finish the job.

Rise screamed "No!" And lunged toward him. He sent her flying against the wall with ease with one arm. Cooper roared and came at him then but Rend was already there, dispatching him with a vicious kick to the head.

Rise saw Cooper sag against the wall some three yards away from her.

Rend looked down at her smirking in triumph.

And then the HellCats came.

And they came in their true form. The size of ponies. Muscled, sleek, clawed, fanged. Some red. Some black like Damask.

And Damask was amongst them. With three more Kittens like her. Though she was the smallest of them and obviously the youngest.

As one of the older HellCats took down Arc, Damask took down Rend.

The other HellCats threw themselves into the battle, fighting beside the Nephliim. The Earth Militia may have been forewarned and prepared for Nephliim, but they were certainly not prepared for HellCats.

The HellCats tore at them with their claws, and bit into them with their fangs. And the militia's enthusiasm for the job at hand waned as the odds turned considerably against them.

Desperately Rise tried to move herself from the wall to help Damask. She and the Old One rolled and tore at each other. But Damask was only a Kitten. From the heat of the battle Scion, the red furred Queen of the HellCats, sensed danger for her youngest.

Too late she leapt, as Rend caught the unsuspecting Kitten with a vicious, curved blade.

"No! "Rise screamed and threw herself the remaining feet at him.

He laughed in her face as he ripped the blade cruelly up the Kitten's side. The baby HellCat cried out piteously in pain and then went limp and silent.

Rise gathered all of her strength and threw herself on him, punching and kicking. She felt the power of the Siren surge through her in the heat of her anger. But it was momentary. Just enough however to divert his attention from the Kitten.

Scion, the Queen, dived in then and opened up a vicious wound across his chest with her claws. He howled and dropped Damask. And the Queen picked her up in her mouth and carried her to safety.

Rise was left with him and too late she realized with horror that all of her Siren power had deserted her again. Rend stood up with her held by the throat as if she weighed nothing. He squeezed tight and she began to see stars before her eyes.

Rend smiled in satisfaction. "Time to die Siren."

Cooper Pierce made one last desperate pull to free the Blade from the Nephliim Leader. It dislodged suddenly with a sickening noise, thick purple blood oozing from the sight of the wound.

He already knew the sweet spot he was aiming for. He didn't need to look again. He threw it.

It took Rend perfectly in the side of the neck.

He howled, his eyes rolling back in his head and his mouth frothing. Rise crumpled to the ground as he dropped her instantly. His eyes frantically scrabbling at his own neck.

Two Militia darted forward, but they did not seek to engage. Simply dragged the Old One to safety.

Cooper raced to Rise. "See I told you I do the saving," he said to her as he helped her sit up." It made her smile which made her cough.

The fallen body of the adult HellCat who had attacked Arc lay close to them and a wave of sorrow filled Rise.

Followed by dread. Whirling in the other direction she saw the still bodies of Balia and Damask. Scion, The HellCat Queen was crouched over them, protecting them, hissing fiercely and scratching at Arc as he tried to get them and to her.

CHAPTER FIFTY-SEVEN

Rise screamed, "No!" And was at Scion's side in an instant. Cooper cursed and launched himself after her.

He took out Arc in a classic flying football tackle as a defiant Rise stood between him and the HellCat Queen, and the bodies she was protecting. Cooper rode him hard into the ground and knocked the wind out of him.

They rolled and Rise held her breath as Arc made it to his feet first. But then another HellCat was on him from behind. Front paws on his shoulders. His fangs sinking deep into his neck.

Arc howled and murmured an incantation. The HellCat cried out in pain and released him before the full blast of the dark magic reached him.

Arc grabbed for the HellCat but it avoided him easily.

And the damage was done. Arc staggered and looked like he would fall. But them the same Militia who had dragged Rend to safety, pulled Arc unwillingly away.

Across the drill yard, Rise could see a craft of some kind. Out of its window the other Old One, the one so beloved by so many of the people of Earth, looked at her steadily and smiled chillingly.

He ran a hand across his neck in a killing motion. And then Arc was in the craft and the doors closed. They took off abruptly. A temporary retreat to tend their wounded and reassess their plans.

"Help me! Please help me!" Rise implored anyone who could hear her, turning her attention back to the wounded of their own.

Cooper staggered over to them. He was almost done for. Still, he ripped a Militia jacket from the nearest body. Ripped it in two again. He shoved one half at Rise, no explanation necessary. She wrapped Damask while he wrapped Balia. Scion hovered close, watching them carefully.

Cooper surveyed the yard. Bodies littered it. And not a few of them were Nephliim and HellCats. Still the majority of them were Militia. It would appear they might have just won the day.

But they needed medics and they needed transport.

The Nephliim agreed. And within moments of him thinking it, the craft descended into the yard. Choppers? If you really knew your choppers, not so much. But from a distance, Cooper surmised they would be Ok.

The Nephliim made short work of stretchering or herding them all into the craft. Rise glanced up at the Veil before she got in. It was a shimmering golden line in the sky. It was still intensely aware of her. And it would wait for her. And her next decision.

Rise boarded the craft and then could feel it no more.

There were busy medics and med-bots on board attending to the wounded. They took Balia and Damask from them.

Rise saw a small team working feverishly on the white haired Nephliim leader. Perhaps there was hope for him after all.

A weary Nephliim soldier sat not too far away from them. He did not need medical attention. He sat with his eyes closed and his head leant back against the gun metal wall of the craft.

Cooper glanced back one more time to make sure Rise was Ok. She had her own eyes closed now and had her own back against the wall. Satisfied he made his way over to the resting Nephliim.

He opened his eyes quickly as he sensed Cooper's approach. Cooper had a sense of the being reading him on some level unintelligible to him.

The Nephliim inclined his head to him and extended his hand. "Friend." Cooper took it and the Nephliim grasped it warmly. He gestured to Rise. "Our thanks. You and the Siren did a mighty job of piercing the Veil only enough so that ourselves could come through."

"Not me," Cooper said. "It was all her." He looked at Rise, and there was a sort of wonder in his eyes. The Nephliim smiled at him.

"I think you did more than you imagined Cooper Pierce. And in any case, are you not the one who first recognized her and rescued her from Moethiica? It is the first sighting of the Veil Sirens which is the important one."

Cooper nodded. Not truly understanding but willing to concede to higher knowledge. "Where are we going now?"

"To the hold in the mountains. It has been prepared for our coming for some time now. Have no fear. You and the Siren, and all who aid you, will be well looked after there."

"Ah," Cooper said. "Resistance1?" He queried.

"Correct," the Nephliim replied.

"Badger. He helped us in the city," Cooper mused. "He was retreating there also."

The Nephliim said nothing, simply nodded and then looked across at Rise.

"Lucky man. Cooper Pierce," he said, a knowing smile playing over his features.

Cooper looked at Rise and then back at him.

"What? Oh no. Godds. I *should* be so lucky." He ran his hand through his hair.

"Really?" the Nephliim said knowing and mocking all at once. "Are you sure about that Cooper Pierce? She risked much for you. Not the least her life."

He stood, before he could answer, clasping Cooper on the shoulder as he did so. "I must go and help the others. We are landing."

Cooper moved carefully back to Rise, only conscious now of the change in the craft's momentum.

He laid a hand gently on her shoulder. "We're landing," he said quietly as he settled in beside her. And she nodded wearily in acknowledgement but did not open her eyes.

Not long after they felt the craft land. There was shouting and a flurry of movement and activity as both wounded and well were herded efficiently off the ship.

When Cooper alighted, the crisp mountain air hit him. The oxygen was so pure, just the simple act of breathing was a rush.

They had landed in a courtyard. Ancient stone walls towered up above them on all four sides.

Large double doors, equally ancient, but fortified with titanium steel from within, opened on to a large, curved, sweeping passageway.

The med-bays were close by and Rise and Cooper followed those who had Balia and Damask there. Scion was close beside them, three other HellCat Kittens now sticking close to her side.

Both Rise and Cooper gasped at the size of the treatment facility. One huge vast room held literally hundreds of beds and all manner of equipment.

A row of private Med-Bays for operating, stasis and the more seriously wounded ranged along one wall.

"So many," Rise said. The wounded they had brought in did not take up even a tenth of the space.

"Yeah," Cooper said, and his voice was grim. "They're prepared for war."

CHAPTER FIFTY-EIGHT

The medics were a long time with Balia and Damask. Eventually someone came to lead both Rise and Cooper away. They had done all they could for them. Put them both in stasis. The HellCat Queen, Scion, and her other Kittens would stay in the Med-Bay with them.

Yes, Cooper and Rise could visit. But *after* they were checked and cleaned up themselves. And after Rise had discarded that hideous Echelon cloak.

Rise looked down at herself surprised. She had not even remembered it was on her.

As soon as she became aware of it, the sensations of it crawled along her skin. She began to pull at it frantically, wanting it off of her.

The Medic and Cooper steadied her. "Come," said the Medic. "We will find a med-gown for you to put on and burn it."

They were separated then while they checked each of them over. Rise was cleared, but Cooper they wanted to keep in the Med-Hall overnight for observation.

That was all they told her as they shuffled her out of there.

The hold proper was massive and confusing.

Solid wooden beams crisscrossed over a large foyer area. Medieval looking light fixtures hung from them by thick black chains. They had held oil and flame in their time. Now soft cleverly crafted bulbs provided the light.

Their light illuminated the foyer area expertly and softly, but left the space above the beams in semi-darkness.

There were humans here. Rise noticed in surprise. All of them looked busy, bringing in boxes and supplies of all shapes and kinds. When they saw Rise, they would stop only briefly to bow their heads to her, and then return to their tasks.

The Nephliim Medic stopped to speak to a human woman and they conversed rapidly in a foreign tongue. He turned to Rise. "This is Osia. She will take care of you now."

Osia grasped her hand warmly. "Thank you, Rise," she said in greeting. Rise nodded, a little overwhelmed, and turned to thank the Nephliim Medic. But he was already headed back to the Med-Hall.

Osia led her across the large lobby and they moved up a large staircase on the left-hand wall.

They turned left on the landing, passing heavy closed doors. At the end of this hallway were another two staircases to choose from.

Osia chose the one on the right. "I will take you for bathing first," Osia explained to her. "And then to your quarters. We have prepared rooms for you both." She looked at Rise, a little unsure of herself. "We weren't sure of...." Seeing Rise's confused look, she decided not to pursue it and instead broke into a broad smile.

"Anyway, they are just across the hall from each other. Easy access!" She beamed and they were on their way again.

At the end of the last hallway they turned into were doors opening on to a huge communal bath and steam room.

Osia led her to the showers first, showing her a range of shampoos, conditioners, soaps, body-washes, everything she would need. Rise sniffed them appreciatively. They all smelt divine.

When the first delicious warm torrent of water hit her, she sighed in contentment. It took with it far more than dirt and blood and grime.

Rise washed herself thoroughly and then started on her hair. When she was done she was reluctant to leave the shower.

But Osia smiled and helped her secure a thick towel around her hair. She led her to a deep sunken, gently bubbling tub. The water was perfect. Warm and soothing. It smelled beautiful. Rise began to feel her skin relax and soften as she sat there, eyes closed, head back against the cushioned edge of the side.

She must have drifted off in it. Next thing she knew Osia was shaking her shoulder gently, coaxing her out of the water and enfolding her in soft warm towels.

They had drying units. State of the art. It dried and moisturized expertly. Ones for winged, Rise noted sleepily. She was in it only a few minutes and she was done. Her dark hair falling about her shoulders, in soft, delicious smelling waves.

Soft warm pajamas and a huge warm robe were waiting for her. A pair of soft, fluffy boots encased her feet perfectly.

On the floor above were their appointed quarters. Osia led her through a cozy lounge room with a fire, to an equally cozy bedroom.

It too was warm and toasty but no fire was evident.

The bed was huge, piled with soft fluffy pillows and covers.

The woman helped Rise out of the robe and under the covers.

It was heaven.

She was asleep almost as soon as her head touched the pillow. But before it took her she reached out a hand and laid it on Osia's arm. "My friends, are they alright?"

The woman patted her arm. "We will find out soon enough. Rest now. When you are awake I will take you to see them."

"You promise?"

"I promise. Now sleep."

Satisfied, an exhausted Rise did so.

CHAPTER FIFTY-NINE

For the first time in many days Rise awoke not with a start, but with dream filled, yawny, stretchy delicious comfort.

But then the reality of her injured friends and the uncertainty of the entire situation came crashing back down on her.

The cupboards and drawers were full of clothes. Everything she would need. She dressed quickly in warm leggings, boots, a tight sweater with a loose, flowing wrap over the top.

When she burst into the lounge area intent on heading straight for the Med-hall, Osia was there to firmly stop her and make her eat.

Rise downed her coffee quickly and they made their way to the Hall.

It was quiet after the hive of activity it had been yesterday. Osia spoke quietly to one of the attending Nephliim who nodded and took them to the med-bay containing Balia and Damask.

Cooper was up and already in there.

He looked tired but vastly improved from yesterday. He sat in a chair, absently scratching the ears of Scion, who sat beside him.

Even sitting, her head was on a level with his own in the chair. In all the events of yesterday, Rise realized she had not fully comprehended how big the HellCats were.

The Queen turned to her and nodded with sorrow laden eyes. Then she turned back to her vigil over her Kitten.

Rise's eyes flicked to the Stasis Chambers. There was only one occupied with Damask. Her heart sank but then she noticed the small, tightly wrapped bundle, curled up in Cooper's lap. It was Balia and it took all of Rise's effort not to pick her up and cuddle her madly.

Which was just as well, as Balia no doubt would have taken it quiet badly, she thought wryly.

Almost as badly as she was going to take the fact that someone had found more pink mittens for her horns.

Perhaps it was the only color they came in? Rise pondered as she took a chair next to Cooper. "How are you?" She asked quietly, not wanting to wake the sleeping Balia.

"Never better," he quipped but his eyes were still strained with pain. He still had more healing to do. Rise could tell.

She looked over at the still form of Damask in the stasis chamber, and dashed a tear from her eye.

She raised her eyebrows in question at him, not wanting to say anything out loud in front of Scion.

Cooper just shook his head. He handed Balia to a waiting Med-Aide and indicated they should leave the room.

Osia moved forward to steady him and get an arm underneath his as he rose and Rise realized with a shock she had no idea how badly he was doing.

She took his other arm. "Cooper, what is going on?"

"I'm fine. I'm fine. They had to operate on me last night is all." He waved her off as if it was nothing.

"And you're up?" she said incredulously. At the same time wanting to hold him and kill him.

She turned around, demanding answers from all of them, any of them.

"Why is he up? Who has let him out of bed?" She looked around accusingly.

Cooper looked at her in horror. A nearby Nephliim Medic tried his best to hide his smile. Even Osia was grinning, though she schooled her face to stoicism when Rise whirled around to look at her.

"Relax, Rise," she said. "He is fine to be up and be discharged to his rooms. He will be weak for little while, but I will attend to him."

"Now, come," she continued. "Our leader Maxiimus's address will start soon."

And she led them out of the Med-Hall and into a large room adjoining it.

There were chairs arranged in rows before a small dais. Many of the injured Nephliim were already seated before it, covered in warm blankets or thick robes.

The uninjured Nephliim warriors stood or sat. They were casually dressed in dark colored combat pants and turtlenecks. Even out of their armor, they were still enormous.

Osia directed Cooper and Rise to seats at the very front of the room.

Without fail, every Nephliim they passed put their fist over their heart and bowed their heads to them.

Neither Rise nor Cooper knew what to make of it or do with it. Sensing their discomfort and confusion, Osia ushered them into their chairs.

A short time later, the white-haired leader, Maxiimus, was wheeled on to the dais. A heavy bandage around his head.

Rise was amazed that he lived, and then also wondered who had let *him* out of his bed Because clearly, he was in even worse shape than Cooper.

She stilled her thoughts. She was a jumble of nerves. And her thoughts were rambling.

The Nephliim leader smiled down at Rise and Cooper. And then he too placed his fist over his heart and bowed his head deeply.

All of the Nephliim in the room followed suit, as did the humans. Who had quietly entered and were now scattered amongst the Nephliim.

Osia held the stance the same as the rest.

Cooper nudged her with his elbow. He was mimicking the gesture. Rise followed his lead. Only raising her head when she heard the voice of the Nephliim Leader.

"My friends, I thank you," he said simply and then turned his attention to the rest of the room.

"Nephliim. Friends. Alliances. Those of you who know me well will be thankful that I do not have it in me for a long speech. And so, this one will be brief of necessity."

There were a few chortles at that and Maxiimus smiled.

"The Veil is pierced, not opened. Thanks to the Siren of the 5th." He nodded at Rise. "Which means it is only us few here for now. Her actions have prevented the worst of the Old Ones from descending to Earth, not only from the other side of The Veil, but also from the other corners of the cosmos. Siren5 you have saved many lives and prevented much evil. I, we, every being and world striving for freedom in the cosmos salutes you."

There were murmurs amongst the others there. Salutes and praises. Rise blushed furiously and bowed her head.

"That was quite a throw Siren of the 5th." The Nephliim Leader smiled, breaking the solemnity of the mood and lifting her eyes back to him.

"I used to throw a lot on Moethiica," Rise stammered. "I had a lot of practice."

"The most unlikeliest of circumstance often prepare us for greatness." He nodded to her and turned back to the room.

"We hold the advantage at this time. However, this will not last. Already two Old Ones and one Echelon walk the Earth. Doing already what is not supposed to be possible under the rules of the game."

"And if they find the other Serpent Diamond then nothing else really matters. They will control the Golden Serpent. Game Over. Well and truly over. I would say they will destroy us all, but I fear that is simply what we would wish for, helpless, under their power."

Cooper looked up at him, realization dawning. "It's what they have been doing all along here, isn't it? What they have us truly mining for."

"Yes," Maxiimus replied simply. "Both in the Earth and in the minds of Earth's inhabitants."

"It could be in either," Rise said, suddenly realizing.

"Yes," Maxiimus replied again. "They do not know. No-one knows where it currently resides. We believe, it jumps, just like the one you both carried, to preserve its safety."

Cooper looked stricken at that. "What of the one we carried? It died in me." He paused, gathering his resolve. "It died saving me. I'm sorry," he said to all of them, as he had said to Rise.

Rise put her hand on his arm and Maxiimus smiled.

"If the Serpent Diamond died in saving you Cooper Pierce, then that is because it was meant to." He peered closer at him from his chair on the stage. "It would not have jumped from the Siren to yourself if you were not vital to its cause."

He turned to Rise. "We removed the blackened diamond from Cooper Pierce last night, Siren of the 5ᵗʰ and discovered it missing a splinter. But I believe you know of that already. Am I right?"

Cooper looked between Maxiimus and Rise in confusion.

She squeezed his arm gently and nodded to Maxiimus. "The splinter was hidden in the lucky charm given to me on Savana9." She confirmed. "I only felt it when I went to put it on and the other diamond was separated from me. It was so faint, but it was there."

Cooper was looking at her in amazement. "That's what you took out of Balia's hair and wrapped around the Nephliim Blade."

"Yes." Rise shuddered, remembering the image of Balia in Arc's cruel hands and her fear that he would have already discovered it.

"It was the Echelon's cruelty and his obsession with the larger diamond that blinded him to what was with the Fae in his possession," Maxiimus mused and then smiled.

"Sometimes their nonsense works in our favor. I like it when this is so."

"Why would they carry the Nephliim Blade?" Rise asked curiously. "And how did they get it?"

Maxiimus glanced quickly at Cooper before he answered.

"It is that Nephliim Blade which closed the Veil Portal, many, many years ago. Hiding ourselves, but also the worst of the Old Ones behind it." He looked down, and when he looked up again, his eyes glistened.

"A Prince of the Nephliim. One of our bravest warriors, chose to make the sacrifice to close the Portal with it and drop to the other side. To live as a human, lost in their game, forgetting everything. But saving all," he concluded and then looked at Rise.

"How the Echelon got that Blade, is a tale only the Echelon can tell." He beamed at them both. "But how we got it back. Now that is the tale for the moment!"

There were cheers around the room at that.

"Now," Maxiimus declared, settling the cheers with his hand. "We rest, heal, recoup. We plan our next move carefully. This is but the first battle in what is like to be a long war."

He looked down and smiled at Cooper and Rise.

"Are you with us Cooper Pierce and Siren of the 5th? Will you stand beside us and help the rest of our people through?"

"Yes," they said it in unison, no hesitation in either of their voices.

And the cheers at that were loud.

And it was not the Nephliim leader that quieted the cheers this time, but wails and cursing from the Med-Hall. They were accompanied by the sounds of many things thrown and breaking. Cooper was reminded for just an instant of a winged Moethiican girl in the bathroom of a small flyer.

But this was not Rise. This was Balia. Alive and well. She had awoken. And discovered her pink horn mittens.

CHAPTER SIXTY

The added benefit to Balia's horn mitten tantrum was that it awoke Damask.

It is something to be said about the power of a Minx Fae tantrum that they can awaken someone from induced stasis sleep.

Fortunately, there were no explosions this time.

Damask would not be leaving the Med-Hall for some time however. The HellCat Queen and the other HellCat Kittens would stay with her there through the worst of it. Balia too.

With her baby awake, Scion finally gave herself over to her grief. It was her mate that Arc had killed. It was her mate, along with her ridiculously brave Kitten, Damask, who had probably saved all of them.

When Rise learned of this she cried for hours.

When Osia came to fetch her after settling Cooper in his rooms, and attending to her other duties for the day, she found her sitting back against the wall of the Med-Bay. Damask was out of her bed and nestled against her mother. The HellCat Queen's head rested in Rise's lap and Rise was gently stroking her. Tears were still falling quietly from Rise's eyes.

Balia snored loudly, cuddled in on the other side of Rise. Someone had tied black ribbons to crisscross around her pink horn mittens and she was slightly mollified. An amused human Hold Attendant had promised to fashion her something in that color palate as soon as there was time.

Osia's heart caught at the sight of them. She gestured in the Aide who had food and medicine for the patients.

Damask was put firmly back in her bed, but only after she got in two substantial licks on both her mother and Rise.

Scion was given a mild sedative in her cream. She needed to sleep and heal her own minor injuries and other hurts.

Rise tucked a blanket over the sleeping Balia who did not wake at all.

She laid a kiss on both Damask's and Scion's heads as she left. Damask purred contentedly and the fast fading, sleepy HellCat Queen nuzzled against her.

"I will kill him," was all Rise said on the way back to her rooms. "I don't care what it takes but I will kill him."

Osia had simply nodded. "I hope you do. Though I think you might have to fight Scion for the honors." She chuckled then. "This Arc is going to be a very sick and sorry Echelon at some point in time me thinks."

"You can count on it," Rise agreed, well pleased with the woman's response.

When they arrived back in her quarters, a meal was waiting for her.

"How is Cooper?" she asked, before Osia left her for the evening.

"Sleeping like a baby last time I saw him." Osia smiled at her. "I'll go check on him now before I retire for the night." She looked at Rise conspiratorially. "He's right across the hall if you want to check on him later."

"I… No, I'm sure he'll be fine. Best to let him rest quietly I'm sure," stammered Rise. Heat rising to her cheeks and making Osia smile even harder.

"Is there word of Badger? She asked quickly changing the subject. The hold had expected him back already for some days now.

"No, I'm afraid not. Sleep well, Rise," Osia replied and made her way out the door.

Rise sighed and prayed for the little creature's wellness.

She finished her dinner. Took a shower. And then settled back in front of the ever-burning fire. Osia had given her a reading tablet. Filled with hundreds of books. Rise picked one at random and began to read.

~ ~ ~ ~ ~

An hour or so later, a refreshed, revitalized Cooper Pierce awoke.

His rooms were virtually identical to Rise. And before the ever-burning fire in his room, a perfectly cooked and heated meal awaited him.

Cooper set about demolishing it with gusto. He was ravenous.

Afterwards he luxuriated in a long hot shower, marveling at the advanced healing capabilities of the Nephliim, and his now practically good as new body.

Maybe better than new. He could not remember feeling this good in a long time.

He looked at himself in the mirror and made up his mind.

"Show no fear," was the mantra he repeated quietly to himself as he crossed the hallway and knocked quietly on the door.

"Come in?" her voice sounded uncertainly, a little drowsily from the other side of the door.

"You should keep your door locked," he said as he moved into the room.

"Cooper?" she said in surprise, sitting up in her chair.

Her long dark hair was shining. Her cheeks looked pink and healthy. It was warm in here too and she had on only a long night shirt.

And nothing underneath it by the looks of things.

He stood staring at her, unmoving. Not saying a thing.

"Cooper," she said again, softly and wide eyed. Standing up from the chair.

"I'm sorry." His voice was rough and deep. "I shouldn't be in here. I'm sorry. I didn't mean to wake you."

He tried to move back out the door and away from her. But the energy sparking between them was too much. He was so aware of her and how naked she was underneath that nightshirt he could barely function.

He already knew she was perfect. Roughly, he pushed the image of the first time he had seen her away from him. He would not bring those images here. Not here. Not now. Not ever. Thank the godds he had been able to save her.

He closed his eyes and tried to breathe his way to calmness.

"Cooper," she said softy again. She had moved right in front of him. Gently, she laid her hand against his cheek.

It was so crazy, it felt like the world had stopped.

He felt some part of himself somersault and slam into some other part of himself.

He cupped the back of her head with one hand and her cheek with the other and he kissed her.

He kissed her like he suddenly remembered kissing her in the flyer. Godds. How could anyone, ever, forget a kiss like that.

The feelings that washed over him as he kissed her were the most exquisite feelings of ecstasy he had ever known.

Kissing her. Just kissing her was better than sex.

And as soon as he thought it he realized just how that might feel. And he had never wanted anyone so badly in his life.

He ripped open her nightshirt in one easy motion. Discarded his own t-shirt to the floor.

Rise wound her hands in his hair and pressed herself against him.

And when he felt her perfection pressed against him, Cooper went over an edge, that there was no coming back from.

He kicked the door closed behind him, took her in one fluid motion to the thickly carpeted floor. He was on top of her and his kisses were hot and hard and urgent.

He felt her hesitate ever so slightly under his new urgency, and he tensed, thinking she would stop him.

But then he felt her drop a shield that she held between them. He felt her open to him.

And he suddenly knew, that to have her, truly have her, he must do the same.

And he did. And suddenly it was easy. And for the first time as he began to truly see her, he began to see himself also.

But she. Godds she was magnificent.

And she wanted him. As much as he wanted her. And that was enough. And he gave himself over to it. To taking her, possessing her, as he'd wanted to do from the very first moment he'd laid eyes on her.

Rise moaned and Cooper gasped at the waves of power he felt from her, crashing against him.

And he could feel her diamond now, spinning, shining ever so brightly, and reaching out to his mind, to connect with his own.

It would be so easy to take it.

But he wasn't like them. He didn't want to take it. He wanted to share it with her, connect their two diamonds, and feed her the same power of his own.

She opened her eyes then and they stared at each other, eyes locked, the thread between them expanded, the waves of energy flowing between them.

And suddenly he knew, that he didn't even need to touch her. That they could both ride these invisible waves together and come hot and hard and heavy. And he knew then what the Pann spoke about when they talked of these things.

But he was here now. And she was here now. And by the Godds he was going to touch her. He would file that other thought away for later. It had possibilities.

He looked down the length of her beautiful body.

"Please, Cooper," Rise said. "Please."

Her saying that nearly undid him.

He pinned her wrists back over her head and drove into her perfect, hot, tight, wetness, hard and deep.

He had no memory of ever being this hard for anyone.

He kissed her as he moved deep and full in and out of her.

His pace quickened. Her nails tore the skin on his back.

Rise screamed, wave after undulating wave from her breaking over him.

And Cooper forgot who he was. He forgot himself.

And they weren't there. They weren't there in that room anymore. They were in a cave. Drawings on the walls. Firelight flickering.

And then there was only them and nothing else in the world.

They were the world.

They were making the world.

They were nothing.

And they were everything.

He came. And he had never come like this before. And she came again with him.

And the echoing pulsing magic of the divine came with both of them.

And they woke something large and cosmic, the vibrations of which, caused just a tiny tear in the Veil in the sky above them.

They felt it, saw it, knew it instantaneously. Their eyes flew open and they gazed into each other, the waves of power still undulating and crashing all around them.

And Cooper did remember himself then. As did the Siren he was still inside of.

"Fark me," he said. "I'm a Nephliim."

"Not just any Nephliim, Cooper Pierce," she replied. "That Blade I threw into the Veil Portal, is yours."

CHAPTER SIXTY-ONE

The war drum beat.

It beat without cease.

It said simply, I am coming for you. And you should probably be afraid.

Most people who heard it were. Which was half the idea. To throw people off guard. Make them lose focus, edge and deep training. Make them do something stupid.

The other half was to empower those who came behind it. Fill their veins with a rush of adrenalin, courage and righteousness. Focus them on the task at hand.

It was so loud up here in the tiny cave. It reverberated off the rock walls. Badger felt his chest pound physically with each beat.

An undulating cry pierced the air, making him jump involuntarily. He stole back as silently and quickly as he could into the shadows.

The creature shot up before his eyes, barely three feet away from where he lay hidden.

He was huge.

His enormous wing span cast shadows over the red dirt floor below. He was oiled and his muscles glistened in the sunlight. His armor was black. Leather and obsidian. He was heavily inked. Mostly war runes.

He hung, seemingly suspended in the air, surveying the training field below him. Badger held still, not daring to move. Not daring even to breathe.

With the same undulating cry, the winged creature banked sharply and sped in an unerring line back to the training field below.

Badger moved frantically out of the cave. He must get back to the others and report on this. It was now imperative they make haste to the Hold and warn the Nephliim.

But in his haste, Badger inadvertently dislodged a pair of sulphur rocks.

The rocks had been patiently trying to work their way loose from this wall of stone for some two million years.

They were ecstatic to have been given such a helping hand towards the end of their tireless journey. They hurtled towards the edge of the cave and tumbled down the side of the rock face with glee, making as much noise as they possibly could to celebrate their newly found freedom.

It was a lot of noise.

It was a lot of movement.

They were a long way up so it was quite a trip down.

By the time they reached the hard-packed red dirt floor below they were well pleased with themselves.

They settled peaceably and contentedly in the hot, red dirt and wondered what the next two million years would bring.

Badger froze.

The amassed winged warriors on the ground, looked up as one to the cave.

Talon, their leader, who had just landed, waved his hand dismissively. "A cave rodent, no doubt. Some random creature. We cannot be jumping at any little thing."

He was bored already with this training session and anxious to get to the night's entertainments.

The Old One's human Militia Leader looked up at the cave thoughtfully for a time and then shrugged. He gestured to his 2IC to take the last of the winged brutes through their paces and finish up for the day.

A short time later, Talon, was well pleased to be done. On his way back into their rocky dwelling, he noticed one of the sulphur rocks glinting strangely in the moonlight.

Absently, he picked it up.

It had a pleasing form. He tossed it in the air and pocketed it.

Its partner was left alone and parted from it, for the first time in several million years, on the deserted training ground floor.

It felt a sharp pang of loss at its star born friend. The tales it had told! The adventures it had been on. Godspeed my friend. It wished it. Godspeed.

And indeed, the star rock was now making speed. And this winged brutish creature would do nicely.

After all these many millions of years, the Original Maker, who had first thrown it into play, was calling to it again.

The star rock was well pleased.

Days later, as the winged brutish thing flew high above the remote Nephliim Mountain Hold, on a scouting mission for his own Masters, the star rock discreetly dislodged itself from his pocket.

It landed far short of the hold itself. But that was Ok. It was a rock. And it was very patient. Someone was sure to find it.

~ ~ ~ ~ ~

In the city, the apartment building of Badger and Resistance1 was raided that night. The Liaison left his men to its ransacking, and came out into the narrow hallway to smoke.

He flicked through his phone as he did so, checking every social media account, all the news feeds.

Most couldn't see it, but there were some more aware than others on Earth. Still, any mentions of the golden, shimmering Veil had been shut down nicely. "A standard weather formation, often occurring in these parts. Just more visible due to the current positioning of a couple of unimportant stars and planets in the night sky. Nothing to see here people. Move along."

The Liaison smiled and pocketed his phone. And still, no-one knew who he was, had guessed his identity. When he was done here, he would make his way to the Mountain Hold, and his old buddy, Cooper Pierce.

After all these years, it would be a pleasure to take care of Cooper Pierce once and for all. The slut Siren and the Nephliim scum under the same roof, would just be an added bonus.

A movement out of the lone hallway window caught his eye.

A neon sign shone through it.

But there was movement behind the neon sign, large and shadow like.

The Liaison peered at it.

"Sir, we're done here."

He turned away only slightly from the sign to his man.

"What? Fine. Let's go then."

He turned one last time to look at the neon sign before he entered the elevator, but all was stillness.

Still, he stared at it intently until the elevator doors finally closed.

He was a nuggety fellow with a wizened face and farseeing, somber eyes. He was an exceptional pilot, a recruiter, a jack of all trades, a loyal soldier.

The Gargoyle, Watcher for the Original Makers, shifted back from where he had studied the Liaison from behind the cover of the neon lights.

He had watched over much from this vantage point over the years.

The Siren of the 5th had sensed him.

Which was fine.

But not this one. Not this one with the farseeing eyes who had almost spotted him. He must warn the others to be more careful. And someone must get word to the Hold immediately.

The stakes of the game had just gone up a level. And Jackdaw, Liaison to the Old Ones, was now in play.

*****

Thank you!

Thank you so much for reading rise siren five. I'm honored to share this story with you. If you would be so kind as to share a review at your place of purchase, it would be very much appreciated. The small act of leaving a review - no matter how short - helps make what authors like myself do, possible.

For new release info and the occasional musing, please join my mailing list at:

www.sarahsofiadelaunay.com